# THE
# WIREGRASS

## ADRIAN HYLAND

ultimo
press

Published in 2023 by Ultimo Press,
an imprint of Hardie Grant Publishing

Ultimo Press
Gadigal Country
7, 45 Jones Street
Ultimo, NSW 2007
ultimopress.com.au

Ultimo Press (London)
5th & 6th Floors
52–54 Southwark Street
London SE1 1UN

    ultimopress

 A catalogue record for this book is available from the National Library of Australia

*The Wiregrass*
ISBN 978 1 76115 004 3 (paperback)

**Cover design** Design by Committee
**Cover images** Background by John Fairhall/AUSCAPE / Alamy Stock Photo; Eagle by Peter Crome / Alamy Stock Photo
**Text design** Simon Paterson, Bookhouse
**Typesetting** Bookhouse, Sydney | 13/17 pt Adobe Garamond Pro
**Copyeditor** Deonie Fiford
**Proofreader** Pamela Dunne

10 9 8 7 6 5 4 3 2 1

Printed in Australia by Opus Group Pty Ltd, an Accredited ISO AS/NZS 14001 Environmental Management System printer.

 MIX
Paper | Supporting responsible forestry
FSC® C018684

The paper this book is printed on is certified against the Forest Stewardship Council® Standards. Griffin Press – a member of the Opus Group – holds chain of custody certification SCS-COC-001185. FSC® promotes environmentally responsible, socially beneficial and economically viable management of the world's forests.

Ultimo Press acknowledges the Traditional Owners of the Country on which we work, the Gadigal People of the Eora Nation and the Wurundjeri People of the Kulin Nation, and recognises their continuing connection to the land, waters and culture. We pay our respects to their Elders past and present.

*To Mary*

*a winter kiss*
*and walking back to the Bluehouse*
*we climb, on an impulse*
*into the icicle chimes of starlight*
*that glitter and ring in the cypress pine*

Kenji Takada (1926–1980)

# CHAPTER 1

Long waves of rain swept through the headlights' arc. Big branches, heavy and wet, came whirling in upon the wind. A blizzard of twigs and leaves and other debris peppered the sides of the car. You could hear the tyres splash through the puddles on the bitumen, the V8 engine roar.

I glanced into the mirror. The Country Fire Authority ute was following close behind. Somewhere behind it was a Greendale patrol car. We'd been playing this wild game of tag since I started my shift this morning.

As we swung round a bend, a messmate gum on our right came crashing down onto the road in front of us.

'Go left!' screamed Lance, beside me.

I hit the anchors but stayed on course and slammed into the trunk.

'Fucken hell,' said Lance.

We stepped out into the rain and inspected the damage – the bull-bar was pushed back, the grille cracked. But the vehicle should still be driveable.

The CFA pulled up behind us. Danny Clarion, the Satellite brigade captain, got out and joined us, a chainsaw in his hands.

'Good job,' he muttered. He was a tall, spare man with bemused eyes and a rolly welded to the corner of his mouth.

'Good job?' replied Lance. 'She ran straight into the tree. What a bloody mess.'

'Well, it is a messmate,' said Danny. 'Rather hit the trunk than the branches,' he explained, nodding at the thick foliage to our left. 'You get that lot coming through the windscreen, they'll be pluckin' pieces out of you for weeks.'

I pointed at the fallen tree. 'You got this, Danny?'

'We got it.'

'Thanks.'

He put the saw on the ground, started it up smoothly. His crew appeared with crowbars and axes, got down to business. Lance and I worked our way around the scene and resumed our journey.

'How far now?' I asked.

'Couple of kays.'

We'd been despatched to an accident on Reynolds Road. There was a driver reportedly trapped in an overturned car, one of the dozens of incidents coming over the radio as the storm battered the Windmark Ranges. People said it was the worst in living memory, but they always say that. It was certainly the worst in my memory, but that wasn't saying much; I'd only been here a few days. Whatever the truth, I could see there were trees and poles down everywhere, roads washed away, sinkholes opening up, flash floods and landslides descending.

I put my foot as far down as I dared. Frogs and fat raindrops bounced off the road. A shadow-cat flew by, scared out of its wits. The clock on the dash said it was almost midnight.

'I do hate driving bells and whistles in a storm,' I commented.

Lance remained silent, his features contorted as he leaned forward and stared at the road ahead, like he expected mace-waving orcs to rise up out of it. His confidence in my driving abilities had clearly taken a battering.

I caught a glimpse of something odd in a gully beside the road and slowed down for a closer look.

'What is it?' asked Lance.

'Thought I saw a wheel.' I stopped, reversed.

'This isn't Reynolds Road.'

'Feller had just rolled his car . . .'

'Yeah . . . in Reynolds Road.'

'Might not have known exactly where he was – Reynolds might have been where he was heading.' I stared down into the shadows. Nothing.

Lance twisted around, his belly lolling over the seatbelt.

'Jess, we have to go.'

'Gimme a second.' I lowered the window and scoped the gully with my Maglite. The wind and the rain came sweeping in. We both got wet laps.

There was a tangle of shapes and shades down there: bushes, tree trunks, a twisting creek, fantail ferns. And a half circle: a wheel in the air.

I moved the beam and a rectangle of metal pipes and plates appeared. The wheel was attached to an overturned car.

Was it a historic wreck or was it the object of our search? I moved the torch again.

Not historic. There was a body halfway out the window.

Lance called it in while I scrambled down the slope. I was relieved to see the body sketch a vague wave as I drew near.

'You right there, mate?' I asked.

He gave a drunken mumble in response.

I helped him out of the car. He was in his thirties, rubber-jawed, red-eyed, breath smelling like the back bar of the Satellite Hotel. He slumped to the ground, groped for his phone, tried to take a selfie, managed to take one of his own feet.

'For the 'surance,' he mumbled.

'Yeah right.'

I gave him the once-over. He seemed okay. I tried a breathalyser but had trouble getting enough breath out of the bloke to take a reading. I was still trying when Lance arrived, panting.

'How is he?'

'Pissed as a public urinal.'

'Ambulance'll be here in twenty minutes,' he said. 'CFA, twenty seconds,' he added, glancing back down the road, along which a set of flashing lights were approaching. Those guys never gave up.

Danny Clarion came surfing in on a black mud wave.

'Just got a call,' he said. 'Tree down at Wycliff Rise.'

'Trees are down everywhere.'

'This one's killed someone.'

Wycliff Rise? I'd never heard of it. Then again, there were a lot of things round here I hadn't heard of. The ranges around us went all the way to Queensland. Half their luck. I was still trying to get my bearings in this part of the world. Main thing I'd learned so far was where to buy the best coffee and pies.

'How far's this Wycliff Rise?'

'Night like this,' said Danny. 'Half an hour.' A tree toppled in the distance. 'One of those hits you, maybe forever.'

I nodded at the car below us, its driver flopped back against the wheel, arms akimbo. Rain fell into his mouth. One of his shoes had come off. 'You know this joker?'

Danny peered at the car, frowned and shone the torch on its driver.

'Jeez, Lenny,' he said. 'Third time in less than a year.'

'Sorry, Danny,' Lenny said, then vomited onto his phone.

The Greendale car arrived, its crew a pair of constables just starting their shift. I wanted to get to Wycliff in a hurry so I handed the drunken Lenny over to them, and Lance and I set off.

A string of washouts and diversions meant the trip took longer than expected. As we rounded a bend I caught an unexpected sight in the headlights: a white horse cantering through the bush alongside the road, a young woman – maybe a girl – in the saddle.

She vanished as swiftly as she'd appeared.

'See that?' I asked Lance.

'What?'

'Girl on a horse.'

He glanced around, but whoever it was, they were long gone.

'You're seeing a lot of things tonight,' Lance grunted. He was a decent enough bloke, but not what you'd call dynamic. He'd been on the job for twenty years and had risen to the heady heights of senior constable. I wouldn't have blamed him if he was pissed off that I'd been appointed officer-in-charge of the Satellite Station, but, if so, he was hiding it well. He told me he hadn't applied, didn't want the paperwork. He and his wife, Wendy, had asked me round to dinner, and he helped me find accommodation, something which, I'd been surprised to discover, was in short supply round here.

* * *

By the time we arrived at Wycliff there were other emergency workers on scene: ambos, fireys, State Emergency Service, police.

The latter was from Greendale – the vehicle was a BMW M3 Competition, the best and newest car in the fleet. That suggested somebody senior. They must have swung round from the north-west. Hardly surprising; there were cops all over the ranges tonight.

Somebody had set up floodlights, a portable genny rumbled. There was a tow truck, orange lights rotating, ready to swoop in and grab the wreck. The operator was out of the cab having a smoke. He hunched into his jacket and stamped his feet as we drove past.

The paramedics were working on what was left of some poor bastard in a Fergie tractor that had been crushed by a falling euca-lypt. The fireys were sawing the tree into bite-sized chunks. They made the final cut and a team of volunteers lifted the main log off and twisted the tractor's metal frame back with a Halligan bar.

The driver was as dead as anybody was ever going to be. I took a quick look at him and shuddered. The upper half of his body was crushed. His thick black hair was slick with blood, his head was pushed back into the roll bar. A smaller branch had speared right through his chest. Strangely, I had a sense of a handsome man, dark-haired, strongly built.

One of the people watching – a man in a high-vis snow jacket and gumboots – turned round. It was Ed Dougherty, the inspector from Greendale. My boss. He was tall, heavy, pale-faced and talking into his portable. Greendale, fifty kays away and on the edge of suburban Melbourne, was our regional headquarters. He finished the call then addressed me.

'Redpath. We're okay here. Get on up to the Leatherwood Crossing. There's a bridge under water there, idiots trying to drive across. One death is enough for tonight. Who you with?'

'Lance Cunningham.'

'He'll know it. Set up a roadblock. Nobody goes through.'

'Got it.'

I paused for a last look at the scene. Tried to take it all in, something I'd learned to do in the Territory. A quick scan, a mental photograph filed away: the angles and glances, the whirling geometry, the anomalies and questions. The ambos, with the help of the fireys, were loading the body onto a stretcher. The SES guys were dragging the logs away to give everybody better access. Chainsaws screamed, sawdust flew. The wind was as sharp as a razor blade.

'Redpath!' The boss. 'What are you waiting for? You're not up in the Never-Never now.'

Was that all I was going to be known for down here? The woman from the Territory. Maybe, until I settled in, forged my own identity.

I climbed up the slope, mud sucking at my boots. Runnels of filthy water poured into every gap they could find. Mud crept into my pants as I slipped, skidded and scrambled up to the car.

I filled Lance in and off we went.

## CHAPTER 2

The Leatherwood Crossing was fifteen minutes up the road. There were a couple of cars parked on either side of a low concrete bridge, their lights illuminating the scene. Three men stood on the near bank gesticulating and pacing anxiously. One of them was flicking a rope into the raging waters.

I looked down the creek. There was a car in there pushed up against a boulder, a woman clinging to the roof. She was only a few metres away, but what metres they were: full of threats and danger, of imminent death. Put a foot wrong and you'd never be seen again. The southern end of the bridge had collapsed and the floodwaters were pouring over it. A cow came rolling by, its legs in the air, briefly, then a terrified head.

'We've called the SES,' said one of the men as we joined them.

I grunted. Fat lot of good that would do. The storm was like a twenty-four-hour tsunami. There were crises breaking out all over the ranges. You were as likely to get a gourmet coffee cart as you were the water rescue team tonight. Lance and I were it.

I studied what was left of the bridge. There was a massive log pressing against the piles, jumping around, revolving. How long it would stay in place – or what would happen when it broke loose – was anybody's guess.

I turned back to the woman in the water. She was thin, pale, with fearful eyes and Gorgon hair, badly tossed about. She yelled what could only be a cry for help. A wave smacked her in the face and knocked her down. Please don't let go, I willed. For a moment, all you could see was an arm clutching the doorframe, then her head bobbed up again, her mouth a frantic O in the foam. She was putting up a fight. But she could well have only seconds left, no matter what she did.

I stole a glance at Lance. Twenty years older than me, twenty kilos heavier, a heart-attack-in-waiting. I grabbed the harness and rescue rope from the boot.

'Anchor me,' I said, slipping into the gear.

Lance protested briefly, then saw my point. He secured the rope to a tree and organised the spectators into a human chain.

I stepped into the water and was immediately bowled over. Bloody hell, it was powerful. I felt like an egg at the bottom of a blender. The cold nearly knocked me senseless. After a minute bouncing my head about on the rocky bed, I found my feet and came up gasping. I copped a lungful of water and did what I could to spit it out. I pushed on into the creek, had to swim desperately for the last few metres.

As I drew close to the car, I heard Lance's voice, a desperate warning.

I looked upstream. The log had broken free from the bridge and was whirling in our direction. I threw myself forward and seized hold of the woman just as the log slammed into the car and sent it tumbling downstream.

When I came up for air I made a frantic signal to Lance, who was already hauling us in. My feet were flailing wildly, finding nothing. The woman struggled briefly, panicking, then went limp, hopefully realising her struggle was only making things worse. The rope felt like the only thing between me and eternity. Finally, I touched the rocky bottom and pushed off. The civilians waded into the shallows and took the woman from my arms. I crawled up onto the bank and collapsed into the mud, lay there, heart racing, breath short.

I looked over to where the others were tending to the woman. She was about thirty, with flattened peroxide hair and numerous tattoos. She was staring up at the night sky, her mouth moving silently.

'How is she?' I asked.

'Fucking ace,' she grated through rattling teeth. A good sign. She caught my eye. 'But thanks.' That was an even better one.

Lance came back from the car with an armful of woollen blankets, a couple of which he wrapped around the woman. He passed me a spare and I leaned against a tree, still struggling to get my breath. My head was throbbing. My tongue tasted of blood, my feet were like lumps of wood.

'How are you yourself?' asked Lance, looking concerned.

'Okay.'

'Ambos are on the way.'

But the next car to come along was Inspector Dougherty's BMW. He pulled over and walked down to where our little group had gathered. I climbed to my feet, then stumbled into the mud, face first.

'You look like a drowned mouse,' he said. 'What happened here?'

'Woman tried to cross the bridge, ended up in the water, boss,' said Lance. 'Jess pulled her out.'

Dougherty turned to me. 'You okay?'

'I'm fine.'

'She did a bloody good job,' Lance threw in.

Dougherty studied the creek. 'Where's the woman's car?'

'Somewhere downstream.'

He looked around, clearly trying to piece things together: the woman under the blanket, the roaring winds, the racing waters, the wet rope. He was a hard man to read, Dougherty: taciturn, blunt. I'd never seen him smile, even when he was welcoming me to the region. His face was pale and pudgy; like his name, it was mainly dough.

'There's an ambulance on my tail,' he said. 'Do you need it, Redpath?'

'Nah – few bruises. Mainly just bloody cold.'

'What time did you two start your shift?'

'Eight this morning,' said Lance.

'Long enough. Get on home. That's if you've got one, Redpath. You found somewhere to live yet?'

'Got a place in Satellite, boss. Moved in yesterday.'

'Then go and get some shut-eye.'

'You got enough crew here?'

'Highway Patrol and ambos are behind me. Fresh teams. They can take this. You get tired, you'll make mistakes.'

Fair enough.

The Highway Patrol car appeared out of the darkness. Dougherty had a word with its occupants then turned back to us.

'You've done a good job. Now piss off, the pair of you.'

That was encouragement enough for my partner and me. We climbed into the car and set out.

My first inkling that all was not right in Satellite came as we entered the town. It was the lights. There were none.

'Bloody hell,' Lance muttered. 'Power's out.'

Hardly surprising. Trees and power poles would be down all over the district, transformers blasted apart, live wires snarling on wet roads.

'Wendy better have a hottie in the bed,' mused Lance. 'Either that or she'll have to do the job herself.'

No hotties in my bed, I thought as I dropped him off at the station. Better find my thermo-nuclear long johns.

I switched the police car for my white HiLux Twin Cab and drove to my house on Shady Grove Road. I pulled up in the driveway and checked it out. No lights. Bugger.

The accommodation that came with the job was a flat above the bakery, but I couldn't see much point in being in the bush if you were going to have to put up with your neighbours' bread-making noises at three in the morning. Lance did a little asking round and came up with this place, a log cabin nestled among the manna gums on the outskirts of Satellite. It was a Forestry Commission summer crew bunkhouse that had been declared unfit for human habitation. That suited me fine; after ten years in the outback, I was barely fit for human habitation myself. Plus I was getting it at mates rates.

The ramifications of the power outage – the prospect of freezing to death – dawned on me as I walked up the steps. The cottage's main source of warmth was a rattly old reverse-cycle unit – power-driven. There was an open fireplace and a rusty

Coonara wood heater in the corner, but I hadn't had a chance to collect any wood yet.

I glanced over the road. My nearest neighbours, across and a hundred metres down the road, were a retired couple named Rocco and Meg Teller. I'd said hello to him but hadn't seen her yet. Apparently, she was often on the road, supplementing their pension by selling free-range eggs all over the district. There were no lights to be seen at their place either.

As I entered the front door a bat swooped around my head.

There was a blur of movement in the kitchen. I swung the torch at it. A fat rat scuttled across the floor, a spring in its step, an apple core in its mouth.

'You're welcome,' I grunted.

When it stopped and smirked at me, I had a shot at it with a boot. The rodent zipped out of the torchlight and sprinted up a corner pole.

The cottage was basically a single room, with a cupboard and a bed to the left, a table and chairs to the right, a tiny wannabe-kitchen and bathroom at the back. The furniture came with the house, as did the ancient Kriesler Bakelite radio on a shelf beside the bed. I presumed it had been left there by some long-gone old man of the trees.

Icy needles of wind were zipping in through the numerous cracks in the walls and windows. A hot shower would be nice, but, without power, neither water nor heat were available. The only water source was a five-thousand-gallon tank filled from the roof, but it needed electricity to pump water up to the house. Actually, there was another water source. As I sat on the bed to remove my remaining boot, a heavy drop of water landed on my nose. I scanned the roof with my torch. There was a leak over the bed. The single blanket was damp. Not much I could do about that right now. I donned my fleeciest pyjamas and thickest socks and draped a couple of coats across the bed. I hadn't got round to buying proper bedding yet.

I crawled under the blanket, clutching my ribs and rubbing my feet together, doing everything I could to generate a little heat. My hair was still damp, my nose a blue icicle, my breath a frozen ghost in the air above me.

My shivering gradually dissipated. The first ripples of warmth began to surface from within.

Please, I whispered to god knows what, give me the gift of sleep. If nothing else, it would be a way to escape the cold. Everything would look better in the light of day. Maybe I'd jump out of bed and go for an invigorating run through the bush or drop into the bakery and buy some breakfast.

My eyes closed. I felt my nerves beginning to unwind, the adrenaline wearing off, sleep stealing over me, seeping out into my limbs.

My eyes sprang open.

What was wrong?

Something had been hovering down in the backwoods of my brain. A disturbing image that only rose to the surface when I began to relax.

Wild winds, wet hair, black bark, blood. A crushed body.

The poor bastard killed by the falling tree at Wycliff Rise.

Something about that scene wasn't right.

I replayed the episode in my head, trying to figure out what had brought me to this pass.

The ambos had their backs to me, doing what they could to give the guy a little dignity. The emergency service workers were dragging the torn frame back with a Halligan bar. Inspector Dougherty was talking into his radio, keeping one eye on the various emergency crews going about their business. The fireys were cutting up the tree, chainsaws screaming, steel-caps kicking. The tow-truck driver was standing next to his vehicle, cap down, collar up, waiting for the all-clear. Half-a-dozen neighbours or passers-by were looking on, their faces grim, their jackets blown about by the wind. Chances were they knew the victim.

One of the chainsaw operators took a break as his mate dragged away the last length of wood.

That was it. The wood, the tree. There was something wrong there. What sort of tree was it? It had rounded leaves and fibrous bark: a red box eucalypt. My young friend Possum Kelly had told me once that it was unusual for them to fall like that. They've got long tap roots, which makes them relatively stable. I sniffed suspiciously. There was something else wrong with the scene, but I couldn't see what.

I shook my head and cursed quietly. This wasn't going to do much for my popularity, but I had no choice. Follow your hunches: that was the only way I knew.

I sat up in bed. The room hadn't got any warmer. I reached for my phone, punched the number with quivering fingers.

'Boss,' I said.

'Redpath,' snapped Dougherty. 'You're meant to be asleep.' An engine roared. He was driving.

'Have Forensics finished at Wycliff Rise yet?'

'Heading for town as we speak.'

'They have to get back out there.'

I heard the engine ease off. 'What!'

Only a solitary word, but the tone spoke volumes.

'Something's not right.'

'Yeah, you.' The engine hushed. He'd pulled over. 'Your little dip in the river must have scrambled your brains. I'll overlook this. Go back to sleep.'

He killed the call.

I lay there for five minutes, shivering, for want of anything better to do. Willing myself to forget it. But I couldn't.

Finally, ever so reluctantly, I dragged my weary body out of bed. The lino was icy underfoot. I tried the lamp. Still nothing. I did a few half-hearted taekwondo exercises in a vain attempt to work a little life back into my bones, then kitted up by torchlight and left the house.

# CHAPTER 3

The wind continued to sweep through the night, but it had a little less fury in it now. I sat in the HiLux and called Danny Clarion, the CFA captain. I'd only met him a couple of times, but I instinctively trusted him. He had an air of no-bullshit about him.

'Still on the job?' I asked.

'We'll be goin' all night.'

'Where are you now?'

'Green Creek. Tree down on a house.'

I heard a scream in the background. Hopefully it was a chainsaw, not a resident.

'Any chance of meeting me back at Wycliff?'

'When?'

'As soon as.'

A long pause, during which I presumed he took a drag of his smoke. 'Is it urgent? We're under the pump.'

'I don't know what it is.'

Another pause. The wind howled. I could imagine it whipping away the smoke, the nicotine streams and embers.

'Sam Kelly spoke highly of you,' he said. Kelly, captain of the nearby Canticle Creek Fire Brigade, was a family friend. 'I'll be there in half an hour.'

I checked the time. Just after five.

I drove out to Wycliff Rise. The tractor was gone, but the bog holes were still there, the tape was still in place. I got out and stood there staring, trying to work out what had snagged in my consciousness. I hoped that being on scene would add more detail.

I walked across and examined the tree.

The fallen section of the trunk was still partially attached to the stump. There were torn shreds where the tree had snapped off. Was it all torn? No, at the base of the split was a small chainsaw incision. Fresh. Was it deep enough to bring the tree down? Not on its own. Somebody must have given it a hand, maybe dragged it down with a winch.

Why would the CFA operator make an incision like that? And if the operator hadn't put it there, who had?

I stood at the stump and looked around, trying to recreate the incident.

What did the ground have to say?

Not much; between the wind, the rain, the emergency workers' vehicles and boots, the site had been trampled into a quagmire. I walked across to the far side of the road and prowled along the churned verges, occasionally getting down on to my knees. Muddy water flooded my boot prints, then my boots. The scene bore all the scars of the chaos that had erupted here.

Skid marks, tyre tracks, runnels and ruts, potholes, bog holes everywhere.

There was a multitude of vehicle tracks. I tried to recall how many there'd been at the job. At least seven or eight. They'd pulled in along the edge of the road, leaving room for the ambulance. The CFA tankers had parked at either end of the site, their beacon lights serving as a roadblock. If there were any civilian vehicles here, they'd been held well back. From what I'd seen of the tow truck, it had kept mostly to the bitumen, doubtless wanting a solid base to work from.

I checked along the opposite edge, slowly and carefully, studying the surface by my Maglite. I'd gone maybe twenty metres when I came across what I'd been looking for: a set of tyre tracks, deeper than the others, at a 45-degree angle to the road.

I made a rough calculation of the distances and angles involved, then crossed over to what was left of the tree.

The fireys had sawn the fallen trunk into short lengths, each a metre or so long. That was the best way to get rid of unwanted wood round here; anything left on the side of the road would be gathered up by somebody keen to avoid the effort of cutting their own.

No one had done so yet, though. There were half a dozen sections lined up along the verge. I went through them, one by one. Nothing. I improvised a crowbar from a length of timber then turned the sections over and examined the undersides, forcing my hands through the chunky mud, scraping it away. I was two-thirds of the way along the tree when I found what I was after: a scarred section where the bark had been torn and a cable had bitten into the wood. I scrutinised it closely. I could just make out a slick of oil and tiny splinters of steel glimmering in the torchlight.

'So what the hell are we doing here?'

I spun round in alarm. There was a shadowy figure on the rise above me.

It was Inspector Dougherty, hood up, hands deep in the pockets of his jacket. He must have parked back along the road. Absorbed by my task, or distracted by the weather, I'd missed his arrival. Still, he moved quietly for a big man.

'Scared the crap out of me, boss.'

'Pays to keep your eyes open, Redpath. Like I said, you're not in the Territory now.'

He didn't look happy. He looked even less happy when I showed him the section of tree trunk at my feet and asked what he made of it.

'Bit of wood,' he replied.

'Look at the marks on it.'

He obliged.

'Bit of scarred wood,' he expanded.

'Scarred by a winch cable.'

'Maybe. Maybe it was a randy possum.'

'Look more closely, you'll see traces of oil and flecks of steel. Someone's dragged it down with a cable.'

Another vehicle appeared, then Danny Clarion joined us. I filled him in on my concerns. After a close inspection of the log, he agreed that the scars could well have been made by a winch cable.

I took them back to the stump and showed them the v-shaped wedge.

'Would your guys have done that?' I asked Danny.

He flicked his smoke away, shook his head and said no, he couldn't see any reason why they would have.

Then I showed them the churned earth where the vehicle with the winch had planted itself.

'Put it all together and you'll see,' I said. 'Somebody prepped the tree – just a bit, so it wouldn't be too obvious. Then they put a winch around it and dragged it down onto the tractor.'

'You're saying this was deliberate?' Dougherty asked. 'Somebody killed the poor bugger with a falling tree?'

'No.'

His brow furrowed.

'Then what the hell are you saying?'

'I'd say he was already dead. Or at least unconscious. Be a bloody inefficient way to kill someone, dragging a tree down on him as he was driving past. Anybody with his wits about him would just stop when he saw the cable round the tree, or jump out of the way. No, they put him in the tractor, positioned it carefully then dropped the tree on top of him.'

I thought some more about the damage done to the body. 'Maybe they even rammed a branch into his chest to make sure he was dead.'

Dougherty cast his eyes across the scene, calculating, assessing. I sensed that he was coming round.

Danny Clarion lit another rolly and blew out a line of silver smoke. His eyes were burning. Death, I presumed, he could accept. He'd have seen plenty of that; I knew he'd been a strike team leader on Black Saturday. Murder was another matter.

'I don't suppose any witnesses have come forward?' I asked Dougherty.

The inspector shook his head. 'We spoke to the locals. Nobody saw the tree come down.'

'When was the body discovered?'

'Call came in around ten pm.'

I tried to recollect the events of the night.

'I saw a girl on a white horse,' I said. 'About a kilometre down the road to Satellite, riding away from the scene. She might have seen something.'

Dougherty turned to Danny. 'That sound like anybody you know?'

'Horses all over the place round here, most of 'em have got teenage girls on their backs. I didn't see any of 'em out and about last night.'

There was a golden glow in the east. Dawn wasn't far off.

I asked if we knew anything about the victim and Dougherty checked his notebook. 'Name's Raph Cambric,' he said. 'His family own the apple orchard at the end of this track.'

I nodded thoughtfully. My brain was automatically shifting into accumulation mode: first gather your facts, then find the golden thread that runs through them.

'What is there in the way of family?'

Danny Clarion obviously knew the victim. 'Father's a widower, but he's more or less retired now. His sons do most of the work. Raph lived in a cottage down at the packing sheds, but the other brother, Jared, lives with his wife and kids in the main house. Raph did a bit of farrier work as well as helping run the farm.'

I cast my eyes up and down the road, trying to get a better sense of the locality, something I've always found essential to the resolution of a crime.

Dougherty asked some pertinent questions of Danny. Did he know of any enemies Raph might have, were there any local or family feuds? His interest was clearly piqued by the fact that support was coming from another local, rather than from the interloper. Danny's answers were all in the negative. He knew the family, had no idea who'd wish any harm on Raph Cambric.

'So what are we going to do now?' I asked Dougherty.

He turned and began trudging through the sludge, back up the slope towards his own vehicle. He returned a couple of minutes later, a roll of crime-scene tape in hand.

'I've called in Homicide,' he said wearily.

He stopped for a moment and kicked up a clump of mud.

'What a fucking night,' he said.

True story, I thought. And it's not going to get any better.

# CHAPTER 4

They began to appear half an hour later: the cavalcade of heavies and experts, the (mostly) men in suits, boots and overalls, more moustaches per square head than a seventies skin flick. First came the Criminal Investigation Unit from Greendale, then Highway Patrol, Forensics, Homicide. Somebody even arranged a morning tea van, full of the kind of crap cops consume to shorten their lives and lengthen their belts.

I gave a statement to the Hommies, explained my observations and conclusions. The sergeant in charge, Calhoun, listened closely then nodded what may have been appreciation.

I spent a few hours on scene, part of a band of local uniforms consigned to the grunt work when the specialists took charge.

The jobs I was given got dirtier and gluggier as the morning wore on. I spent a few hours scrambling down among brambles and boggy wombat holes, foot-slogging through the sludge and the mud, trudging around the neighbourhood knocking on doors in search for witnesses. Needless to say, I didn't find any. They were an insular lot round here. *Deliverance* country.

My only notable moment came when I lifted a log and
snake leapt out, striking wildly before slithering away at pace.

Dougherty disappeared, but came back around eleven.

'You still here?' he exclaimed when he spotted me digging
mud out of my boots.

'Haven't been released yet.'

'I'm releasing you now.'

'This is my region, boss. I like to know what's going on.'

But he told me to go home, take a couple of days off. He
was right, of course. I'd been on the go for nearly thirty hours.
You lose your concentration after a while.

I grabbed some sandwiches from the van and drove back
to Satellite. My heart sank a little as I rolled into town. Still
no power. Everything was shrouded in semi-darkness. Semi-
darkness, I was beginning to realise, was par for the course
round here, even in the middle of the day. The tall trees came
right up to the edge of town, seemed to almost smother it.
Satellite would be a hell of a place to be if – when – a bushfire
hit. I'd been in a bushfire a couple of years before and didn't
want to be in one again. It had been worse than I'd imagined.

Satellite was a small community – maybe five hundred
people, as many again in the surrounding hills. It had been
a mining and timber town in its heyday, but the gold had
long since dried up and timber was going the same way. The
community's main sources of sustenance, as Lance succinctly
put it, were drug dealing, dole bludging and the old age pension.
There was a store, a school, a stockfeed, a cop shop – and a
pub. A trio of desperadoes were sitting in the gutter outside
the latter, beer cans in hand, faces bright with grog blossom.

I pushed on to Shady Grove Road. The rain had stopped but the bed was still soaked so I dragged my swag out from where I'd dumped it in the shed and curled up inside it.

When I woke it was dark outside. I checked my watch: six thirty in the evening. I'd slept all afternoon. I must have been more exhausted than I thought.

I wondered how the investigation was unfolding up at Wycliff Rise. The incident had left an unpleasant taste in my mouth, a stirring of anxiety in my bones. I realised what was worrying me: the level of organisation. This was no random incident. It had been carefully planned. Whoever was responsible had covered their tracks in a manner that suggested a ruthless intelligence at work. It was a miracle I'd spotted the anomalies I had, a fact that was doubtless due to the years I'd spent working with Warlpiri trackers in the Territory.

I considered phoning Dougherty, but rejected the idea, worried about the reception I'd receive.

Bugger it, I thought, it's my turf. I'm responsible for this town and its surrounds. If there's anything going on, I need to know about it.

\* \* \*

I drove my HiLux back to the crime scene at Wycliff. By the time I got there, though, the place was deserted. I got out and walked around but found nothing other than a few shreds of tape and a lot of trodden, sodden earth. Everybody had packed up and pissed off. I couldn't blame them. A clap of thunder crashed through the heavy mountain air and the rain returned with a vengeance. The sky was full of mad, mauling winds and flying ice.

I ran for the car and sat there for a moment, shivering and listening to hail bounce off the roof. I closed my eyes, breathed deeply and carried out a little self-examination. The results were not good. My fingernails were filthy and broken, my hands were numb, my stomach was growling like a camp dog. I felt shithouse, my general decrepitude magnified by hunger and fatigue. I thought about the condition and contents of my kitchen back in Satellite. A can or two of beans, a loaf of bread. Beans on toast. Hmmm, possibly cold beans on wet bread. I didn't know if the power was on yet, and the roof was a sieve.

New plan. I started up and headed for Ryan's Road, the quickest way to Windmark, the biggest local town. With a bit of luck, the pub kitchen would still be open. If not, I could nip up to the nearby Canticle Creek and do some freeloading off my father, who lived in a snug little house there.

The darkness flew by, its depth somehow intensified by the red glow from the tail-lights in my wake.

## CHAPTER 5

Idid my best to drive carefully, but it had been a long couple of days and I may have slipped into autopilot. The rain hammered unabated, visibility was shit. I was a minute down the road when I caught sight of a strange object – a rock? a fragment of wood? – in the middle of the bitumen. I slammed on the brakes, but it was too late. I was going to collect it.

Then, somehow, a shadowy, shrouded figure flew in from the left, snatched up whatever it was and landed in a heap on the far side of the road. I gasped. Had I hit it?

I grabbed my torch, jumped out and rushed back to the scene.

There was a man in a dripping oilskin jacket climbing to his feet, cradling something in his arms.

'Are you okay?' I called as I drew near.

He leaned forward and gently placed an oval object on the dirt verge. Four stumpy legs appeared, then a head, knobby and wobbling. I watched as the turtle tried to make sense of its surroundings, then trundled towards a roadside ditch.

The creature seemed calm enough, but somewhere deep inside it was doubtless thinking: *What the fuck just happened?*

The animal's eccentric saviour glanced in my direction, his face glistening. I shone the torchlight onto him. He might have been in his late thirties, with a scowl and an array of cuts and abrasions across his face.

The glisten was intermingled rainwater and blood.

'Sir,' I said, reaching for my phone. 'I'm calling an ambulance. Are you injured anywhere other than your face?'

I moved closer to him but he angled a suspicious glance at me.

'No need for an ambulance.'

'I'm a police officer,' I said. 'You've sustained at least one injury that I can see. I need to know if there's any more.'

'I'm fine,' he said, picking a hat off the ground and putting it on his head. He shook himself and an arc of water – or worse – whirled away. 'I'd be better if you'd drive more carefully. There are all sorts of creatures out on the road at night.'

'Sorry about that,' I said. 'At least let me look at you.'

He didn't say no, so I gave him another shot of torchlight. He held his head back while I examined him. There was a cut on his forehead that appeared to be the source of most of the blood. Other than that, he didn't seem too bad.

'Can I ask your name?' I asked.

'If I can ask yours.'

'I'm Jesse Redpath.'

'Nash.'

'Do you know where you are, Nash?'

'Standing on the side of Ryan's Road with a bossy woman manhandling my head.'

'I need you to tell me how you feel,' I pressed. 'Are you experiencing any pain? Dizziness? How's your neck? Your head? Your teeth?'

I saw his tongue move. 'Still there.'

I raised his arm and felt his pulse. It appeared to be beating normally.

'Strong hands,' he commented.

I held them up. 'Squeeze,' I said, then grunted when he did so. He had strong hands himself. And an interesting face when it wasn't scowling.

'You didn't actually hit me,' he explained. 'I just crashed into the ground with more force than I should have.'

I told him I'd be a lot happier if he'd let me call an ambulance, but he shook his head.

'Appreciate your concern, but I'm not going to hospital. Not for this. Can't leave the property just now. Lot of storm damage, fences wrecked, flooding down by the creek.'

'Where is the property?'

He swept out a hand.

'All round us. The house is just up the road.'

I felt something brush against my leg and jumped. It was a dog, a wet, weathered old border collie.

'Ah, there you are, boy,' said Nash, pushing a hand through his sodden fur and giving him a pat. 'This is Flinders.'

'What were you and Flinders doing,' I asked, 'out in the elements on a night like this?'

'Been repairing a dam wall that collapsed in the storm. Had to do it quick or I could be out of water come spring.'

'You don't have a car?'

'Went out in the tractor, but the creek rose so quickly I was cut off. I'll come back in the morning and get it out.'

I gave the matter some consideration.

'You seem okay,' I said. 'But I'm still not sure . . . Do you live alone?'

'No.'

'You've got family?'

'I've got Flinders,' he said. The dog looked up expectantly.

I couldn't leave this guy out here on his own. If he walked a hundred metres down the road and dropped dead, it would be on my head. When I offered him a lift, he hesitated briefly, then accepted. He climbed in beside me. The dog jumped onto the back seat and shook himself. He was a smelly old boy.

'So what were the police doing out here?' Nash asked as we drove.

'You haven't heard? We had an incident earlier on.'

'I've been busy all day. Storm caused a shitload of damage. What was the incident?'

'Feller killed by a falling tree.'

He frowned. 'Who was it?'

'Raph Cambric.'

'Jesus. Raph?' His jaw dropped, and he glanced through the rear window with a look that was difficult to read; it might have been alarm, might have been sympathy. He took a deep breath and rubbed his temples.

'You knew him?' I asked.

'Not well,' he said with the air of one who didn't know anybody well. 'But we're neighbours. My southern boundary is his northern one. We talk when there's a need.'

Jeez, cheery sort of neighbour this guy would be. I peered at the road, pushed some hair out of my eyes and stifled a yawn.

'Shift over?' he asked.

'Long bloody shift. Been going for days.'

He seemed to relax slightly, or maybe realised how rude he'd been and wanted to make amends. 'You've got a hungry look about you. I couldn't tempt you to a bowl of soup?'

I considered the offer. The pub kitchen could well be closed by now; other options were thin on the ground. I took a closer look at him. He had trustworthy eyes, from what I could see of them under the hat. They were dark and wide: outdoor eyes, accustomed to measuring and reflecting distances, looking for threats or opportunities.

'What sort of soup?'

'Flexible,' he replied.

I shrugged. Why not? If he did turn out to be a creep, chances were I could handle myself. But he didn't feel like a creep. A few hundred metres down the road he indicated a driveway. I turned into it and pulled up in front of a white weatherboard farmhouse nestled in a grove of cypress pines.

# CHAPTER 6

'What do you grow?' I asked as I stepped out of the HiLux and peered off into the darkness.

'Kangaroos and gum trees, mainly. A few apples to pay the bills. Sunflowers and corn, when the wombats don't squash 'em and the deer don't eat 'em.'

Nash climbed out and walked to the door. Flinders and I followed suit. The first thing that hit me as we entered the house was its warmth. This was the warmest I'd felt since I left the Territory.

'Wow,' I said. 'Central heating?'

'Insulation,' he said. 'Lots of insulation. And good stoves.'

Nash hung his jacket on a hook beside the door and his hat – a battered Will and Bear with a long, impressive feather in it – on a stand. He flicked a switch and the room lit up. It had a slow-combustion kitchen stove, a blackwood table, a blue couch and an open fireplace made of cobblestones and slate.

In the light of the room, he turned out to be a clear-cut, dark-haired man in a thick woollen jumper and Hard Yakka work pants, with a dirty face and scabs on the back of his hands. He was slim, broad-shouldered, with an air of the magnetic storm about him.

The dog slipped in behind us and flopped onto a bed near the back door. Nash went into the bathroom, came back a minute later, rubbed, scrubbed and lightly bandaged. He said I was welcome to use the bathroom myself, which I did.

He pulled a pot from the fridge, put it on the stove and revved the fire there. Then he did something similar to a stack of wood in the open fireplace. In seconds, it seemed, the room grew even warmer.

'My god, I wish I had a house that could do that,' I said. 'Mine feels like winter in Antarctica.'

'It's all in the design,' he said.

I stood with my back to the fire looking out over the house. It was a sturdy, no-nonsense dwelling, with soft yellow lights, bare walls and a red oriental rug on the floor.

'Did you design it yourself?' I asked.

'The heating system I did. It's hydronic, underfloor. Borrowed a few ideas, stole more. Power's out, but I've got solar panels and batteries. I like an open fire, but this one's really more for staring into than for warming the room.'

He threw on some more wood and gave me what may have been intended as a smile. Maybe I'd misjudged him. He was reserved but loosening up.

'I haven't seen you around,' he said.

'Only been in the area for a week or so.'

'Wild welcome. Where have you come from?'

'I've been down in Melbourne, doing a transition course at the Police Academy. Before that I spent seven years with the Northern Territory Police.'

He raised a brow, then noticed the soup was bubbling. He dished up a bowlful, serving it with grainy, buttered toast.

'This'll bring you back to life,' he said.

I took a spoonful.

'Have to run you over more often.'

Nash sat in a seat opposite the fire and stretched his legs. He seemed to somehow reflect the warmth of the room. As did the soup: it was thick and hot, with red lentils and chunky potatoes, green onions, broccoli. Surprisingly delicious.

When I'd finished I stood up and ran a hand across the mantelpiece, struck by its mass. Ironbark perhaps? It felt as smooth, hard and heavy as a river stone. There was a framed photo on the mantelpiece: a creek tumbling down a ferny gully with a fallen log forming a natural bridge across it.

'Where's this?' I asked.

He glanced at it. 'North-west of nowhere. Probably just a figment of my imagination.'

Wherever it was, he clearly wanted to keep it to himself. I took a closer look at the photo and noticed a large bird on the far side of the creek, partially camouflaged. It was perched on the centre pole of a rough wire shelter and staring at the camera with an imperious disdain.

'What's with the bird?' I asked.

'It's a wedgie. Name's Pauli.'

'Pauli?'

'Called him Poorly when I first met him – that being how he looked. He'd been whacked by a car then attacked by a fox. I was trying to make sure the fox didn't come back and finish the job.'

Nash's natural reserve was definitely fading. This was a subject with which he felt at home.

'Did you succeed?'

'Shot a couple of foxes nearby. Then I built that shelter over him – just bush posts and chicken wire, but it did the job. The bird had a fractured ulna. Eventually let me treat it. A fortnight later I was able to let him go.'

I was taken aback. 'You sat there watching him for two weeks?'

'More or less. I got to like it. Made a little hide nearby, kept an eye on him. After a while the bird trusted me enough to eat the strips of rabbit or rat I left on the post.'

'When was this?'

'Year or so ago.'

'And do you and Pauli keep in touch?'

'I get up there from time to time and he seems to recognise me. Returns to the feeding post when he sees me coming.'

Nash offered me a cup of tea, then served it up with a piece of pleasantly crusty fruitcake. I leaned back against the hearth and took off my jumper, asked more questions about the bird. I'd never met anybody who'd rescued an eagle before. He made me smile when he spoke about the bird's struggle to regain his independence, Pauli's anger and frustration at his situation. He made me laugh when he described the way Pauli used to exaggerate his injuries to elicit sympathy, sneak food, angrily attack him and then gently peck an apology. He almost brought a tear to my eye when he described the bird's eventual return to the skies: clumsy at first, then soaring as he found a thermal.

'They can see them, you know,' he said, eyebrows rising.

'See what?'

'Thermals. They spot bugs and leaves rising in them from miles away. Their vision stretches into the ultraviolet, so they can detect the UV light in a rabbit's urine from the sky. I find that difficult to comprehend.'

So did I, but what I could easily comprehend was how much the bird meant to him. And I wondered what had made Nash the man he was. The ring of isolation around him was almost palpable. The eagle, I suspected, was as close as he came to companionship. The house was a solitary man's abode. There were no family photos, no personal mementoes, no posters or artwork, no sign of a woman or child. Just that photo on the mantelpiece.

Maybe I was imposing upon his solitude? I finished the tea and stood up.

'I better be on my way,' I said. 'Thanks for the meal, Nash.'

As we moved out onto the darkened porch a bolt of mega-lightning flickered in the distance. Pitchforks of pure energy lit up the night. His eyes were like pools of oil with a glimmer of phosphorescence.

He gave me a sideways glance and I felt a connection. More than connection. I almost fell in love. Maybe it was just lust. Maybe it was curiosity. Or madness. Who knew? Whatever it was, it had me by the throat, it flowed between us like an electric current.

What the hell was in that glance? Some metaphysical force? A black hole into which I couldn't help but tumble.

'Will I see you again?' he asked.

'Sure. In fact . . .'

I leaned forward and kissed him on the mouth. Carpe diem and all that crap.

Nash raised a brow. 'That how you do things in the Territory?'

'Not normally.'

I kissed him again and he pulled my body into his. His chest felt hard, his jaw rough and pleasantly whiskery. His breath was redolent of paperbark and mint bush, his hair and hands of loam. I slipped my tongue into his mouth and took pleasure in what I found there.

I turned my head away and blinked. Hang on, woman, I said to myself. What are you doing? Hitting on a guy you just met. This isn't you. You barely even know his name. Nash. Was that a first name or a family one? You know nothing about him other than he builds warm houses and likes dogs, that he rescues eagles and would risk his own life to save that of a turtle.

The lightning flashed again. Maybe I absorbed something of its energy and speed, its electrostatic hunger for connection. Bugger it, I thought. Who cares? You haven't had a man in years. We're in the middle of nowhere. Nobody will know about it except him and you. If it leads to bigger things, great. If it doesn't, what have you lost? I held him close, ran my hands down his back, his dirty work pants and the contents therein. He did something similar to me. His hands were like worn saddle leather, hard and smooth, comforting. We dirty-danced each other back into the house and out of our respective clothing.

Somewhere in the ensuing tête-a-tit we ended up on the rug in front of the fire. I straddled him, guiding him into my body then rocking, triggering a wave that grew into a tsunami, a dazzling burst of light.

Time, self, all sense of the separation of body and mind, disintegrated under the wave.

But then the light changed, narrowing into ominous beams that swivelled around the room with a puzzling intensity and a chorus of noises that almost seemed human. Then they were definitely human, the men who owned them yelling in my ear. The dog barked and attacked somebody. The room was full of people.

Christ, I thought, what's going on? This can't be happening.

A gloved hand threw itself around my shoulders. I whipped it forward and slammed whoever it belonged to into the floor then jumped to my feet. Was this an ambush? Had I been set up?

Another blackened figure came at us. If it was an ambush, Nash wasn't in on it. He seized our latest assailant and wrestled him to the ground.

I kicked out at another attacker, connected, followed up with a double punch, likewise. Somebody grabbed me by the waist and dragged me down. How many of them were there?

Then discernible words emerged from the chaos.

'Armed police!'

I stopped.

Nash didn't. He jumped at the closest cop, swept him off his feet and threw him into a bundle of his mates.

'Nash,' I yelled. 'Settle down! They're police.'

He showed no sign of stopping, moving towards another of our assailants, so I tripped him and sent him sprawling.

'Sorry, Nash, but they're on our side.'

A cluster of coppers jumped onto him, held him down and wrangled him into a set of cuffs by torchlight.

They were in the process of doing the same to me when the room lit up and a heavy man in a black jacket and Kevlar vest was standing at the door with one hand on a light switch.

He stared at me, bug-eyed. I knew him well enough to know that he had a way with words, but right now most of those words had deserted him.

'Evening, Neville,' I said. 'Couldn't spare me a blanket, could you?'

'Jesus Christ,' he exclaimed.

'Let her go,' he said to his crew. 'She's one of us – worse luck.'

# CHAPTER 7

Detective Senior Sergeant Neville Wallace, from the Homicide Squad, dragged a coat from a hook near the door and passed it over to me.

'What the fuck are you doing here, Jesse?'

'Kind of asking the question and answering it at the same time there, Sarge. Whatever I'm doing, it's my own business. I was invited. What are you doing here?'

He chewed hard on a piece of gum and gazed around the room with an expression somewhere between astonishment and disgust. And maybe a trace of unease – whenever Wallace and I had interacted in the past, the results had been complicated at best.

'We came to arrest your . . . friend. Heard you'd started working in Satellite. Didn't expect to come across you in flagrante delicious.'

I looked at his team, half of whom were still wrestling with Nash while the other half were perving at me. I clapped my hands at them and the perverts looked away. The dog, obviously a gentle soul, was looking at the newcomers with interest and a friendly tongue, his earlier aggression forgotten.

'Couldn't you have just knocked?' I asked Wallace.

'Course we knocked,' he said. 'And identified ourselves. But with all the bloody yelling and groaning going on in here, we thought somebody was being murdered. This bugger does have a history of it. So in we came.'

I sniffed, gathered up my clothes and my dignity and went into the bathroom.

By the time I came out, the arresting officers had removed the cuffs and were holding Nash while he climbed into some clothes. One of them was reading him his rights, three others were gripping him tightly. I listened with dismay as they told him he was being arrested on suspicion of involvement in the murder of Raph Cambric. They led him out towards a waiting van. I noticed a pair of examiners entering the garage. Nash looked round, seemed lost, overwhelmed. I was a little confused myself. I turned to Wallace.

'He killed the guy on the tractor?'

'Looks that way.'

Nash was halfway down the path, bending to adjust his shoes by the light of the assembled cars.

'I presume,' I said, 'you've got something vaguely evidentiary to go with all this macho door-busting?'

'Aside from the fact that your boyfriend's a convicted killer whose prints were found on a chainsaw file at the Wycliff crime scene and who was heard making threats against the victim a few days ago, no, not much. We might have more by the time we've finished examining his house and car.'

Jesus. Nash was a convicted killer?

'Who did he kill?'

'Before Raph Cambric? Nash was a police officer. A detective constable who went rogue and killed a feller up in Horse Thief Creek.'

Horse Thief Creek? I'd heard the name. A small town, somewhere back up in the Windmarks.

'Who was the victim?'

'Name was Leon Glazier.'

'When was this?'

'Seven years ago. Nash has spent six of the years since then on a custodial supervision order. Banged up in the nuthouse.'

This was getting weirder by the minute. The feller I'd flung myself at was a killer, a cop and a psycho? He hadn't seemed like any of those things. He'd seemed kind of nice, if a little reserved. Was my bullshit detector that out of whack?

There was a shout from outside, then a chorus of frantic voices. Wallace spat out a curse and ran to the door. I followed, reaching the verandah in time to spot Nash racing for the bush on the far side of the drive. Wallace was yelling orders and waving his arms around like a windmill in a cyclone. One of his elite squad lay spreadeagled on the ground.

'Thorney!' yelled Wallace. 'Get off your arse and after him.'

Thorney, a heavy guy with an even heavier moustache, struggled to his feet and joined the pursuit.

Something about the ease with which Nash glided over the uneven ground had me doubting his pursuers' chances, and so it proved. He was limping, must have been injured in the struggle, but he had the home ground advantage and was outpacing his pursuers. Just before he disappeared into the darkness, he glanced back, caught my eye and mouthed what almost looked like a plea for understanding – with a dash of despair thrown in. Then he was gone.

Wallace was bellowing like a bull with a lance up its arse, but it was obvious that his efforts weren't going to affect the outcome. In another couple of minutes the pursuers came back, jumped into a car and raced away, siren and sergeant screaming.

Good luck, I thought.

# CHAPTER 8

Wallace came and stood alongside me as one of the cars came racing back; one of its occupants picked a helmet out of the mud and the vehicle hurtled off in the wrong direction.

'Hand-picked most of the useless bastards,' he said with an exasperated glare. 'They didn't even have him properly cuffed!'

He turned his attention towards me. 'What's your story, Jesse? Heard you were back in Victoria. How do you know this guy? You must have only been in the district for a few days. Did you meet him last time you were down?'

'No, just recently.'

He sniffed. 'How recently?'

I shuffled uncomfortably. 'Oh – quite.'

He peered at me. 'How'd you get to know him?'

I fumbled around, looking for an explanation.

'We met over a turtle.'

He blinked.

'A turtle?' he echoed. 'I can't even remember the last time I saw a turtle. Where was this turtle? At the zoo? A Chinese restaurant?'

'Just out there,' I said, nodding at the road out front. 'It was on the road. I almost ran it over. Nash made a determined effort to save it.'

'I see. Very Buddhist of him. And you thought you'd show your appreciation by fucking him. When was this?'

'Er, what's the time now?'

His brow arced as the pieces came together. 'Jesus.' An expression of bewilderment – rare in the Wallace world – moved through his features.

'We just got chatting,' I added in a pathetic attempt at explanation. 'He gave me a cup of tea and a piece of cake. One thing led to another.'

'I can imagine. I mean, a cup of tea and a piece of cake. What else could you do?' He shook his head. 'This is a side of you I haven't seen before. Anyway, you'd better get your story sorted. It'll come out at the trial.'

I swallowed. 'You sure there'll be a trial?'

'I'm not sure the sun's coming up tomorrow. But I'd rather be in my own shoes than Nash Rankin's.'

So that was his name. Nash Rankin. It suited him. Wallace turned away.

'I'm outta here,' he said. 'Places to go, manhunt to organise. Fuck-up to explain.'

He went into the garage and spoke to the forensic examiners, who were taking a particular interest in Nash's vehicle. A long fellow in short overalls and blue shoes rummaged under the tonneau cover and emerged with a chainsaw.

'What am I supposed to do?' I called to Wallace from the porch.

'Feed the fucking dog! In fact, keep it. And get out of the house. The techies'll be starting in there next.'

He climbed into a car and roared off into the night. I stood there for a minute or two, brooding. Then the cold bit into my exposed skin and drove me back inside. I looked around the room, wondering what my next move should be. I closed the fire gate, put away the food, replaced a few items that had been knocked over in the ruckus.

One of them was the photo from the mantelpiece.

I took another look at it, then, acting on an impulse I didn't understand, slipped it into my pocket.

I whistled Flinders, who fell in beside me. By the time we went outside, the rain had returned. I climbed aboard the car. The dog jumped up and sat on the seat beside me, did some serious reeking. The examiners were still at it in the garage. One of them adjusted his hood and walked towards the house.

I set out for Satellite, the sky pelting angry black missiles at the windscreen.

Half an hour later I was sitting in the car in front of my house, frowning. The power was still out. I gave my head an irritated shake. Unbelievable. Power supply down here was worse than it was back at Kulara, the Territory town I'd come from.

I dashed up the path and fumbled with the lock. The dog, accustomed to the opulent warmth of Nash's house, sniffed at the shack disdainfully, but followed me in and sat next to the cold stove. Any port in a storm. I gave him some bread and milk, which he ate begrudgingly, then he looked up at me, big brown eyes pleading.

'Sorry, feller, that's it. We'll find you something meaty in the morning. There's a rat in the roof if you're interested.'

I climbed into my pyjamas then into the swag.

I lay there for a minute or two, rubbing my body, trying to generate some warmth. After a while things settled down and I stared at the roof.

The move to Victoria was going well.

On the plus side, I'd had the best (well, only) fuck I'd had for a year or two, Wallace interruptus notwithstanding.

On the minus side – just about everything else. The sex had turned out to be with a crazy killer who was presumably just looking for inside information. As well as that, I'd been battered and bashed by coppers and rocks, I'd been half-drowned, snap frozen and smothered in mud. I'd been landed with a smelly hound.

And, worst of all, I'd made a fool of myself in a manner that would doubtless reach the ears of every police officer in the district. Hell, in the state. Great way to start a new job.

Things could be worse, I countered. At least I had a roof over my head.

A drop of iced water splash-landed on my nose.

I reached for my torch and looked up. The ceiling leak was spreading. There were half a dozen more that I could see.

Bugger it. I was past caring. I pulled the canvas cover over my head and closed my eyes.

# CHAPTER 9

When I woke up, the dawn was doing its best to break and the dog was at the door wanting outsies.

I let him out then stood on the verandah eating an apple and drinking icy water from a metal cup. There were frozen leaves on the path, icicles hanging from the gutters. Time to get a little heat happening. I rummaged through the shed for some dry wood. The few scraps I found were too big for the Coonara. I dumped them on the front lawn, then poked about the bush near the house and found some more that weren't too wet. A few minutes more and I had a bonfire blazing on the grass. I dug the billy out of the tray of my twin-cab, gathered together the wherewithal – tea, biscuits, jaffle iron, beans, borderline bread and mouldy cheese – and made some breakfast.

'Not bad,' I said as I demolished a cheese and bean jaffle. 'Not bad at all.'

I threw some wood onto the fire, some food at the dog and reflected again upon the events of the night before.

I should have felt pleased with myself. I'd helped catch a killer. Sort of maybe.

But there was something wrong – and it wasn't just that I'd been caught red-cheeked. It was the look on Nash's face as he was disappearing into the bush.

That fleeting glance spoke to me of a lot of things: despair, confusion, a desperation to avoid the lock-up.

What it didn't speak of was guilt. It wasn't the look of a killer. I've come across a few of those in my time, and none of them looked like that.

Was he a loner? Sure. Damaged? Probably. Unstable? Certainly – he'd spent years in a mental health facility. But that turtle . . . Not to mention the soup, the warmth, the eagle, the dog. You can tell a lot about a person from their dog. Most things, actually. It's no wonder Donald Trump never wanted one.

Flinders, reading my mind, snuggled up to my feet and started gnawing his paws. I gave him a good rub, which he seemed to appreciate. We were still sorting out each other's tricks and expectations.

My thoughts turned to his absent owner. There was a bit of life left in my phone, so I did some searching. There it was, in an old copy of *The Age*. The story was just as Wallace had said. Seven years ago a serving police officer, DC Nash Rankin, had been found unfit to stand trial for the murder of one Leon Glazier. A psychiatrist described him as psychotic, with limited prospects of long-term recovery. He'd been committed to a forensic mental health hospital and had apparently spent the years since then in the acute care network.

I would have been a newly minted constable in the Territory at the time. If I'd heard about it, I mustn't have paid it much attention. I searched some more, but the press coverage was minimal. It was as if everybody involved had wanted to keep a lid on it, maybe because there was a sense that the perpetrator had already suffered enough in his life. There was a fleeting reference to the fact that he'd had a traumatic childhood in an extreme cult.

I put the phone down. The psychiatric diagnosis was maybe the most surprising aspect of the story. As a frontline officer in a small town, I'd had a lot to do with members of the public – and the occasional colleague – in different stages of psychological distress. Nash was clearly a recluse, but I'd seen nothing to suggest a history of psychosis.

A blue Isuzu ute with red P plates came cruising down the road. Looking for someone? The vehicle pulled up in front of my house, then reversed into the drive.

The tray was loaded with fresh-cut firewood.

The driver's door opened and my young friend Possum Kelly jumped out and strode towards me, the usual bounce in her step, the usual smile breaking out across her face. She was wearing jeans, jacket and polished Blundstone boots, her tangled black hair flowing out from under a green beanie.

'Hey, Poss,' I said. 'When'd you get your Ps?' She'd turned eighteen a couple of weeks ago.

'Yesterday.'

'Amazing,' I said, embracing her enthusiastically. 'And the car?'

'Same. Been saving for years.'

'My god, you're all grown up.'

Flinders loped up to her, tail wagging, tongue lolling, keen to join the party. Here we go, I thought. A meeting of two like minds.

'You got a dog!' Possum beamed, giving him a dodgy kiss on the lips.

'Strictly short-term, believe me. No room for pets round here.'

The passenger's door opened and Possum's mother, Lucy Takada, appeared. She gestured at the load.

'House-warming present,' she said. 'Literally.'

'Thanks,' I said, giving her a hug. 'Did you cut it yourself?'

'It's some of the stuff that blew down in the storm,' Possum explained. 'Plus a bit of dry stuff from home.'

'I presume your brigade was flat out?'

'Worked our little arses off,' she replied. 'Even the big ones,' she added, doubtless thinking about the rear view of some of her colleagues.

Possum had joined the Canticle Creek Volunteer Fire Brigade the year before and was now a qualified firefighter – not that she'd seen much in the way of fires yet. It had been ice, wind and water damage for the most part, but the CFA was nothing if not multi-tasking.

'Can I offer you some breakfast?'

A few minutes later we were sitting on logs round the fire, hoeing into jaffles and flicking cheesy crusts at the dog, who snatched them from the air with a startling proficiency, like a chameleon zapping flies. Lucy's contribution to the repast was a scrumptious apple and walnut cake.

'How's my old man getting on?' I asked her as I ate.

'Happy when he's working, restless when he's not.'

'Like always.'

My father, Ben Redpath, had been living in a cottage on the family's property in Canticle Creek for a year now, helping rebuild a house that had been destroyed by a bushfire. And painting, of course. A landscape artist, he'd been assiduously capturing the changing face of the bush as it recovered from the blaze. He'd lived in the Northern Territory for decades, was well known for his paintings of rocks and minerals, but the year before he'd had a stroke. When he came out of hospital he accepted Lucy and Sam's invitation to move into the cottage. He seemed to be flourishing in his new environment. I suspected his newfound enthusiasm for the lush Victorian Highlands had added years to his life. He loved the Territory, but it was hard work, all that heat, booze and questionable company, for a man of his years.

'We heard there was some poor fellow killed by a falling tree up at Wycliff,' Lucy said.

'And that it wasn't an accident,' Possum threw in. She always knew the score. 'Did you get caught up in that?'

Where do I begin? I wondered. At least the question suggested they hadn't yet heard about my own inglorious involvement in the debacle.

'There was an arrest,' I said. 'Didn't last long. The arrestee was last seen heading for the hills with the Keystone Cops on his tail.'

'The which cops?' asked Possum.

'Never mind.'

'And which hills?'

'Whatever you call the hills north-east of Wycliff.'

Mother and daughter glanced at each other.

'Maybe up around the Wiregrass Valley?' suggested Possum.

'I imagine so,' replied her mother.

Their local knowledge was infinitely greater than mine. I went inside and found a topographical map and the photo I'd filched from Nash's mantelpiece, then asked if they recognised the location.

'Hard to say for sure,' said Lucy, taking a close look at the photo. 'But from the look of those rough tree ferns – Cyathea, aren't they, Poss?'

Possum agreed. She was in the first year of a degree in Environmental Science and Botany at Melbourne and knew her flora.

Then she spotted the eagle in the background. 'That's weird,' she said, pointing it out to her mum. 'The way it's looking at the camera so placidly.'

I explained that the bird had learned to trust the photographer, who'd helped it recover from an injury. Lucy said that added weight to her view that the picture was taken in the Wiregrass Valley. There was a sizeable community of raptors up there – she'd seen goshawks, peregrine falcons and wedge-tailed eagles. She speculated that they sought shelter in the Wiregrass when their natural habitats were impacted by human activity, most commonly logging and farming – or fire. The birds of prey were well equipped to survive the conflagrations that regularly afflicted the area, taking to the skies when many a smaller species was overwhelmed.

I unrolled the map and found the Wiregrass, a remote off-shoot of the Windmark Valley, some twenty kays to the north-east.

'Looks rough,' I said, struck by the jagged ridges and spurs, the tightness of the contour lines, the limited signs of human activity.

'I've been hiking up there,' said Lucy. 'It's old mining country, about as rough as you get round here. And dangerous. Lots of abandoned shafts and rockfalls. Is that where you reckon your escapee was headed?'

I shrugged. 'Could be swanning around the Gold Coast by now. All I know is that he ran into the bush, heading north – but he did have this photo on his mantelpiece and he seemed fond of the bird.'

Possum glanced at me suspiciously, clearly wondering how close a look I'd had at this wanted man. She was always encouraging me to spice up my love-life, but I doubted whether a homicidal maniac was what she had in mind. I changed the topic, reluctant to say much more about my social intercourse with the man in question.

Possum and Lucy stayed for another hour. We unloaded the wood, then I gave them the grand tour of the estate. That took about thirty seconds. It was composed of a simple cabin on an acre of weeds that was fighting a losing battle against the encroaching tide of wattle and dogwood. Monstrous manna gums towered over everything.

Lucy cast a critical eye over the faded fascia boards and window frames, her arms folded.

'Could do with a good coat of paint,' she said.

'Could do with a good wrecking ball,' Possum added.

When we went inside, Lucy ran a hand across the bed and scowled up at the ceiling.

'You'll want to get that drip fixed,' she said. 'I'm sure Sam would be happy to do it when he gets a moment.' Her partner, Sam Kelly, was a builder when he wasn't being captain of the Canticle Creek Fire Brigade.

'I'd appreciate that,' I said. 'If he comes across my body in a block of ice, tell him to donate it to polar science.'

Eventually they made to leave. Lucy headed for the Isuzu, but Possum lingered for a moment and looked me in the eye.

'Not your usual effervescent self,' she said.

'It's just your bloody Victorian weather,' I said, though even as I spoke I was wondering why I bothered. There was no defence against Possum Kelly when something piqued her curiosity. She kept her ear so close to the ground it probably had footrot. And she had cop connections; her friend Karly's father was the sergeant-in-charge at Windmark. She'd know about my ill-fated tryst within minutes of getting back to Canticle Creek – if she didn't already. She kissed me goodbye, told me it was good to have me back in town. As they departed, I noticed a light come on at Rocco and Meg's across the road. There was one at my place too. Power was back on.

When they'd gone I decided to split some wood, something I do when the shit's in the vicinity of the fan. Some of it I left by the front door, most of it I stacked in the shed.

Half an hour later the shed was full and I was sweating. The dog came over and had a sniff around. I gave him a pat, then stopped, took a deep breath and looked out over my domain. Light, warmth, water, friends, a faithful canine companion: what more could you ask for?

# CHAPTER 10

I left the house early the next morning, before things had a chance to thaw out. I packed food, maps, a machete, camping gear – and the photo.

I stood for a moment on the front step. The clouds were low and mean, the muddy rubble on the road was piled high and the edges were crumbling but at least the rain had eased off. Rocco Teller, my neighbour, was up early, digging out the gutters in his drive. I gave him a wave.

As I boarded the HiLux, I whistled up Flinders, who leapt into the passenger's seat with a proprietary air.

'Don't get too comfortable,' I warned him. 'This is just a temporary gig.'

He gave me a big, sloppy grin and wagged his tail.

Getting to the Wiregrass didn't take long – maybe half an hour – but exploring the valley itself proved to be a much trickier exercise. It was wild, remote, inhospitable. The river at its base – the headwaters of the Windmark, according to the map – wound in and out of a series of steep land formations, sometimes within sight of the road, more often not. There were gullies every few hundred metres, most of them with water of some description – creeks and streams, a river, a trickle – running along their floors. As Lucy had warned, it was old mining country, riddled with crumbly shafts and quicksilver trails.

I was concerned to spot at least three or four police cars cruising around the district. There was even a helicopter making an ominous appearance overhead. Wallace was a cunning bastard. Was he thinking along the same lines I was? He may have spotted the photo on the mantelpiece, or heard about the raptor angle from somebody else. One thing I knew for sure: he'd be pissed off at having a prisoner escape on his watch and would do everything in his power to remedy the situation.

I mounted at least a dozen little expeditions during the course of the day, trying to match the places I came across with the one in the photo. I made my way down serpentine trails and watercourses, hacked a passage into thick scrub, startled wallabies and lyrebirds, stirred up stroppy pigs and kangaroos. I had to jump out of the way once when a beefy sambar deer came pounding down the track.

None of the locations were quite right. They didn't have that feel. They were too steep, too shady, too dense, too open. The main thing I gained was an appreciation of just how rugged the country was up in the Wiregrass Valley. A step in the wrong direction and you could vanish into a tangle of woolly wattle or cat's claw, never to be seen again. Thick vines twisted and clung to the messmates and mountain ash, giving the impression that they'd mummify you if you gave them half a chance.

It was getting on for dusk and I was thinking of chucking it in for the day when I drove over a narrow wooden bridge and the dog gave a low bark and put his paws up on the window. I glanced to my left and spotted what could have been a hollow, partially grown over, in the bush.

I pulled over and made a close inspection. Flinders made a closer one. He disappeared, then I heard him crashing about the undergrowth and barking, saw pigeons flutter up in alarm, heard a cockatoo screech. I searched in that direction. There was a track there. It was overgrown, long out of use, but a definite trail, running alongside a spidery creek that flowed down to the Windmark River. The odd chopped mossy log or carved step suggested the trail had been hacked out of the bush by some long-gone tree-feller or gold miner.

There was an arrangement of acacia branches over the entrance that didn't look natural. I dragged them back and walked onto the track. The dog returned and tagged along beside me, seemed to think he was showing me round the neighbourhood. A hundred metres in I paused to absorb the scene. The country was definitely opening up. You could almost call the area in front of me a clearing. There were black polished boulders, fallen logs, patches of wallaby and wire grass. The ground was carpeted with moss and rotting wood, with fallen fronds, fungi, lichen.

I compared it to the photograph.

There were neither eagles nor shelters to be seen, but this looked very much like the location in the photo. Maybe the same place seen from a different angle? Or somewhere very near. The vegetation, colour and light were almost identical.

What now? Beam a Bat-Signal into the sky?

I thought about Nash, the dark emotion in his eyes, the ease with which he evaded his captors and disappeared into the bush. His affinity with that high-flying eagle.

I'd never catch a man like that on my own, not unless he wanted me to.

The winter mist was growing heavier in the gullies. The sun had vanished and there was a bitter edge to the air. Time to decide. Stay or go? Mental coin toss. Stay. Never in doubt, really. I went back to the car, cleared a path and drove into the clearing. I didn't want any of those police patrols to spot my vehicle.

A quick scavenge through the bush produced what I hoped would be enough wood to see us through the night. As it grew dark I made a small fire, then unrolled my swag, put the billy on and watched it come to the boil. The night came stealing in swiftly, the last vestiges of the day almost scuttling from the air.

A brush bronzewing uttered its mournful call. I couldn't see it, but I'd learned to recognise that creepy, crepuscular hoot. I pulled some sausages out of the esky, chopped up a few tomatoes and onions, added some corn and fried the lot. If the smell of that didn't bring Nash out of the bush, nothing would.

I ate a hefty portion of the sausage dish, drank some tea and finished the meal with a piece of Lucy's apple and walnut cake.

I pulled a rug around my shoulders and listened to the sounds of the bush at night: crickets and curlews, possums, frogs, a big bass owl in the distance. Sugar gliders swooped and chattered about the upper branches.

I tightened the rug, threw more wood onto the fire.

It took maybe an hour before I detected it: the slight change in the susurration of the night that told me I wasn't alone.

Flinders pricked up his ears and gave a slight whimper. Then he slunk off into the bush.

There was a rustle in the undergrowth, then I heard the dog panting and bouncing about. He emitted an excited yelp. I sat there for a few minutes then spoke in the direction from whence the sounds had come.

'There's food in the frypan, Nash.'

Silence.

'This isn't a trap. I'm on your side.'

There was a noise off to my left. Then another, further away. Was he leaving? No, he was moving back towards the road, scoping the area, making sure I was alone.

Another delay. More noises off, then Nash stepped out of the darkness and walked towards me. I noticed he was favouring his left leg, limping heavily. His upper body was wrapped in a blanket but his footwear – a pair of ancient sneakers – looked completely inadequate for winter in the Wiregrass. The past couple of nights had been bitterly cold and he wouldn't have risked a fire.

He followed my gaze.

'Best I could do,' he said. 'Hello Jesse.'

'Hey, Nash. What's with the limp?'

'Soggies mangled me on the way out.' The soggies were the special operations officers he'd escaped from.

We locked eyes; just for a moment, but that was enough to re-establish a connection. He came and stood on the far side of the fire, the reflected light glowing on his brow. What had looked like a blanket from a distance was a piece of tarpaulin. Then I recognised the hat he was wearing – the one with the feather.

'You've been back to the house!' I said.

'Snuck back in later that night.'

'Weren't our friends from Special Ops watching?'

'There was a car in the drive, but they were busy with their Big Macs and I know the secret entrances. I'm attached to this feather. Had it since I was a kid. About as close as you get to a lucky charm in a life like mine.'

'Shithouse job it's done so far.'

He smiled. 'Maybe, but imagine if I hadn't had it . . .'

He swayed momentarily, and shivered. The lines on his face seemed to have grown deeper and dirtier, become more engrained. They were like scars. He coughed, a deep, hacking rasp that rattled his thin frame and bent him over.

'Not your usual bouncy self,' I said, thinking about how he'd made his house a haven of comfort and warmth, how much he must have been missing it. 'Have you eaten?'

'Bits and pieces.'

I gestured at the frypan. He came and sat on the other side of the fire. I handed him a plate then dished up the rest of the meal. He ate it voraciously, barely pausing for breath. When he'd finished I lay back in the swag and raised a corner.

'Come in and warm yourself.'

His eyes continued to flit suspiciously. He was a cautious character, reluctant to put himself into a vulnerable position. Then again, given what I knew of his history, he had good reason to be.

'Offer doesn't stand all night,' I said.

He came round the fire and climbed in behind me.

'Bloody hell,' I yelped. 'You're freezing. Stick to your own side, thanks.'

He did his best to oblige then asked how I'd found him.

'That photo of the eagle on your mantelpiece. The hide's somewhere near here, isn't it?'

'A few minutes along this track.'

He went quiet, then put an arm around my waist. I felt his tension ease slightly.

'What's going on, Nash?'

He took a long time to answer.

'Buggered if I know. I feel like a pig being swallowed by a python.'

'They're saying you killed your neighbour.'

'I didn't.'

'Doesn't look that way. Unless you've got a doppelganger out there with your fingerprints.'

'They found my prints at the crime scene?'

'On a chainsaw file.'

An exasperated sigh emerged from the darkness.

'I was set up. Either that or I'm going insane.'

I decided not to go down that avenue. It would keep. But he chose to add more.

'I presume by now you know my history?'

'Some.'

'That first incident – Leon Glazier, the one they put me away for – I'd been in a bad way for weeks before it happened: confused, blacking out, experiencing hallucinations. No idea why. People were giving me weird looks. I knew I wasn't seeing things the way everybody else was. I even began to wonder if I had killed Leon, though I had no recollection of it. But this time, it's different – it just doesn't make sense. I've been clear-headed for months, years. Ever since I got out of Ravenhall. I thought I'd been rational – by my standards, anyway.'

'You seemed pretty rational to me. That's why I'm here. Do you know anybody who'd want to frame you?'

I heard his tongue click.

'Lots of candidates. I grew up in a world you had to fight your way out of, full of holy rollers and junkies.'

'That's a weird combination.'

'They were a weird group, an evangelical church. People called them the Revelators.'

'What the hell is a Revelator?'

'Somebody who reveals a hidden truth.'

'Sounds hard to argue with – truth being a little open to interpretation. And was there a head Revelator with his fingers in the till? Or the pants? There usually seems to be.'

'His name was John Patmos, though it was his wife who wore the pants. Guin, her name was.'

I may have detected a slight tremor running through his body.

'Where did the junkies come into it?'

'The church ran a drug rehab program in the Windmarks. My mother came to it as a patient, ended up working for them. I escaped as soon as I was old enough, but god knows what kind of baggage I'm carrying. Or what enemies I made. Then I was a police officer, which was almost as bad. You pick up a lot of ticks and leeches along the way. People knew me, my reputation and rap sheet, living up at Wycliff on my own. Maybe somebody figured I was a convenient patsy.'

His voice faded. Anonymous creatures shuffled through distant leaves.

'Come back in with me,' I said. 'If you're innocent, I'll prove it.'

'I don't know that I'd survive another stretch inside. There are people in there who'd cut your throat just because you were a cop.'

'So what's the plan? Sneak around the mountains living on thistles and creek water?'

'For a while, yes. I can't go back inside. It does things to my head. I had enough of that as a child.'

'The holy rollers or the junkies?'

'Both.'

I let that go. Hopefully there'd be plenty of opportunities to learn more.

'There were a lot of police vehicles cruising around out there today,' I said. 'Does anybody else know you're up here in the Wiregrass?'

He hesitated. 'Not that I know of.'

'You seem a little uncertain.'

'At first light this morning I was making my way down a back road, had this feeling that somebody was looking at me. Soon afterwards I heard a shot. Figured it was hunters. You get 'em round these parts.'

'It probably was,' I said, though the comment added to my concerns. A hunter could have heard there was a man on the run, spotted Nash and passed word on to the authorities.

We lay there quietly. Despite the fact that he was a wanted man, I liked the warmth of his breath upon my hair, the touch of his mouth against my neck. I liked the firelight, the starlight, the ghostly smoke. I liked his rough-hewn personality.

He drifted off to sleep with his arms around me.

# CHAPTER 11

I took a moment to figure out where I was and who the body snuggled up against me belonged to. The air was damp, rich with the smell of rotting wood and winter fungi. My breath came out in icy clouds. A blue-black ant struggled through the mud before my eyes, dragging a lump of something many times its own size. You couldn't help but admire its persistence.

I needed to move, to feel the blood circulating through my body, but I was reluctant to expose myself to what looked like a freezing morning. I gave it a few minutes then crept out of the swag and into my pants and boots.

Nash was still breathing heavily, snatching at air in sharp, shallow gasps. I let him rest. He looked like he needed it.

What had he said last night? The hide was further along this track. I followed it for maybe a hundred metres, Flinders tagging along beside me. He obviously knew the way. There were spider webs across the track, dew drops and morning light glimmering on their quadrilaterals. The country had been burned by a bushfire in recent years. The tree trunks were scorched and some of the ground was still coated with a layer of ash. There were even traces of vitreous material, where the sand had been blasted into glass. But new green shoots were surging out of the ashes and hunting for light. Fire was clearly an essential element in the natural cycle up here.

I came across a tiny wooden structure – an overgrown cubbyhouse, really – in a tree overlooking a gully. I climbed up into it. There was a sleeping bag in one corner and a food stash – a packet of Vita Brits and a tin of peaches – in another. There was a set of climbing equipment hanging off a peg on the wall. I examined the gear with interest. It was designed for ascending trees: there were ropes and spurs, a harness and a throw line. I was familiar with most of it. I'd done a high-angle rescue course in the Territory, even assisted with the odd real-life emergency.

I crawled to the front of the structure and looked out through an opening there. Fifty metres away, across the creek, was the improvised wood and wire shelter I'd seen in the photo. Beyond that was a magnificent mountain ash, maybe sixty metres in height, with a scattering of acacias around its base.

Halfway up the ash was a huge nest, a couple of metres wide, bristling with sticks. No sign of its occupant, but somehow that made the eagle's presence more powerful. You could feel it. The nest held a commanding view, both of the valley below, with its mazy mists and waterways, and of the streaky winter blue above.

Some words came to mind. 'That stormy white but seems a concentration of the sky . . .' Dad had muttered the line once as we watched a flock of swans lift off from a waterhole in the outback. He said it was from a poem by the Irish poet, Yeats, describing a flock of swans rising from a lake in Galway.

This was a different bird on another continent, but the meaning and significance were the same. Nash's eagle was a concentration of this place, the focus of its buffeting winds and thermals, the centre point of its angles of attack, its lines of sight. It was the kind of totem a desperate man would cling to. A desperate, decent man; he hadn't turned to drink, or drugs or violence to cope with his troubles, as so many had before him. He'd turned to the natural world. That was what had drawn Nash to the Wiregrass Valley, to that lofty creature: he'd seen them as a symbol of the tranquillity he was searching for.

But how fragile was his paradise? How long would he last up here? He wasn't looking good. He was shivering and limping, short of breath, feverish. I thought about the police parties I suspected were combing the hills and valley. Wallace wasn't stupid. If I could find Nash, so could he. There were already choppers on the prowl. How long till they brought in the dogs or drones? How long would Nash be able to evade them? If his pursuers did apprehend him, his flight would go against him, maybe lengthen his sentence or prejudice a jury.

'Morning Jess.'

I looked down. It was Nash. He'd abandoned the tarp and wrapped himself in one of the blankets from my swag, but he still looked like he'd been through the wringer.

I swung down and gave him as warm a hug as I could muster. I felt him tremble against my shoulder, then he turned his gaze to the valley before us.

'Any sign of Pauli?' His voice had gone raspy overnight. He was definitely coming down with something.

'Nope.'

'He'll be out there somewhere,' he assured me.

An unseen helicopter churned through the clouds to the south-east. I caught Nash's eye, struck by the flicker of anxiety as he glanced up in the direction of the sound.

I stepped towards him and touched his brow.

'You're feverish,' I said.

'It's nothing. Been coming on for a couple of days. Picked up a cold when I was out working in the storm.'

I looked him in the eye.

'Nash, are you sure you've thought this through? It's only been a couple of days, and you're already looking wrecked. You need help. A doctor, maybe a spell in hospital. And then there's Neville Wallace,' I added. 'He's got his flaws, but when he gets his teeth into something, he doesn't let go. He'll track you down: choppers, dogs, drones, whatever it takes.'

He stepped back and emitted a sigh.

'Maybe it would be best,' I continued, 'if you came down to Windmark with me now? I'll do what I can to help: get a lawyer, speak up for you. And I'll try to find out who set you up.'

He turned away, folded his arms and contemplated the trees before us. Not the mountain ash, I realised. He was looking at a smaller wattle alongside it.

'Last night,' he said, 'I may have sounded a little bitter about my childhood. But it wasn't all bad. Near the front gate of the property was a beautiful golden wattle. When things got rough, Shiloh and I . . .'

'Shiloh?'

'My big sister. We'd climb into the upper branches and sit there for hours. We even made a little tree house of sorts, if you can call a few planks hammered together a house. The magpies would perch and sing around us and we'd join in with them. The choughs would cluster and rustle in the upper branches at night. Sometimes the eagles would soar overhead. That was where I found this eagle feather.' He touched his hat. 'It was our solace, that tree, those birds. Even today, as an adult, when things are going bad, I can still find it, buried in my memory.'

He coughed heavily, then raised himself up. 'Okay,' he said. 'I'll go down to Windmark, hand myself in to Vince Tehlich. He's always been decent.'

He took my hand and kissed it.

'I couldn't have done this before I met you, Jesse. It's a relief, knowing there's someone on my side. That hasn't happened much in my life.'

He turned and hobbled towards the camp.

I felt the resolve hardening in my heart. There was no way I could let him rot in gaol. And the only way to prevent that was to find out what really happened, both at Wycliff Rise and, years earlier, at Horse Thief Creek.

# CHAPTER 12

I insisted he sit and rest while I packed up the camp. In a few minutes we were on our way, Flinders dribbling on the back seat. We drove slowly down the mountain, the roads mostly quiet, the mist slipping eerily by. A school bus emerged from a side road, chugged along in front of us. The kids spotted the dog and waved; the dog waved back – sort of. Nash pulled the blanket tight and rested his head against the window. He may have nodded off. But then, a few kays out of Windmark, I spotted a police roadblock ahead. I could see at least three officers in tactical gear manning it. There were several cars in attendance, one of them parked among the trees on the left-hand side of the road.

I muttered a curse and reached for my badge.

'I'll tell 'em we're coming in,' I said, hoping there'd be somebody there I knew. They waved the bus through, then gestured at us to turn in.

I wound down the window. A constable I didn't recognise walked towards me.

'Morning,' I said, raising my badge. 'I'm in the—'

That was as far as I got. The passenger's door flew open and a fourth officer appeared. He must have been in the car under the trees. He had his weapon drawn and his fist raised. He grabbed Nash by the throat then dragged him out of the vehicle and slammed him to the ground, all the while yelling at him to keep his arms behind his back.

'He's coming in of his own accord.'

A couple more officers ran round to that side of the car, added to the pile on. In seconds they had Nash trussed up and tightly secured, his ankles shackled, his wrists cuffed.

The first cop looked up at me with a sneer. It was Thorney, the member of Wallace's crew who'd been upended during Nash's escape. He wasn't taking any chances this time. Nash tried to find his feet, but Thorney put a knee into his back.

'Lay off him,' I called, but they gave no indication they'd heard me. Thorney landed another couple of blows with such force that I realised he was still smarting over Nash's escape that first night. He was raising his fist for another serve when a figure stepped in, seized the fist, dragged its owner aside and pushed him away.

'That'll do,' he growled.

It was Wallace. He must have been the other occupant of the car under the trees.

'How's it going, Nash?' he asked.

Nash looked like he'd just been hit by a road train. I ran to his side.

'He was coming down to turn himself in,' I yelled at Neville. 'Would have by now if your thugs hadn't attacked him. He's not well – he needs a doctor, not a shellacking.'

Neville carried out a cursory examination, agreed with me and called an ambulance. They were there in a few minutes, racing out from the Windmark station. They decided Nash was suffering from a fever and hypothermia then announced they were taking him into the Windmark Hospital. Wallace told a couple of his crew to accompany them. 'Not you,' he barked at Thorney when he moved to join them. 'I want him to get there in one piece.'

'What am I supposed to do?' asked the officer.

'Take a hike. While you're at it, you might think about what you'll say to the investigators.'

'What investigators?'

'The ones who'll be asking you why you couldn't arrest an injured prisoner without assaulting him.'

I noticed Nash's hat on the ground. 'Wait a second,' I called to the paramedics as they guided the stretcher through the rear doors. I scooped up the hat and put it on his head. Even as I did so, I wondered if this was a wise move. They'd only take it off him when he got to the remand centre. That might make things worse. He caught my eye and gave me a grim smile as they closed the door.

The ambulance pulled away, a police car on its tail. Thorney followed on foot, not without a hostile glance in my direction. I returned the favour. Wallace noticed.

'What are you smirking about?' he asked. 'You're not exactly in the clear yourself.'

'What have I done?'

'You mean apart from sleeping with a fugitive and being caught driving him round the countryside? I dunno, but we'll think of something. How did you manage to track him down when the search parties and choppers couldn't?'

'I used my brain!' I snapped. 'And his dog.'

Flinders, on cue, jumped down from the back seat and joined us. We watched the various emergency vehicles leave the scene, then Wallace pulled a Big Mac out of his coat pocket. He took a bite and joined me at the bull-bar, chewing nosily, apparently planning to eat and interrogate simultaneously.

'This isn't right,' I said.

'I agree.' He examined the burger. 'Tastes like Styrofoam.'

'I mean what's happening here.'

'Have to agree with you there. Aiding and abetting a fugitive, conduct unbecoming. What have you got to say for yourself?'

'I was trying to resolve the situation – peacefully.'

'So you say.'

'Don't be a smart-arse, Nev. There's something odd about this case.'

He threw the remnants of the meal into his mouth, swallowed it whole and smacked his lips.

'Seems pretty straightforward to me: we got motive, means, evidence – much of it thanks to you. Anyway' – he shrugged – 'outta my hands now. We'll see what the prosecutor says.'

He began to walk back towards his car.

'Neville,' I said.

He kept going.

'We've been here before!' I yelled.

That stopped him. He paused, turned, caught my eye.

He knew what I was referring to. The last time we'd worked together on an investigation, I'd solved it, he hadn't. For the first time since this episode began, a hint of something other than smug self-confidence flitted across his face.

'You think you know this bloke?' he snapped.

I gave him a surly shrug.

'You know him from an hour or two in the sack,' Wallace continued. 'I know him from the job, the way I know any crook. That's what I do.'

'Sounds like a boast, Nev. Maybe it's clouding your judgement.'

He came closer and turned up the volume. 'I've studied the files, examined the evidence, talked to his old colleagues. The evidence for the Wycliff incident is piling up and it's all going one way. There were traces of wood from the tree that killed Raph Cambric on a chainsaw in Nash's car. We found his file and boot prints at the scene. The victim's brother reported Nash had been arguing with Raph the day before. And then there was that first killing, Leon Glazier up at Horse Thief Creek. I wasn't on the case, but I know the people who were. I looked at it carefully. They had witnesses, motive, means, evidence. Why Nash did it, I can't say, but I've very little doubt that he did.'

I began to reply, but he rode roughshod over me.

'You been doing this as long as I have, you get a nose for these things.'

I shivered, maybe from the cold, maybe from being on the receiving end of a Wallace diatribe. I'd been there before.

'All I want is the truth,' I said. 'And I don't feel like I'm getting it. Not all of it, anyway. What more can you tell me about Nash's background?'

He ran a hand across his jaw, then snorted and leaned back against the bull-bar. The dog sidled over and rested his head on Wallace's foot. That was one smart dog. The senior sergeant gave him a perfunctory pat and calmed down a little.

'They say he was a decent copper,' he said. 'Conscientious. Maybe too conscientious. Started to get obsessed with the job. Especially crimes against minors. Seven years ago, he had a complete breakdown.'

'What did that involve?'

'Delusions, confusion. Voices in his head, from what I heard. Not my department. All I know is that he went overboard on a couple of arrests, assaulted one of his colleagues. And in the end he killed someone.'

'Yeah, you told me. Feller named Leon Glazier. Can you give me any more about that?'

He glanced at the road, down which Thorney was sullenly trudging.

'Seems the two of them knew each other as kids. Grew up as members of some kooky church.'

Interesting. So Glazier had been a member of the Revelators as well.

'Nash came across Glazier's name as a person of interest in a child sexual images ring,' Wallace continued. 'That must have got his blood up. He went to Horse Thief Creek to have it out with Glazier, and the having it out ended up with Glazier getting a bullet in the head.'

I rested my chin upon my hand and gave all that a moment's consideration. It sounded reasonable, but so does a lot of bullshit at first glance. Somebody could still be framing Nash. I thought about the Wycliff murder. It wouldn't be that hard:

steal something from his shed, plant material from the crime scene on his property. There'd been no direct witnesses that I'd heard of yet.

Despite Wallace's pugnacity, he was still an astute judge of character. I asked if he'd known Nash personally. Maybe the feelings I had for Nash were blinding me to the dark side of his personality.

'Our paths crossed a couple of times,' he replied. 'He was Criminal Investigations in Greendale, I was Homicide in the city. I certainly knew about him after he went down. Everybody did. I spoke to the lead investigator at the time. The case was rock solid. Crazy was the only defence he had left.'

I tried to explain my doubts but found the task harder than I expected. What it boiled down to was little more than gut instinct – not much of a counterweight against the mountain of evidence Prosecutions must have had to see a police officer banged up for six years.

To give him due credit, Wallace did hear me out. But in the end, he shook his head and stood straight.

'Justice,' he said as he walked away. 'You know me, Jess. He'll get it.'

Justice? I thought. That's a convoluted concept if ever I met one.

As Wallace drew close to his car a wood pigeon shot up from the grass at his feet and startled him with its whirring wings. He tottered briefly then fell into the mud. He glared at the vanishing bird, then looked at his dirty shoes, his muddy elbows and knees, the anger building. The natural world was an alien environment to Wallace. He'd be more at home if his enemies came at him bearing broken bottles and butterfly knives, covered in scars and blood.

He swung back to me.

'Christ, Jesse,' he snarled. 'Nothing's ever straightforward with you around, is it?'

'That's just nature's way of keeping you honest, Nev.'

He shook his head in a manner that set his jowls wobbling and departed.

# CHAPTER 13

What now? If Nash had experienced some kind of psychotic episode and killed his neighbour, there wasn't much I could do except offer him support.

But if he was being set up, two possible explanations arose.

One – he was the fall guy and the intended victim was Raph Cambric. Or two: Nash himself was the target. But did that make sense? Why would you go to all the trouble of murdering one man just to frame another? That led to a third possibility: somebody was trying to get rid of the pair of them.

If Nash had been set up, was the incident connected to his former profession? How had he put it? As a cop, you pick up a few ticks and leeches along the way.

Or did it spring from childhood? He'd described it as something he'd had to fight his way out of, fraught with holy rollers and junkies. Wallace had also made mention of the 'kooky church'.

Whatever the truth, I needed help. And there was only one place I could think of to get it. I was a newcomer down here, but I had made a few friends on previous visits. I drove towards Windmark, hoping that news of the latest instalment of my self-immolating career hadn't come through yet.

I put the foot down.

* * *

'God no,' Vince Tehlich groaned when I came in the front door of the Windmark Police Station. The senior sergeant dropped his head into his hands. 'Tell me it isn't true,' he pleaded.

I hadn't put the foot down far enough.

I don't know why I bothered. Gossip flies through the police force faster than a sunray through space.

There were a couple of constables in the room. 'Hey, Jesse,' said the first, Jace Gradey, whom I knew and liked. 'Katie Page,' said the second, who apparently knew me, if only by reputation. A probationary, she was young, blonde and staring at me with what might almost have been awe, which was a worry.

Vince certainly wasn't staring at me in awe. He raised his head and twisted his face into something resembling a wet rag.

'You've only been here five minutes . . .'

I stepped closer to him.

'You going to let me give my side?'

'I just spoke to Nev Wallace. You've been caught shagging a wanted man, then chauffeuring him round the countryside. There couldn't be a *your side.*'

I did my best to explain. I told him how I'd bumped into Nash out on Ryan's Road and struck up a friendship. If Vince's eyes rolled back any further they'd be looking at the bottom of his brain. When I told him I'd gone up to the Wiregrass to persuade Nash to turn himself in, he frowned.

'And you didn't think to run this by your colleagues?'

'It was my day off. I just went up there to have a look around.'

He still didn't appear convinced.

'Come on, Vince,' I said. 'You know me better than that. I've got my faults, but bullshitting isn't one of them.'

He sighed, swallowed, looked around the room. Pale blue walls, wanted posters and windows heavy with wintery sky looked back at him. The wind outside was picking up. A woman on the footpath was fighting a losing battle with an umbrella. The child at her side was fighting a losing battle with his temper.

'My office,' he said. 'Katie, Jace,' he said to the constables, who were pretending to work while keeping an ear on proceedings. 'Make yourselves scarce.'

They did so, grabbing their jackets and heading for the door.

'Area familiarisation?' asked Katie.

'Bakery,' replied Jace.

'And word of this doesn't get out of the building,' Vince called after them.

Jace gave a mock salute and left.

'Getting cheeky, the boy,' I said.

'About time,' Vince muttered as we entered his office. He took a chair and asked what I was after.

'I'm looking for information on Nash Rankin.'

'Why are you asking me? From what I've heard, you already know more about him than I ever will.'

'I got the official version from Neville Wallace, but it just doesn't feel right,' I said. 'You know how I tackle a problem like this.'

'How's that?'

'By instinct.'

He leaned back in his chair and turned his eyes to the ceiling.

'Yeah, yeah,' he admitted. 'You're like Doc Watson flatpicking a lead break.' An appreciation of country was one of the few things Vince and I had in common, though we were on opposite sides of the Venn diagram. He was traditional, I was alt. I liked Sierra Ferrell, he wanted some of whatever she was smoking. We overlapped somewhere out where Johnny Cash ran into Slim Dusty.

During the complicated silence that followed I licked my lips. He noticed.

'You had breakfast?'

I shook my head.

'Come and I'll introduce you to our latest recruit.'

I followed him out to the kitchen, where he showed me a deadly little DeLonghi coffee machine.

'Wow – where'd you score this?' I asked.

'Lost and found,' he replied. 'Somebody lost it, we found it.'

'Somebody?'

'Nobody we need worry about. And Katie made some ace cookies.'

He gave me one from the jar: it was fat, rich, full of oats and nuts and dark, drizzled chocolate. I took an extra one. 'For the road,' I explained.

In a few minutes Vince and I were sitting on the back verandah talking about the Wycliff incident and watching a flock of lorikeets squabble over god knows what in the overhanging she-oaks. One of the cheeky buggers was eyeing off my cookie. I told it where to go.

'So you really think there's a possibility that Nash was framed?' Vince asked. 'Not just once, but twice? I know we get a lot of lightning up here in the hills, but in all my years here I've never seen it strike twice in the same place.'

'It's just an idea, but I can't abandon it until I know it's wrong.'

I took a sip. The coffee was good. Smooth and powerful, a heavy-hitter.

'So,' I continued. 'Shoot.'

And shoot he did. He said he'd known Nash Rankin, though not well, before his downfall. He'd had a reputation as a good copper. Maybe too good – too intense, too eager to get results, unwilling to compromise or bargain. He'd started out in uniform at the Greendale Police Station, transferred to the Criminal Investigation Unit when his appetite for arrests became obvious. He was never one of the good old boys, down boozing in the bar or sneaking freebies at the brothel. And he wasn't a thug, or on the take, or meth. Nor was he your community cop, out talking to schools and service clubs, coaching the local footy team. He was a loner. Intense, moody, guarded. But he made arrests – lots of them. And they led to convictions. His main weapons were persistence, intelligence and a relentless hunger for justice. He played a role – albeit a minor one – in several major investigations. His star was on the rise. The bosses liked him.

It was a year or two into his promotion to the CIU that things started to come unstuck. His personality changed, cracks appeared, went seismic. He began getting agitated by small things, worried that individuals unknown and unseen were out to get him. He blacked out once in the station, assaulted a colleague, went over the top bringing in a couple of crooks.

'Who was the colleague he assaulted?' I asked.

'His partner – and immediate superior, Dan Starcevic. Starcy. The senior sergeant in Greendale. He didn't want to press charges, insisted that it had been a misunderstanding. They'd been close, and he knew Nash was unwell.'

'Is this Starcy still around?'

'He's retired now. Spends most of his time in a shack out bush. And before you say it, no, he doesn't need any grief from the likes of you.'

Dan Starcevic. I made a mental note to track him down. Even if he'd left the force, he could be a useful source of information. He was the first person I'd heard described as being 'close' to Nash.

'What about these crooks Nash assaulted?'

'I was busy running my own show, but memory tells me one was a drunk phys. ed. teacher arrested for grooming and abusing young girls. Nash said the guy swung a punch and he was defending himself. But a complaint was made, went on his record.'

My first reaction was to think, well done, Nash, but I put that aside.

'Then there was the domestic up in Hawksborough. Feller bashed his wife, fractured her skull. Nash roughed him up bringing him in, the guy tried to get him charged.'

So far, I thought, Nash was travelling well.

'He was already under investigation for those incidents, then he went and killed this bloke up in Horse Thief Creek.'

He gave me the story, much of which I'd already gleaned from Wallace. Apparently, Nash found evidence that his old friend Leon Glazier was involved in a child pornography circle, went up there to confront him. There was an altercation and the guy ended up with a bullet in the head.

'What are the chances Nash was set up?'

'Slim to non-existent. There was a witness.'

'Nev mentioned that. Who was it?'

'Old bloke next door. Saw Nash rock up to Glazier's place and bang on the door. He heard a yell, then a scuffle and a shot. When everything went quiet, the neighbour went over and looked in the window. Found Nash semi-conscious on the floor, Glazier dead – by Nash's gun.'

'So this neighbour didn't see the actual shooting?'

'Heard it, and he had no reason to lie. He was just a harmless old codger. Hommies aren't stupid, Jess. I'd leave it be if I were you. Gonna give yourself a world of hurt.'

I finished my coffee and stood up. 'How's Karly going?' I asked.

'Doing well,' he said. 'Loving the work.' His daughter, Karly Tehlich, was in her second year of a building apprenticeship with Sam Kelly, Possum's father. The question had an ulterior motive and both of us knew it; I was reminding Vince of his debts. A couple of years earlier I'd saved Karly's life.

Whatever its ethics, the question did the trick.

Vince told me he'd look through Nash's case records, have a word with a few old friends in low places, see what he could dig up. That was as good as I could have expected. Vince had worked in the area for twenty years, knew where the meta-phorical bodies were buried, had buried a few of them himself. He'd have a multitude of contacts, snitches, debts to collect, favours owed.

I lingered for a last hint of the coffee's rich black aroma, stole another cookie for the road – it was a very long road, I explained to Vince – and drove down to the Windmark Hospital.

# CHAPTER 14

I presumed Nash would still be in emergency, but they'd already admitted him. His room wasn't hard to find: it was the one with a police officer standing guard. A handsome fellow, he was engaging in lively banter with a female nurse who appeared to be enjoying the company.

I identified myself to them both. The officer's name was Auty. He was a local, not one of Wallace's unsavoury crew. Vince had phoned to tell him I was coming. I glanced through the open door. Nash was in bed, shackled to the frame, semi-recumbent. His mouth was open, his eyes were closed, but his face, with its bruises and wounds, appeared strangely luminous in the morning light.

'How's he going?' I asked the nurse.

'He's really been in the wars,' she replied. 'Hypothermia, a virus. Throw in a sprained ankle and an array of cuts and abrasions and you get the idea.'

'And when he's released?' I asked Auty.

'He'll be taken straight down to the remand centre.'

I asked if I could have a minute or two alone with him, and they agreed. From what she'd seen of him, the nurse told me, he was a restless patient but there was nothing to suggest he was a risk of either fight or flight. He'd been given analgesic drugs, which would have sedated him. I went into the room and closed the door behind me.

His eyes opened as I stepped towards him.

I kissed him lightly.

'Jess,' he rasped.

'How you doing?'

'Been worse.'

'The nurse just gave me a rundown of your condition. Good thing you came in to civilisation.'

His reply was little more than a whisper. 'Ask me how civilised it is in a few days. What do we do now?'

I shrugged. 'First we get you back onto your feet. I don't suppose you've got a lawyer?'

'I'm suspicious of people who've got their own lawyer.'

'Fair enough, but we better find one. Hopefully you'll get bail. Then we do our best to figure out what actually happened to Raph Cambric.'

He stared out the window with a hungry look in his eyes, as if he were searching for answers, or maybe a raptor to carry him off to some desert isle.

'Why are you doing all this, Jess?' he asked. 'I imagine it's putting your career at risk.'

'My career's always at risk.'

I took his hand and kissed it.

He still looked like a condemned man waiting for an overdue axe.

'This may seem a little odd to somebody with a history like yours,' I said. 'Maybe it doesn't fit in with the future you've imagined for yourself – but I like you, Nash. You better get used to it.'

He offered a wary smile in response, but seemed to be waiting for the catch. He was still waiting for it half an hour later, casting suspicious glances at the door and windows when I gave him a goodbye kiss and left.

## CHAPTER 15

I'd just pulled up in front of the house when I received a call from Inspector Dougherty telling me a complaint had been made about my performance and I was suspended – on full pay, thank god – pending the results of a Professional Standards investigation. The investigator would be in touch within a week. Lance Cunningham would run the station in my absence.

'You'll get written confirmation of all this shortly,' he added. 'And you'll be contacted by a member of the Police Association, who'll support you at the hearing if you want them to. But I should say up front that one of the conditions of the suspension is that you're forbidden from having contact with any of the witnesses in the case – and that includes Nash Rankin.'

That was a bugger, but hardly surprising. They didn't want us swapping notes or concocting alibis.

'Where's your weapon?' asked Dougherty.

'Still in the safe at the station.' I hadn't got round to organising one for my home yet. Given the structural soundness of the home – not to mention my career – I probably never would.

'Make sure it stays there. And Redpath . . .'

'Yes?'

'That night of the storm, you did well.' There was a rustle of static. 'If there's a way out of this mess, we'll find it for you.'

I was touched. 'Thanks for that, boss.'

When he'd signed off I sat there staring at the glowering sky.

Suspended. That hadn't taken long. It wasn't exactly a surprise, but it hit me harder than I expected. The authority of this job gets into your bones. You become accustomed to it: the respect, the camaraderie, even the abuse – they bond you to your colleagues. And, when you were on a task like the one I was on now, it was bloody useful. I felt like Nash's eagle, a creature of the sky laid low with a broken wing.

If Nash had killed Raph Cambric, he was a brilliant actor. Or was he? I tried to recall his reaction when I first mentioned his neighbour's death that night in the car. Had it really been news to him? He'd been alarmed, wary of something. Was that the natural reaction to a local tragedy or had he suspected there was a power of trouble coming his way and worried that I was its harbinger? Impossible to say. It had been rainy and dark, he'd been wearing a hat and jacket, his face was streaked with blood.

He was a peculiar character, Nash. And yet, despite my reservations, I'd felt attracted to him. Powerfully attracted. Still did. God knows why. What dangerous instinct drew me towards such a man? He was trouble. Troubled. You could smell it. But there was more to him than that. I sensed, deep in his core, a mulish refusal to compromise his values that amounted, almost, to courage.

I rang Vince Tehlich and told him about my suspension, asked if he could let Nash know that I wouldn't be able to have any direct contact until the situation was resolved. While I had him, I asked Vince if he could recommend a lawyer and told him I'd be happy to pay. He said he had a few ideas, that he'd get back to me.

When I entered the house the bloody rat was on the bench. He made a break for it, scuttling across the floor and up into the roof. Then he sat among the beams grinning at me. I wondered if I was giving him due credit. Maybe he was some kind of native animal, a phascogale or a bush rat? I took a closer look at him: long, black tail, prominent ears, disgusting little incisors. Nope, he was your regular rodent. *Rattus rattus*, the black rat, habitué of gutters and slums all over the world, purveyor of death and disease, host of parasites and slayer of native wildlife.

I wasn't accustomed to rats. We hadn't had them in the Territory, though the cockroaches there would have given them a run for their money. I decided to give my lodger a name: Rupert. Figured it might make him a little less obnoxious. I had another go at him with the boot. I missed, but at least he vanished from the rafters and I didn't have to look at his ugly face for a while.

I prowled around the house, restless, hungry, drumming a little tattoo on the walls. Flinders was smart enough to steer clear. I wanted to do something, but what? I had no authority. Anything untoward on my part and the suspension could escalate into dismissal.

I needed a distraction. A book? Fuck that. Something physical. I looked around, then up, my attention caught by an enormous Tasmania-shaped stain on the ceiling. 'You'll do,' I muttered.

I grabbed a few tools, went outside, scrambled up onto the roof via a convenient tree and spent an hour crawling around on my hands and knees hammering loose sheets of iron down and battering the battens, improvising seals with strips of material, tightening the roof screws. As I worked I grew increasingly conscious of the enormous messmates and manna gums towering over me. I paused to gaze up at them, found myself hoping I wasn't at home when one of them decided to come down. Who'd build a house here? Crazy. Who'd rent one? Me. Just as crazy.

When I'd smashed and screwed everything that was due for a smashing or a screw I climbed back down, went inside and surveyed my handiwork.

A trickle of black water ran onto my face.

Bloody hell. I punched the wall. The house was like Hal, in *2001*: out to get me.

I took a deep breath. This wasn't working. I couldn't just sit here and wait for the law to do its thing. That might never happen. There was room for only one event in my mind right now: the Wycliff incident and Nash Rankin's role in it.

I considered my options but could only come up with one, and it was the cliché to end all clichés: return to the scene of the crime. No doubt my superiors would hit the roof if they found out, but what did I have to lose? Just the roof, which was a wreck already. Or my career – likewise. I grabbed the keys. Flinders responded reluctantly to my whistle, but eventually dragged his weary old bones out to the car and up into the passenger's seat. He looked like he was missing his boss. So was I. We made a despondent duo as we drove up to the place where Raph Cambric had met his end.

## CHAPTER 16

Flinders and I spent half an hour poking around the site, trying to discover if it had anything more to tell us.

It didn't, but as I stood at the northern end of the scene, I heard a diesel chugging and caught sight of a tractor working its way across a paddock at the end of the lane.

The brigade captain Danny Clarion had told me Raph's family had a farm down there. There'd been mention of a father and a brother.

I drove down to the paddock, pulled up alongside the fence and gave what I hoped was a friendly wave to the driver. He responded. Inspector Dougherty had warned me off talking to witnesses, but as far as I knew, this guy wasn't a witness.

The machine drew to a halt and the operator climbed down from the cab. He walked across the paddock with that slow *where's-the-horse?* gait men tend to settle into in the bush. He was in his thirties, wearing an oilskin jacket, a blue beanie and a look of mild suspicion.

The suspicion diminished when I introduced myself, giving him a quick glance at my ID and nothing about my current employment status.

He pulled a blade of grass out of the ground, chewed it slowly and asked how he could help me. He'd obviously grown accustomed to talking to cops over the past few days.

His name was Jared, and yes, he was Raph's brother. He lived with his wife, Marcie, and a mob of kids in the main house on the property. He seemed puzzled that I was out here asking more questions about the incident.

'We heard you'd arrested Nash Rankin for it.'

'We have, but there's a few things we need to clarify. You reported that he and your brother were arguing the day before . . .'

Jared said he hadn't heard the argument himself, but Raph had mentioned it to him that evening, said Nash had been really pissed off. I asked what the dispute was about.

'Rats,' he replied.

'Rats?'

'Vermin. We had to poison them. Nash thought we were putting the wildlife at risk.'

No surprise there. I'd seen enough of my own little housemate to know the rats were up and about. And it fitted with what I'd seen of Nash's predilections. If he'd jump in front of a speeding car to save a turtle, god knows what he'd do if one of his precious raptors was under threat. I'd heard numerous stories over the years of birds of prey dying after ingesting poisoned rodents.

'And were you putting them at risk?'

He shrugged. 'Maybe, but we had other priorities – like putting food on the table. There's a plague of rats round here, eating us out of house and home. Wreaking havoc in the orchard, getting into the sheds, even the house. One ate my fucking boots last month.'

'Jesus – tough rats.'

'Well, it had a serious go at 'em, anyway. We have been trying other solutions – clearing, fumigation, monitoring nests, shooting the bloody things. Believe it or not, most of us on the land don't actually want to kill native wildlife. Raph said all that to Nash, but apparently he wasn't listening. All he was thinking about was his birds. Very admirable, sure – but to kill a bloke over it? He must have been off his rocker. And not for the first time, from what I heard.'

I couldn't argue with that. Nash was definitely an eccentric. Maybe he had gone over the edge. But I needed to explore other options.

'You can't think of anybody else who might have had a grudge against your brother?'

Jared shook his head. 'I suppose I would say this, but Raph was a decent bloke. Kept to himself, but he had no enemies that I know of. The odd punch-up on the footy field, maybe, but that was years ago.'

'Nothing more recent?'

He contemplated the distant treetops. 'We have had a couple of run-ins with hunters, but they seemed okay when we talked to them. Couple of kids on trail bikes. I certainly don't know anybody with cause to carry out a crime like this.'

A Subaru drove into the yard around the house. A horde of kids jumped out and swarmed in every direction. Some of them tore out handfuls of grass and ran down to the horse yard, where a trio of horses vied for their attention and grass. A woman stepped out of the driver's seat and glanced at us.

Jared gave her a quick wave as she wrangled the youngsters into the house.

'Curriculum day,' he explained. 'Marcie took 'em to the flicks in town.'

'Raph had no family of his own?'

'Nope.'

'Girlfriend? Boyfriend?'

There was a momentary hesitation.

'Like I said, he kept to himself . . .'

That hesitation needed following up on.

'You don't sound as sure about that as you've been about a few other things.'

He pulled the beanie off and scrunched it with his thumbs, kicked at the dirt with a boot heel.

'I don't know if he was in a relationship or not – certainly there was nobody he introduced us to . . . but there might have been a spring in his step a while back.'

I gave him a puzzled look, pressed for more information.

'Marcie noticed it,' he explained. 'He started sprucing himself up – shaving every day, brushing his hair, taking long walks when he didn't used to.'

Walks? That suggested somebody local.

'Then, a few weeks ago, things took a nosedive. He disappeared for a week, wouldn't say where he'd been. But he seemed distracted and down, on edge.'

'How long did he stay like that?'

Jared gazed at the sky. His eyes followed a flock of cockatoos that angled overhead and settled in the treetops. 'Probably up until the time he died. That might have been why he was in an argumentative mood when Nash had a go at him about the rats. Normally they got along okay. Marcie figured, if Raph had been seeing someone, maybe it hadn't worked out.'

This Marcie sounded like she'd be worth talking to. Not right now, though. She had her hands full. Down at the yard the horses shuffled and stamped their hooves, hungry for more. The kids had come back out of the house and were off the leash. The more spring-heeled of them were climbing onto fence posts and leaping onto the horses' backs. A big old draughthorse stood there patiently absorbing the assault and munching on a biscuit of hay.

'Those were Raph's horses,' Jared said, following my gaze. 'He raised 'em to be gentle.'

We chatted for a few more minutes, but when I noticed him glance back at the tractor I left him to it and returned to my car. What had I learned? Not much. Raph Cambric was a private man, had kept to himself, worked hard. Him and every other farmer around here. He might have been having an affair, but if he had, it had ended weeks ago. He'd been brooding over it.

I drove around to the immediate neighbours to see if they could add anything to the picture of Raph I was building in my mind, but nobody had much new to offer. Everybody knew the Cambrics, everybody liked Raph – as far as I could tell. They weren't a very expressive lot round here. Mostly they were laconic farmers – beef and dairy, a couple of orchards and wineries – with muddy boots and weatherwise demeanours. A few of them mentioned that they'd played footy or gone to school with Raph. Several people commented on the fact that he was gifted with animals, could settle a restless horse with a touch of the hand, calm an aggressive dog with a stern look. That tallied with what Jared told me. A lot of them employed Raph to shoe or trim their horses, said he did good work.

The only one who had anything original to offer was a hard-nosed character in a weathered leather jacket who pulled up on a Triumph Classic at a cottage on Goodwin's Lane. He introduced himself as Stefan Heller, didn't appear to fit the local farmer mould. He rented the place, worked as a welder in Windmark and had flashing, blue eyes, slag-burned hands and a blunt manner. He said he'd had a couple of conversations with Raph about bikes. I hadn't seen Raph as a bikie, but Stefan said he rode a Kwacker 5000 he'd restored himself. The pair had talked about making a daytrip into the hills. That never happened, but Stefan said a few months ago he'd spotted Raph racing along the river trail with a woman riding pillion.

I asked if he recognised the woman but he shook his head. It was getting on for dark and they were fanging it. He hadn't lived round here for long, didn't know all the locals.

'Could you describe her?'

'Long, dark hair, slim, maybe in her late thirties. She wasn't wearing a helmet.' He glanced down to where I assumed the river lay. 'One thing struck me though: she was laughing.'

## CHAPTER 17

I was still in bed the next morning when I heard a car pull up in front of the house. I made it to the door just as Vince Tehlich reached the top of the stairs. He had a cardboard box in his hands. I offered him a cup of tea, but he said that this was a lightning visit. Being spotted in my company was more than his job was worth.

He did come in for a moment, though, putting the box on the table and looking around the room.

'Nice place,' he said wryly.

'Just a roof over the head,' I said. 'Mostly,' I added as a drop of water splashed onto his face.

'I got a lawyer for Nash,' he said, handing over a card.

Her name was Betty Stagg. He assured me she was good, the best in the district. 'I oughta know,' he said. 'She's given me a few thrashings over the years. Pain in the arse when you're trying to get a conviction, but if I were in trouble, she's the one I'd want on my side. I've already spoken to her – and to Nash. She's meeting him this afternoon.'

'At the hospital?'

'The remand centre. He's being transferred as we speak.'

He gestured at the box, which was full of manila folders.

'Everything I could dredge up from Nash Rankin's last few years in the job.'

'Wow.'

He told me he'd focused upon Nash's time with the Criminal Investigation Unit. That was where he'd been working at the time of his fall from grace. No guarantees, but if he'd made any enemies bitter enough to hold a grudge over so many years, I'd likely catch a glimpse of them in these folders.

'Thanks for that,' I said. And I meant it.

Vince extracted from me an oath that I'd never let on where the documents had come from. He warned me to be careful with them, to conceal them when I was leaving the property or expecting company. Then he left me to it. I cleared and dried a space on the kitchen table then settled down to peruse the collection, jotting down anything of interest in an A4 note-book. I was only ten minutes into the task when I paused to send him a text: 'thanks mate brilliant work'.

He must have called in every favour and collected every debt he was ever owed. He'd gone over every significant case in which Nash had been involved, done a load of cutting and pasting, attached extra information – press clippings, records of evidence and witness statements, photographs – wherever it seemed relevant.

I pushed on, fascinated. The notes displayed the full range of criminal activities you'd expect from a police district in which the outer suburbs collided with the country. From the brick-venereal wastelands of Greendale itself, there were B and E's, sexual assaults, child abuse, vehicle theft, domestics, and drug busts. As you moved further out bush, the offences put on their elastic-sided boots and followed suit: there was stock and machinery theft, the interception of drug couriers and the busting of labs and illicit tobacco operations. No mention of mafia or outlaw motorcycle gangs, for which the lord be praised. They were stratospheres above my pay grade.

From time to time I was moved to come across personal glimpses of Nash himself – a signature here, a handwritten note there. There were several reports in which his efforts had been singled out for commendation by his superiors. He'd clearly been a hard-working member. Of particular interest were those occasions when he'd brought his local knowledge to bear on major cases: there were several homicide investigations, the busting of a child pornography ring and some significant fraud cases in which he'd liaised with the Feds.

I stood up and gazed out the window. I was having trouble linking the diligent operator evident in the reports with the troubled individual I'd encountered on Ryan's Road. Something had really gone awry.

There was so much information here, almost too much. How was I going to hone the word-hoard before me into a manageable document? I had to think strategically or I'd drown in a mass of detail.

Perhaps I'd best begin by looking at those cases in which I could detect unanswered questions or evidence of incomplete investigation. This was far from foolproof, of course. If whatever happened to Nash had been related to the job, it could have sprung from the briefest of interactions: some late-night loon he'd booked driving home from the pub, a vengeful puppy-breeder he'd reported to the RSPCA. There was no shortage of disturbed people out there.

But did that really make sense? I thought about the deliberation that had gone into the Wycliff incident, if it was a set-up: killing one man and framing another, all on a conveniently wild, windy night. Surely this was no random wacko?

With a bit of luck and a lot of elbow grease, the files should give me an insight into Nash's activities at the Greendale Criminal Investigation Unit. And maybe even into his mind. Hopefully, I could find some anomalies in these old cases, a clue that had been overlooked, a suspect still out and about, a fault or fracture line that would steer me towards the truth.

I thought about my old mate from the Territory, Danny Jakamarra, and his approach to tracking. The trick, he'd explained to me once, was to look for anything out of place. Danny's eyesight was worse than mine. But so well did he know the desert, the relationship of its cadences and inclines, he could see where things ought to be, not just where they were.

That was the level of insight I needed, but before I could achieve that, I had to get to know the lay of the local land, and the files before me were an integral part of that process. I returned to the table and got back to work, skim-reading and scribbling anything of interest into my notebook.

Time slipped by. When I checked my watch, I was surprised to find it was late morning. I'd been at it for four hours. My body felt stiff and sluggish, my eyes were seeing floaters. I stood up and stretched my back and neck. I did a set of taekwondo drills, then went for a run around the twenty-minute circuit that curved out into the state forest around my house. Running through the bush and its multitudinous smells – the good and the bad, from the native bees' nest to the fresh deer shit – seemed to clear the decks of my mind, make room for new ideas. Flinders plodded along behind, occasionally taking time out to examine a cubic wombat turd on a log or an echidna with its head in the roots of a muddy stump. He was still getting to know the locals, but he was clearly a bush boy.

As I ran past the neighbours' place, I saw a white van pull out from a shed at the back of the property and turn onto the road. I caught a glimpse of a woman at the wheel. The elusive egg lady, off on her rounds. She gave a curt wave as she drove past, but I could barely make her out through the tinted windows.

I sprinted the last few hundred metres home then sat on the front steps, panting and patting the dog when he eventually joined me. Maybe that was the way to cope with this freezing Victorian weather: all I had to do was keep running for the next three months.

I thought about the pile of paperwork waiting inside.

You have to start somewhere, some inner voice whispered. Choose the top three.

I went inside, resumed my seat and skimmed through the notebook.

Three cases floated to the top of the slush. I figured they must have had reasons of their own for doing so. I turned to the middle of the notebook and wrote them out, giving each a double page and a spontaneous nickname. I often do this when I'm tackling an overwhelming challenge. Seeing the facts laid out on a generous spread of paper with a new name and a host of arrows and signs somehow breathes life into them, highlights connections, gives them a structure that makes it easier to see if something's missing.

I read the three case names out loud.

*The Jeremiah thug.*

*The fat financial advisor.*

*The creepy priest.*

In each case, Nash Rankin had played a peripheral but crucial role which could have roused the wrath of some unknown co-offender still lurking in the shadows.

I read over the three cases and wrote out anything that caught my eye: unanswered questions or inconsistencies, suspects still on the loose, lines of enquiry that might have been overlooked.

I glanced at my watch. Almost one. I felt like company, even if it was only company observed from a distance. Being in the proximity of other people often helps coax things out of my brain. There was a light rain falling, but that was okay: light rain was about as good as it got round here.

I dropped the notebook into my backpack, then remembered Vince's admonition about keeping the files under wraps, so I hid them under a pile of clothes in the chest of drawers. Flinders knew something was afoot and was happy to join me as I strode into the town of Satellite.

## CHAPTER 18

The walk was mainly puddles and mud for the first five hundred metres, then patchy concrete as we hit the scruffy outer houses of the town. If I do get thrown out of the force, I decided, maybe I'll set up a lawn-mowing business – there was plenty to be done. Then again, would anybody have the money to pay me?

Flinders hesitated when we approached the swinging doors of the pub. There was a perky, porky terrier reclining by the entrance, its balls dangling like a set of second-hand punching bags. The two dogs sniffed each other out but didn't find much to get excited about so they plonked down and contemplated life from the ageing canine perspective.

There were maybe a dozen people in there, which seemed a decent crowd for a winter's day in Satellite. I wasn't the only one in need of a little warmth and nourishment. A trio of old-timers were in the back bar lapping up their first for the day and shouting at each other, whether in anger or deafness was hard to say. The general air was one of beef, beer and flying phlegm. A raucous roadworks crew were hacking at their steaks, a rubber-eyed drunk was trying without success to chat up a couple of checkout chicks from the store. A fellow in a moth-eaten lumber jacket and an unravelling beanie bit into a bun with broken teeth.

But the fire was crackling, the jukebox was pumping out Cold Chisel – 'Flame Trees' – and Annie J was firing up the espresso machine. I'd only been in here a couple of times, but that was enough for her to get to know my habits.

'Spotted you coming down the path with a thirsty look on your face,' she explained as she poured my coffee. 'Are we eating or just drinking?'

'Both,' I said.

Libby Walker, Annie's partner in life as well as business, appeared in the doorway of the kitchen. 'Hey, Jess,' she called, then she spotted my companion. 'Dog yours?'

'No, he's just a boarder,' I assured her. 'He is a border collie, after all.'

She smiled and flicked a couple of bones at the animals. 'The usual?'

'Yes thanks.' The past couple of visits I'd had the beer-battered fish and it was bloody good. Apparently, it had become my 'usual'.

She returned to the kitchen.

I took a seat by the fire and a sip of the coffee. Both warmed the cockles. The Satellite pub was small and cosy, with smoke-stained, wooden panels and clerestory windows that, at least during the day, delivered the multitudes of light you need to survive in a timber-shrouded town like Satellite. The pub was one of the few buildings in town to survive the conflagrations of Black Friday in 1939 and Black Saturday seventy years later.

Legend had it that whenever a threat loomed, the entire population rushed to defend it. The same, alas, could not be said of
the cop shop – had that been under threat, they would have set
up the folding chairs and passed round the popcorn.

When I'd polished off the meal I stood at the window and
looked out over the town. Satellite had a winter-green patina
to it this afternoon. The river made its way through the town
moodily, like a trail of tears shed by the snow-capped crags in
the distance. The church was a huddle of hilltop spires looming
over the misty valley. A big blue twin-cab pulled into the car
park and disgorged a stringy quartet of long-necked timber
workers. One or two of them glanced my way suspiciously: word
of my occupation was getting round.

The coffee machine was roaring like a Force 10 gale, with
Annie at the controls. 'Another one?' she signalled.

'Why not?' I shrugged. Her coffees had a way of vanishing
down your throat and reappearing in your synapses and neurons,
giving new energy to whatever you were working on.

I returned to my table and started going over my notes. Annie
delivered the coffee and glanced at the pages in front of me.

'A working lunch, is it, Jess?'

'Just writing up some case notes.'

'I presume you were caught up in the Raph Cambric business?'

I swallowed. 'Kind of.'

'Poor old Raph. But poor old Nash as well,' she said. 'I'd
always thought he was a decent bloke.'

I looked at Annie with new interest. 'Do you know him well?'

'Dunno that anybody knows Nash well. I'd see him round,
sure. Come to town every week or two, stock up on supplies, pick
up the mail. Occasionally he'd even drop in for a drink, but he

kept to himself. He'd sit by the fire or out on the verandah, depending on the season, drink a slow beer then disappear. I felt sorry for him. Poor bugger couldn't win. One half of the town hated him because he'd killed that feller up at Horse Thief, the other half felt the same because he'd been a cop.'

'Has he lived round here for long?'

She shook her head. 'I heard he inherited the farm from his grandpa, Matty Rankin. Now there was a decent old bloke. Used to come in here for a pie and a beer every Friday. Died a few years ago, but the place was abandoned until Nash took it over.'

I wondered why the inheritance had skipped a generation. What became of Nash's parents? Did their presumed involvement in the 'kooky church' have anything to do with it?

I asked Annie if she knew much more about Nash's family background but she shook her head. She'd heard that Matty had had a daughter, and that there'd been a falling out. She'd been a teenage tearaway, then she got into drugs and, even worse in Annie's eyes, god-bothering.

'Do you know anything about the god-botherers?' I asked her.

'Jesus, honey, I wouldn't have the foggiest. They're all the same to me. God and I have a rule of mutual ignorance: I ignore him and he ignores me.'

I asked if she could tell me more about the death of Leon Glazier at Horse Thief Creek, but she shook her head. She hadn't known him, but she suspected some of her patrons would have. He'd worked in IT, been the go-to man for any local Luddites trying to work out which end of the computer was which. She said she'd ask around.

'Thanks,' I said, returning to my notes. 'Appreciate it.'

# CHAPTER 19

Three headings, three historic cases. The serial killer, the runaway financial advisor and the creepy priest.

The first was the most infamous. Jeremiah Kursk. Ten years ago, Nash had been following up on a load of stolen copper wire which, according to a tip-off, had been spotted in the yard of a Greendale wrecker named Jeremiah Kursk. The stolen wire hadn't amounted to much, but Nash noticed a couple of things which aroused his suspicion: a HiAce van similar to one reported in the vicinity of an unsolved disappearance the year before, and a floor in the rear of the van that looked out of alignment, might have been false. He was also struck by the look of alarm in Kursk's eye when he first looked over the vehicle.

He passed his concerns on to the Homicide Squad, who widened an investigation that eventually saw Kursk serving a forty-year sentence for the abduction and murder of three women.

He was in the slammer for life, couldn't have been involved in the Wycliff incident. But some of the evidence – the statement from a witness who got away from Kursk, the manner of the abductions, the detection of mystery prints in the vehicle – suggested there'd been at least one other person involved in the murders. Kursk had never admitted his own involvement, much less anybody else's.

He was invariably described as a loner, but among the documents was a newspaper clipping that suggested this hadn't always been the case. Fifteen years ago he'd won a prize in the State Fullbore Rifle competition, and the headline read: ALL IN THE FAMILY. In the accompanying photo were two other men. On his left was a man of a similar age with the same surname: Edward Kursk. I wondered why Vince had included him. Was he a suspect?

There was a brutal similarity about the trio, manifested in their sharp beards, shaved heads and cold eyes. The source of the coldness, instinct told me, was the older man on the right. Theodor, the father. He was stooped, battered about by time, running to fat. But there was the same penetrating white light in his gaze, the same bleakness in his smile, a similar rifle in his hands.

I did a little exploration online. There was plenty about the infamous Jeremiah, but precious little about his brother Edward. I did find, however, a man of that name listed as the proprietor of a tow-truck company in Bloomfield, a hairy-chested industrial suburb south of Greendale. The company, Smash and Grab Towing, was listed as the sponsor of a speedway demolition derby. There was a blurry photo of Edward Kursk handing over a giant cheque to a guy in a purple racing suit and a melanoma hat on backwards.

I moved on to my next candidate. Paul Burstill, a financial advisor from the outer eastern suburb of Glen Waters.

The accompanying photo was of a smirky man with a set of jowls like a bullmastiff's. Nash had apparently encountered a cluster of elderly locals who'd invested their life savings in Burstill's Self-Managed Super Funds scheme, only to find their funds vanished and their financial advisor going the same way. Some of them had lost their homes. When Nash reported the matter and the Fraud Squad came knocking, Burstill's elusiveness turned into complete disappearance, a mystery that was resolved only when a fat man with a fake beard was rescued from the lifeboat of a sinking yacht out east of Batemans Bay. The vessel had been heading for Greece, and its owner was given a five-year sentence that ended a couple of years ago. According to the files, his most recent job was as a shift supervisor in a waste recycling plant in Glen Waters.

I turned to the last page, my third suspect. The photo that went with this one was of a thin man with thick lips and a wintery smile. The creepy priest. Maybe the worst of them all. Ronald Laws had been the chaplain of Weymouth Ladies College, a private school in Melbourne's leafy eastern suburbs with an outdoor education campus in the high country north of the Windmarks.

Nash had attended the suicides of two teenage girls in as many months. New to the CIU, he'd noticed, from photos in their rooms, that both had spent time at the outdoor education campus. Nash made further enquiries and began to hear worrying rumours about the school chaplain, one Ronald Laws. He reported his suspicions to the Sex Crimes Squad, who launched an investigation which eventually saw the chaplain convicted and given a seven-year sentence for sex with minors. Since his release, he'd found employment as an accounts payable clerk with a medical management company in Box Hill.

Each of the three offenders blamed Nash for their incarceration. Kursk alleged he'd planted the evidence in the van. Burstill said Nash had interfered with a legitimate scheme which, in the long run, would have made everybody involved rich. Ronald Laws screamed in court that Nash had coached the witnesses, that he himself had been nothing more than a comforting shoulder for troubled youth to cry on. That there'd been more body parts than shoulders involved was confirmed later when it emerged a third girl had had an abortion.

According to the files, Burstill and Laws were still out and about, and Edward Kursk had never been inside.

I decided to check them out, face to face. Tomorrow.

# CHAPTER 20

I was up early. I did a brutal taekwondo workout, fortifying myself for what I knew would be a heavy-duty day. I made a coffee and sat looking over a map of Melbourne, wondering where to begin.

Start at the bottom, I decided – the pervert priest – and work your way up. At least he worked in a nice, clean office. I wouldn't have to get my hands dirty. I wasn't so sure about my soul.

I buried the files back in the bottom drawer and whistled up the dog. He sprung up from the hearth, tail wagging. The house didn't have a yard and I couldn't leave him on a chain all day so he'd have to come with me. Besides, he was growing on me. And he seemed to have a better situational awareness than I did.

We set out for Box Hill – and Ronald Laws.

An hour later we pulled up in front of a streamlined, triple-storey office building of tinted glass, granite columns and luminescent steel cladding. The company was called Hawley and Sons.

I told the dog to stay put and made my way towards a rock-jawed security man who took himself way too seriously. He scrutinised my ID to within an inch of its life and directed me into a vast foyer. It had crimson carpets, sofas designed to discourage malingering and a receptionist of similar purpose: she had eyes like a basilisk. When I asked for Ronald Laws, she put a call through to some back office. A full five minutes crawled by before a side door opened and a man stepped into the foyer.

He seemed disconcerted by my presence, adjusting his tie and tugging at his collar. I wasn't sure what an accounts payable clerk did, but it clearly didn't involve many visitors.

'Ronald Laws,' he said, not offering to shake my hand. I wasn't complaining; I didn't want to shake his. His eyes were a mess of tics and flickers, his lips as tightly pursed as a cat's backside. From the colour of his fingertips, he wasn't a smoker, but he looked like one would do him the world of good; he was staring at me like a myxoed rabbit.

I almost eliminated him from my list at first glance. He was deflated, balding, hunched forward, maybe in his late sixties. He'd selected his wardrobe from the bargain rack at a back street op shop: a sloping-shoulder suit and a worn shirt with winged collars and a sauce-splattered tie. I was taken aback. This was the dreaded abuser of Weymouth Ladies? He had as much personality as a deflated sex doll. I could barely imagine him making his own lunch, much less carrying out a crime like the one at Wycliff Rise. Stomping about the bush dropping trees on people, manhandling chainsaws and winches? Framing Nash?

Hardly. If this guy wanted to frame somebody, he'd be doing it with accounting software packages or poisoned pen letters.

Anyway, no point leaving without giving him a once-over. He could have hired a hit man.

When I showed the ID, Laws gave a sideways glance at the security man, who hadn't taken his eyes off me. He suggested we move to a meeting chamber further back in the building. He escorted me down a corridor and into the room – leaving, I couldn't help but notice, the door partially open. Being on the sex-offenders' registry must have taught him a thing or two. He motioned me to a chair on the far side of a broad oak table and took a seat himself.

The interview began smoothly enough. I asked him how long he'd worked at Hawley's, how he was adapting to life on the outside. His answers were monosyllabic, wary, his gaze flitting about the room like a honey-drunk butterfly. I asked him about the business and his role in it. He said the company managed every aspect of the modern medical practice – billing, budgets, payroll, recruitment. They had offices in Sydney and Brisbane, over five hundred clients, even owned a couple of private hospitals and carried out important research. He was a member of the team responsible for processing invoices and reconciling the ledgers here in the Box Hill office.

The conversation went as well as could be expected – until I asked him about his movements on the previous Tuesday. He clicked his tongue, shook his head and went still. A red flush crept into his temples.

'Can't help yourself, can you?' he snapped.

I raised a brow.

'Excuse me?'

'I've paid for my crimes – so called – ten times over. But people like you – zealots – you'll never let it rest. You keep turning up, going over old ground, twisting the truth to fit your own ends.'

He caught my eye, and, just for a moment, I got a glimpse of the subterranean anger that must have underlaid his appalling crimes. Maybe I shouldn't discount him as quickly as I'd been inclined to. There was a bit of bite left in the old dog yet.

'Sounds like what you said in court about Nash Rankin,' I said.

'Who?'

'The officer from Greendale who first investigated you.'

'Well, he's had his comeuppance,' he shot back. 'He was of a similar bent, always putting his own disgusting tint on things, on the blessings of human interaction. You're all cut from the same cloth.'

He paused, breathed deeply. His fingernails drummed on the table.

The action must have given him the space he needed to collect himself. He sat up straight, ran a distrait hand through his comb-over and requested I repeat the question. He gave clipped, precise answers to each of my questions then waited for the next one, clearly willing the interview to be over.

I asked him again about Nash, but he said he hadn't given the man a moment's thought in years. He'd never heard of Raph Cambric, had a vague recollection of the name Wycliff Rise but had never been there.

I pushed a little harder about his movements on the day of the storm. He said he'd worked in the office during the daylight hours, then gone home to his apartment. He'd dined on a take-away chicken and a glass of wine, watched television. He swore he'd been nowhere near the Windmarks for years, was endeavouring to get what was left of his life back on track. He was grateful to Hawley and Sons for giving him another chance. Almost against my better judgement, I found myself believing him. When I asked if anybody could confirm his alibi, he suggested his employer, at least for the office hours. He gave me the name and number of the relevant HR person.

Eventually Laws said he had work to do, suggested I find my own way out, muttered a farewell that felt more like a good riddance and disappeared through a door at the back of the room.

As I approached the foyer, another man appeared from an adjoining office and asked if I had a moment.

'Ms Redpath? Kane Lochran. Corporate Governance.'

He was a smooth, buff fellow with a bespoke blue suit and a direct, almost flirtatious smile that wasn't reflected in his eyes. I was surprised to notice that he was wearing Nike trainers. He followed my look. 'Just up from the gym,' he explained. 'I'm wondering if you have a moment? Our managing director would appreciate a word.'

He said it in a manner that didn't invite dissent. I was starting to worry that news of this visit might find its way to my bosses, but I could hardly say no. Lochran had a military brusqueness about him. He escorted me down a corridor to a lift that whisked us up to the third floor and into a plush executive office occupied by a plush executive.

'George Hawley,' he said, rising from the desk and ushering me into a chair opposite his own. He looked to be in his sixties, thin-lipped, craggy-faced, with a confident grip and a suit that would have cost a month of my wages. On the wall behind him were photos of men in white coats with other men who looked like politicians or captains of industry – some of them were even recognisable. Lochran hovered in the background.

'Father or son?' I enquired with a smile, nodding at the nameplate on Hawley's desk. It was gold-embossed, custom-made and had his name prominently displayed under the company's logo – a blue crown with triple spikes and the words 'Hawley and Sons' woven into it.

'Neither, I'm afraid. Hawley and Sons was founded by my uncle, Jonathon. Now, alas, no longer with us. But the business remains in the family, something we're proud of. That and the fact that we've been delivering quality healthcare to the people of this nation for over forty years.'

He leaned across the table and extended a hand. 'Could I have a look at your ID, please?'

I handed it over. Hawley had a pleasant enough demeanour, but I sensed there was a shark circling below the surface. Hardly surprising. You'd need a lethal streak to rise to the top of a business like this. He studied the card for a moment, jotted a note on a pad then cut to the chase.

'I couldn't help but hear you came for a chat with Ronald Laws. Could you tell me what it was about?'

I started to tell him it was a private matter, but he cut me off.

'We're fully aware of Ronald's past, if that's what you're worried about. It's the reason he's working here.'

He explained that the firm had, for many years, been an active participant in Jump Start, a corporate philanthropy program designed to give newly released white-collar criminals a chance to get their lives back on track.

'Ronald's background is about as white-collar as they come,' he said. 'But we're more than happy with the way he's performed his duties. He had a background in bookkeeping before he joined the clergy, and he did further studies in IT and medical management while he was inside. For a man of his age and history, that's quite remarkable.'

I assured him I was pleased to hear it and that I wasn't here to give anybody grief.

'There's no suggestion of a relapse, is there?' he asked with an air of concern. 'We regard Ronald as one of our success stories and I'd hate to see that change. He's not the most . . . dynamic individual on staff, but when he's doing his work he's diligent and reliable.'

'There's no problem,' I said. 'I was just looking for some background information on an issue connected to his previous life.'

His brow moved downwards.

'You can't tell me any more?'

I shook my head. 'It's a police matter.'

He leaned back in his chair and studied me for a moment. 'Okay then, we'll leave it there. But Ronald's health – both physical and mental – is delicate. I'd hate to see you stirring up his demons.'

I told him not to worry, that I could see no reason why I'd need to be bothering him again. I said it with a slight sense of unease. Hawley's main motivation was clearly the wellbeing of his employee. They were committed to this Jump Start program. Fair enough; it sounded like a worthy venture. But if my bosses got word of my visit today, I'd be deeper in the shit than I already was. If the photos on the wall were anything to go by,

Hawley was the kind of character who'd have a range of heavy hitters in the medical, legal, even political circles on speed dial.

I left soon afterwards, then sat in the car going over what I'd just experienced. The visit hadn't gone as smoothly as I'd hoped, especially its finale.

I was still trying to make up my mind about Ronald Laws. He was a weird cat: evasive, bristling, flickering with buried emotions. Hawley and Sons deserved a medal for taking him on.

As I pulled away from the car park, I remembered a slight anomaly in the conversation with Laws. He'd said he hadn't given Nash a moment's thought since the trial. But before that he'd commented that Nash had 'had his comeuppance now'. What was he referring to? If he knew about Nash's history and incarceration, maybe even his recent arrest, he'd clearly given the matter more than a moment's thought.

There wasn't much I could do now except add it to the image of the case I was building in my head.

I've heard people compare the solving of a crime to the completion of a jigsaw puzzle, but, to me, it isn't so much a jigsaw as a portrait. Maybe my understanding was shaped by growing up with the kind of art my father painted. He created intricate landscapes that were subtle, elusive, glancing – and based on solid science. Every mineral depicted, every lithic fragment, every fossilised mollusc had a reason for being there. That seemed to be the perfect metaphor for the kind of investigation I was engaged in now. I couldn't relax until it achieved the sense of balance and completeness those paintings gave me.

I pushed on to my next port of call.

## CHAPTER 21

Smash and Grab Towing Services. I found them in one of the ramshackle back streets of the Bloomfield industrial zone. The flamboyant sign at the entrance read: SMASH AND GRAB – ANYWHERE, ANYTIME. There was a brick office out front and a gravel yard in which half-a-dozen trucks were parked out back. In the centre of the block was an open-gable metal shed containing more vehicles and equipment.

Flinders was a quick learner. He waited patiently in his seat while I went into the property. I came across an unholy trinity of men standing around conversing in the forecourt of the shed. Two of them were in outdoor work wear, with an air of high-vis and low tolerance about them. The third was wearing a black winter jacket and jeans. He was obviously in charge: you could tell from the raucous energy of the laughter that shot up from the group like water from a depth charge when he cracked a joke. I hoped it wasn't about me.

'Morning gents,' I said as I approached. 'I'm looking for Edward Kursk.'

'That'd be me,' said the joker. 'Neddy will do.'

He was in his late thirties, strongly built, with a ginger beard and buzz-cut, a head like a rocky outcrop and brickbat hands.

When I identified myself and asked if he was Jeremiah's brother he put his hands in his pockets and told the others to make themselves scarce. They headed in the direction of the trucks. One of them, a stringy fellow who looked like Maggie Thatcher in drag, glanced back at me with an expression of bleak malevolence.

'I take it you're not here about a tow job?' asked Kursk. The humour that preceded my arrival had vanished.

'Do you know a man named Raph Cambric?'

'Nope,' he said without pausing for thought.

'What about Nash Rankin?'

He stared at me for a moment and sniffed the air. It was rich with diesel and grease and a hint of distant abattoir. I thanked the lord I hadn't come here in high summer.

'He was at your brother's trial,' I added.

He locked his shoulders. His chin jutted forward, his feet followed suit. 'Always comes back to that with you lot, doesn't it?'

'I don't know why that should surprise you. The things he did . . .'

The ginger buzz bristled.

'*He* did – not me.'

Thoughts of fruit never falling far from the tree shot through my brain. Fortunately they had the sense to stay there. There was something deeply discomfiting about this guy. The way he instinctively moved towards me at the mention of his brother. The flare in his eyes, the fists in his pockets.

The gravel was rough and spiky under boot, blue metal aggregate with dirty rainbows in its oil stains. I felt suddenly vulnerable, standing out there on the bare ground, alone, unarmed in civilian clothes and car, talking to a serial killer's brother. Wondering if he were one too. I looked around. Nobody else in sight. There was a scabbed and battered rottweiler in a cage, barbed wire on top of the cyclone fence. This was no place for the weak or the tender-hearted.

What the hell. I've never thought of myself as weak or tender-hearted. Generally I just charge in with my eyes open and my fists closed, hoping a few of my blows will connect and that I won't cop too many in return. I've got away with it so far.

'Mind telling me where you were last Tuesday night, Mr Kursk?'

'The night of the storm?' He told me he and his crews were flat out that night, with breakdowns, smashes and flooded vehicles all over the region. They were still playing catch-up. I asked what time he got home that night, and he said it wasn't until dawn the next day.

'Can anybody vouch for that?' I asked.

A quick shake of the head. 'I live alone.' That didn't surprise me. You could almost see the trail of damaged women and cringing dogs stretching out behind him.

One of the trucks rattled out through the gate, kicked up an arc of mud. The rottweiler slavered and snarled at me through the mesh walls of its cage.

I turned back to Kursk. 'You keep in touch with Jeremiah?'

He narrowed his gaze and chewed on something, possibly a piece of tungsten.

'We're family. You stick by each other.'

The rotty picked up the vibe, let fly with a volley of frustrated barks.

'What's this all about?' asked Kursk. 'Who is this Rankin? Not that I care – I've got nothing to hide.'

'You know his name. I presume you attended Jeremiah's trial.'

Something dawned in his eyes. 'He was the local arsehole who went poking round the yard while Jem wasn't looking? Trespassing, breaking and entering. Jem always swore that shit was planted.'

'Lot of shit to plant,' I countered. By the time Forensics had finished, the van had given them the material evidence – a blood-stained button, a set of prints from one missing woman, some hair from another – that formed the basis of the case against Kursk.

A pathetic little ray of sunshine struggled through the clouds, thought better of it and went away.

'Have you been up to the Windmarks recently?' I asked.

Kursk glanced at the vehicles remaining in the yard.

'Depends what you mean by recent. We go anywhere we're paid to. But I spend most of my time behind a desk these days.'

There was a clangour of hammer on metal from the shed. The rotty scratched at the gate and tore at the lock with its incisors. I took a closer look at the lock, a little concerned about its flimsiness.

'How long have you had this business?' I asked.

'Ten years.'

'So you were running it when your brother was on his spree.'

He took his hands out of his pockets and shot a hostile glance my way.

'I don't like the tone of that question.'

I stepped away, beyond his immediate reach. Maybe I should change tack. I wasn't winning any friends round here. 'Mind if I have a look around?' I asked politely.

He crossed his arms and spat onto the ground.

'I'll take that as a no,' I said.

'Take it any way you like, but unless you got a search warrant, you can piss off. I've got work to do.'

He turned and headed for the office, his big boots crunching through the gravel.

I took his advice and pissed off – at least as far as the car, where I sat for a few minutes thinking. The most troubling part of the conversation was when he'd said that in his world, you stuck by your family. Did that include when they were killing people?

'What do you reckon?' I asked Flinders as we drove away. He wasn't saying much, but five minutes into the drive, as I was turning onto the highway, he emitted a low growl. I glanced into the rear-view mirror. It was busy back there. Trucks, cars, utes of every description, motorbikes, B-doubles. And white delivery vans – oh so many white delivery vans. They were the worker bees of the nation's economy.

But nothing out of the ordinary did I spot. Nobody lingering too close, no unwarranted changes of pace, no surreptitious eyes sliding in my direction.

If there was somebody on my tail, they were a damned sight better at this business than I was.

In a few minutes I came to a roadside cafe. I pulled into the parking lot and sat there, watching and waiting. Something had set my antennae twitching. Was I being followed, or was it just the afterglow of Neddy Kursk's winning personality?

I studied the passing traffic for a full five minutes.

Nothing.

Settle down, I told myself. You won't get anywhere if you go jumping at shadows. I tied Flinders up outside the cafe then went in and ordered a burger. I took a seat by the window, where I could keep an eye on the dog and the car park. The diner was buzzing; maybe twenty people came in while I was there and most of the seats were taken at any one time. When I'd finished the meal, I ordered a coffee and studied my notes on the case. The coffee was weak and watery and the notes weren't much better.

Time to start on a mind map?

Nope. Too early. I'd been in situations like this before. I have a tendency to overthink, to get bogged down in possibilities and potential, overlook the obvious. What I needed was more detailed information. Hard facts. All I could do was push on, accumulate, sift and sieve. Keep talking to people, look into dark corners.

If there was somebody on my tail, I'd spring them sooner or later.

# CHAPTER 22

According to the files, Paul Burstill, the runaway financial advisor, was currently working for a company called Wilde Wastes. The owner of the company was listed as a Max Wilde, and the depot was located deep in the industrial heart of Glen Waters, half an hour south.

I located and drove to the address, gave the dog a bit of toast I'd flogged from the cafe and went in. The place was presentable enough from the street – a red-block office, a spruced-up sign – but as you came closer the façade fell away. The office was pokey and locked, with dusty windows and a bolted door. There was a mountain of material – cans, plastics, cardboard – sealed in bales and stacked along the back fence. The heart of the enterprise was a forty-metre corrugated iron shed from which a chorus of metallic noises was emerging. There was a chemical sting in the air, the ubiquitous dog on a chain and numerous scraps of rubbish scattered about the gravel yard.

I approached the shed and looked in. A delivery truck was backing away from a drop-off zone at the other end of the building, an excavator was busily scooping the recently dumped material onto a conveyor belt tended to by a row of employees in blue overalls.

The sound system was pumping out jangly, guitar-based music which – like most of the workers – was of African origin. They were making the most of it, jumping around to the beat as they plucked items from the belt and threw them into metal containers.

Standing off to one side and definitely not jumping to the beat was a big, bearish man in a loose grey dust coat. He was talking to a squat guy in khaki overalls. The one in the coat was Burstill. I recognised him from the photo in the file. He was wearing thick glasses, clodhopper shoes and a fistful of grease in his thin black hair. He was heavily jowled, with racoon rings around his eyes and a stomach rolling like a wave – tidal – over his belt. He had fat red cheeks and pursed lips, like a man playing an invisible wind instrument.

He passed a manila envelope over to the guy in overalls, who turned and made his way towards a truck loaded with blue drums at the end of the bay.

Burstill looked at me, warily at first, then with a low-level hostility when I showed my ID and said I'd like a chat. He wiped a handful of sweat from his brow and rubbed it onto his coat. He must have been the only person sweating in the state that day. Maybe it was more than sweat; both his eyes and his nose were dripping. He had a head cold and wasn't happy about it – although he looked like he'd be only too pleased to send a little of it my way.

He asked one of the crew to mind the shop then led me into an office which looked out over the sorting area.

'Do we really have to do this now?' he complained as he eased his rear end into a chair. I got a whiff of whisky as he leaned towards me. 'We're flat out here.'

He wasn't wrong. Another truck came in and dumped a load as we watched. The blokes on the conveyor belt upped the ante and the volume of the music.

I assured Burstill it wouldn't take long.

I began the interview with what was becoming a routine set of questions: the where, what and how. I wasn't expecting much, and that was what I got. Talking to him was like wrestling with a clothes horse. He was evasive, curt, aggrieved, giving blunt non-answers and moaning about 'the system', without ever explaining what he meant, which system. I hadn't expected much more. This visit was just the opening shot: it was all about fleshing out the profiles, panning for gold but not raising my hopes of finding anything other than dirt.

I asked him about his movements on the day of the storm and wasn't surprised to hear there hadn't been many of them. He'd been at home, in bed, with the flu. He remembered the night well: the power had gone out and he'd been stumbling around his apartment searching for the Strepsils with a torch. He seemed confused at being asked about some sort of violent incident, and I could understand why. There'd never been any suggestion of physical violence in his history, despite his size. There was a slow, ponderous vibe about the man, as if he had mud, rather than blood, trundling through his veins. If he did swing a punch at you, you'd have time to finish your drink and get out of the way before it landed.

The liveliest thing about Burstill was the glob of snot poking out from his right nostril. A full-bore, pear-shaped gorby.

It showed no sign of going away. I studied my notebook, giving him a chance to remove the offending item, by means of a quick sleeve if nothing else, but when I raised my head the bloody thing was still there. It hung around for the duration of the interview. Occasionally he'd give a disgusting little suck and it would shoot back up the chute, but it never completely disappeared. Maybe the blob was deliberate, a technique he'd developed to put inquisitors off. Credit where it was due. I'd come across all sorts of defensive strategies in my time: anger, evasion, obsequiousness, lies. I'd never come across snot.

I asked a few questions about the company, and he said the owner, Max Wilde, was a cousin who'd offered him the job to help him out. 'Bit of a comedown,' he grumbled.

What do you expect? I thought. A gold medal? He was faring a lot better than the elderly couples who'd lost their homes because of him.

I asked about the threats he'd made against Nash at the trial, but he said he'd just spouted the first thing that came into his head, hadn't thought about the outburst, or the man who'd been the subject of it, for years. He glanced out at the workshop, where some of his employees were smirking and glancing in our direction. His scowl deepened, his wheezy lungs gave an asthmatic rattle. He protested that he'd done his time, had already received more than his fair share of punishment. He repeated the claim, made during the trial, that the police had disrupted a legitimate scheme which would have made the fortunes of all involved. He suggested that he'd been framed by 'jealous business rivals with political connections' and that all he wanted was to be left in peace. Again, I was struck by the sense of entitlement, his anger at the injustice of his treatment, his whingeing about the system.

Another truck came in and dropped off a load. Burstill stood up brusquely, said he had to get back to work and escorted me to the door. I wasn't complaining. It was a relief to be out of his presence, not to mention the sight of his snot.

That was another waste of time, I reflected as I walked back to the ute. Bastard gave me nothing. Was that because he had nothing to give, or was he covering something up? He wasn't happy about being interviewed in front of his employees, but who would be?

# CHAPTER 23

It was late afternoon now. That was enough for day one. I went back home, made a cup of tea and sat out on the verandah, thinking about what I'd learned from the day's exertions.

Not much.

There were some shady characters out there, some people brutalised by the threshing machine of modern life, but that was hardly news. There were some leads to be followed up, some insights to be fleshed out: why Kursk was looking so defensive, what were the financial arrangements behind Burstill's business, could Laws possibly be as ineffectual as he seemed?

The sun was going down in flames. After a while I looked up and gazed into an opalescent western sky, the kind that made you feel very small.

My meditations were shattered when something whizzed viciously overhead and slammed into the wall. I dropped to the floor, reaching for a Glock that wasn't there. I glanced up. There was an arrow – a crossbow bolt – still quivering, buried deep in the wooden boards. I heard a rustle of leaves and a metallic clank in the bushes on the other side of the road.

Just because they missed once didn't mean they'd do so again. Or that the next one wouldn't be a bullet.

I leapt for the door, rolled into the house. Then went straight out the back and into the bush. Anger gave me wings. If I could catch this aspirational assassin, maybe I could find out what was going on round here.

I crept away to my left, beginning a semi-circle that I estimated would bring me round to where the arrow had come from. I kept to the animal trails, moving as quietly as I could, as swiftly as I dared.

When I reached the road, I paused, scrutinising the scene in front of me. All seemed quiet. Then I heard a burst of laughter further down Shady Grove Road. I spotted a boy on a bicycle – no, two boys on two bicycles – whizzing across a gap in the bushes. They were belting along the walking track that ran alongside the road to town, their bikes rocking.

I sprinted back home, scrambled into the car and drove down the dirt track behind the house until I reached a spot where I hoped I'd be ahead of them.

I jumped out, ran through the scrub and around a low hill until I came to the road. I concealed myself in the bushes beside it.

I'd been there for all of thirty seconds when they appeared: two boys, twelve, maybe thirteen years old. Slower now, figuring they'd made their escape. Still laughing, the cheeky little buggers. The boy in front had a crossbow slung across his shoulder, the one bringing up the rear had rich red hair and a face full of freckles.

I waited until the archer was almost level with me, then leapt out, dragged him from the bike and pinned him to the ground. This went well until, fooled by his youth, I dropped my guard and he took a piece out of my hand. I flipped him over and ground his head – especially the teeth – into the dirt. The gingernut swerved around us and kept going, without so much as a backward glance. Great friend.

The boy on the ground struggled and yelled: 'Get off me, you dirty cop! What do you think you're doing?'

Interesting. He knew who – or at least what – I was. Was that what prompted him to take a shot at me?

'It's called making an arrest,' I said. 'Something you better get used to if you're going to run round trying to kill police officers.'

I asked for his name and address. It took some persuading, but eventually I got a single word. 'Bailey.' He looked up and around, furious, desperate, then despairing as he realised the trouble he was in.

'Where do you live, Bailey?'

More protestations of police brutality ensued, but in the end he told me he lived on Buckley's Track and what his father would do to me when he found out about this assault. I made him load his bike onto the tray of my ute and found the track on my GPS. It was just out of town, a kilometre along the road to Wycliff. I considered my options: straight into Satellite for a rocket from Lance Cunningham or home for a deep and meaningful with his parents?

The latter. I'd have a word with Lance myself, once I'd got a fix on the family situation. Given what I'd seen of the boy thus far, I couldn't imagine it would be a good one.

Which may have been why, as we approached what Bailey said was his family home, I was surprised to find a capacious, modern homestead, beautifully maintained, on twenty acres of prime pasture. The house was made of chiselled grey blocks, with high gates, a gravel drive and green grass. There was a quartet of horses in winter rugs – two chestnuts, a white and an elegant bay – grazing in a paddock framed by ironbark posts and white rail fences.

'You really live here?' I asked as I pulled into the driveway.

'You think I don't know my own house?' The boy was sounding tetchier – or maybe more anxious – with every passing second. His breaths were shallow and fast, his hands were shaking.

I kept a close eye on him as he wheeled his bike up the path, half expecting him to make a run for his real home at the ghetto end of town, but he stayed close to my side as we approached the door. I kept the crossbow in my hands and braced myself for a confrontation, wondering what sort of family would produce a child who ran round taking pot shots at police officers. I was almost relieved when the door was opened by a teenage girl. She was thin, pale with a long dark plait and a quiet, wary demeanour. She was dressed in an ill-fitting dress with a beige woollen jumper. Around her neck was a gold chain with a rose-shaped pendant dangling from it.

She flashed a troubled glance at Bailey and asked how she could help me. I told her I was the police and I needed to speak to his parents. She took a sharp breath and stepped back.

'They're not here at the moment.'

'Can you call them? We need to talk about Bailey. And you are . . . ?'

'His sister. What's the problem?'

'He just tried to kill me with his crossbow.'

Her eyes flared defensively. 'I doubt that. If he really wanted to kill you, you'd probably be dead. He's a very good shot.'

'We were just mucking round,' the boy exclaimed. 'Trying to put the wind up her.'

'We? You were with Jake?' she asked.

He glared at the ground.

'I'll take that as a yes.' She ran a hand across her cheek and looked towards the distant town. 'And you fired at the police officer?'

Still no response.

'You do realise,' I asked the boy, 'that it's illegal for you to own or operate a crossbow?'

He gave me little more than a surly stare and a curled lip. The lock of thick black hair dangling over his forehead only added to his angry expression.

'When will your parents be home?' I asked the girl.

'I'm not sure,' she replied.

She chewed a nail and rested a hand on the doorknob, subtly suggesting she wanted to go back inside.

'I can handle this,' she continued. 'I'll lock the weapon away. I'm sorry my brother's been misbehaving. I can assure you it won't happen again.'

I told her it wasn't that simple. This was a serious legal matter and I could only discuss it with a parent. If I couldn't do that, I'd have to confiscate the bow and take Bailey into the station at Satellite. Once I did that, it would be out of my hands. He'd most likely be charged.

She sighed anxiously but saw I wasn't going to budge. She glanced down the road from town. 'All right then. Our father's at work but he should be home soon.'

It was cold out there on the doorstep. Icy clouds were coming out of my mouth, my feet were going numb. Night was closing in. But the girl clearly had no intention of letting me inside. She folded her arms and squared her feet.

'What's your name?' I asked her.

'Lucinda.'

'Could I have your dad's name and number, Lucinda? I'll give him a call.' I didn't want to be standing here all night.

'Please,' she persisted, 'I'm sure Bailey will never do anything like this again. It's not him, it's this town. The boys he runs around with. They have some very negative attitudes towards the police . . .'

'Sorry but I definitely need to speak to a parent. Where does your dad work?'

'In a hospital in Melbourne.'

'He's a doctor?'

'The CEO.'

I took in the swanky house, the manicured lawns. That made sense.

'I see. And what about your mum?'

The trace of a shadow flew across her face. 'She's gone to care for a sick relative in Queensland. She used to be a nurse. But I can sort this out with Dad. I know he's been worried about Bailey, and when he's anxious he can get angry. Bailey's been a bit off the rails lately.'

I frowned. Off the rails? He was off the planet.

A car appeared in the distance, drew closer and indicated a turn into the drive of the house.

Lucinda surprised me by suddenly clutching my hand.

'Please,' she said, 'don't tell our father what Bailey did. He's not supposed to be running round with the local boys. Or using the bow. Dad will be furious.'

What was going on here? 'Are you saying you're worried about your father? Is he mistreating you? Is he violent?'

The roller door went up and the car – a maroon BMW – cruised in to the garage. Lucinda caught my eye. 'Please . . .' she mouthed, desperate now.

I hesitated, sighed and handed the bow to the boy. 'Put it wherever it lives.' He looked surprised, slipped inside. The driver emerged from the garage moments later. He was in his late forties, dressed in a smooth blue suit with a light scarf around his neck. He was thin, with auburn hair and a lined face, sharp cheekbones. He strode along the path that led to the door.

I turned and greeted him.

He narrowed his eyes, clearly not happy about a stranger speaking to his kids. I flashed my badge.

'I'm with the Satellite police. LSC Redpath. Jesse.'

'Craig,' he said, shaking my hand. 'Is there a problem?'

Lucinda caught her breath.

'No, there's no problem. I'm just checking the roads,' I lied. 'We've had reports of flood damage to some of the bridges and crossings out this way, after the storm. We need to know the public can get through safely.'

I caught Lucinda's eye, felt her relief. Bailey reappeared.

'I'd have thought that was a VicRoads responsibility,' Craig snapped.

'The repairs are, but if there's a risk to life or limb, we need to know about it.' I smiled. 'I'm new in town,' I added by way of additional explanation. 'Taking the opportunity to do a bit of area familiarisation, meet the locals.'

Craig stepped away and eased off a little. He cast his gaze out towards the road.

'I see. Well, sure, there's quite a bit of damage between here and Wycliff – culverts blocked, shoulders washed away, potholes everywhere. Water's over the road in places – the turn into Dunham Road's the worst. Up the top end of the valley. Wouldn't want to hit that in a hurry. It can turn to black ice overnight – lethal, I imagine.'

'Thanks for that, Craig,' I said. I stepped back and looked around the property. The horses shuffled in the distance. 'Nice place you've got here. Have you lived in Satellite for long?'

'Just a year or so.' A thin smile. 'Tree-changers, you might say. But we do have family – long-established – in the area.'

While we were talking, Lucinda and Bailey retreated into the house. Craig cast a quick, suspicious glance after them then cut the conversation short.

'If there's nothing else . . .'

I took the cue. He wanted me gone. I had no desire to complicate things for the kids, so I thanked him for his time, wished him a good evening and left. As I headed back to town, I found myself puzzling over the encounter. I hoped I'd done the right thing. The father seemed reasonable, but who could tell? He'd given me the bum's rush at the end there. I felt slightly uncomfortable about the encounter. I like things to balance but something here was off kilter. There was a palpable tension running under the surface of that family.

\* \* \*

I dropped into the Satellite Police Station and caught Lance just as he was about to go home. He seemed pleased to see me, joked that he'd finally achieved the officer-in-charge position, even if it was only acting. Lance was more amused than anything else by my situation; he laughed about the incompetence of our superiors, said he was confident I'd done nothing wrong, would be reinstated soon.

We talked a little about the case. He'd been aware of Nash Rankin prior to the Wycliff incident, but had never had cause to be concerned by him. I didn't tell Lance about my ongoing enquiries, the material from Vince Tehlich. Decent enough bloke as Lance appeared to be, I had no idea of the tribal affiliations at play around this region, and I didn't want to risk him being seen as a party to my illicit activities. The less he knew about them the better.

Lance was concerned to hear about Bailey and the crossbow. He said something about it never raining but always pouring when I was within cooee. I hadn't got the surname of the family but when I mentioned that Bailey's accomplice was a ginger-haired boy named Jake, he said that would probably be Jake Perry, whose older brothers had had numerous run-ins with the law over the years. He knew the house on Buckley's Track – it had belonged to a retired surgeon who died a couple of years ago – but not the current owners. He said he'd make enquiries, do what he could to find out if there was anything going on with the family.

Bailey's antagonism towards the police was a concern. I couldn't help but wonder where that came from. Lucinda had mentioned that her brother wasn't supposed to be mixing with the locals. The boy must have been running wild while his parents were away. Maybe he'd decided to improve his status in the local pecking order with his crossbow skills. Then again, Lucinda hadn't exactly been the soul of affability herself, leaving me freezing on the doorstep, refusing to cooperate.

It was well past Lance's knock-off time. He invited me back to his place for dinner, but I said I needed an early night. I bade him good evening, then stood for a minute on the front steps of the station looking out over the town. A car drove past, its tyres hissing on the wet bitumen. A fox darted across the road ahead, a fleeting red flame in the headlights. Beyond the streetlights was the dark forest, looming over the community, hemming us in. What was going on in those wild, lonely hills? What secrets did they hold? God only knew. It was a strange place, the Satellite district. The mines had gone, the timber was going, but the characters remained, like marine creatures stranded by an ebb tide.

That sounded like a recipe for trouble.

# CHAPTER 24

I was fifty metres down Shady Grove Road when I caught a glimpse of a passing truck in my rear-view mirror. It was rolling along the main road, heading east. I drove a little more. There were heavy vehicles of one sort or another running all over the ranges: fuel tankers, cattle trucks, roadworks vehicles, water carts. But for some reason, this one was playing on my mind. I cursed quietly. It had been a long day, a warm bed and a hot meal were beckoning. But I couldn't relax until I'd scratched the itch.

I turned around and headed after the truck. In a few minutes I caught sight of it up ahead. It was a Hino flatbed with drop sides and a high lift tailgate, heavily loaded with blue drums. As it went round a curve, I caught sight of the name painted on the side panel. Wilde Wastes. The company Paul Burstill worked for.

What was in those drums? Presumably some sort of liquid waste: hydrocarbons, solvents, chemicals, whatever. I recalled seeing a similar vehicle in Wilde Wastes' yard, Burstill handing an envelope to the driver. What was it doing up here? I had no idea what the state did with its liquid waste, but surely the treatment plants weren't out in these green rolling hills, among the tourists and wineries?

Did I have time to distract myself with another investigation, especially one that was more than likely a wild goose chase? No. Then again, given the character of the company's foreman – avaricious, amoral, aggrieved – maybe it would turn out to be more than a wild goose chase. Perhaps there was a connection to the Wycliff incident. Raph Cambric could have spotted one of the trucks running round the hills, asked the same sort of questions I was, made the mistake of confronting the driver.

I held back, doing my best to keep some space between the truck and my ute. If it turned off to some treatment facility, well and good. I'd go home and warm myself by the fire. But it didn't. It kept going, through miniscule places I'd barely heard of: Guilders Glen, Dingo Springs, Waterman Gorge. The driver was keeping well under the speed limit, obeying all the rules, crossing the t's and dotting the i's. The bush on either side of the road was as black as bitumen. There were other cars about, but the further north-east we went, the more the traffic thinned out. I kept well back, worried that he'd spot me. If the driver was involved in anything illegal, surely he'd be keeping a lookout? He gave no sign of it though, moving steadily through the hills.

Finally, twenty minutes past the no-horse town of Saddleback, he turned right onto a dirt road. I almost missed him, just catching a glimpse of his red tail-lights as they vanished round a bend. I pulled into a siding a few hundred metres along.

I waited there for a moment, giving him time to check that he wasn't being followed, then turned around and crept back.

The dirt road was called Heffernan's Lane. I considered my options. There was no sign of the truck, but that didn't mean much. He could have turned into one of the surrounding properties, or he could still be rattling down the lane, heading for somewhere really remote. Maybe the driver lived down there and was taking the truck home for an early start?

I got out and stood on the roadside, watching and listening. My dilemma was resolved when I heard a hiss of distant air brakes and spotted a set of lights working their way down a valley to my left, maybe five hundred metres away.

I left the car and took the dog, worried he might be in danger if I left him there alone. Useful as he was, he was no rottweiler, and god only knew what these buggers were up to or what lookouts they had posted. We came to what was presumably a farm gate. No, not a farm. The dilapidated sign at the front said WOODGRAIN SAWMILL. There was a smaller notice on the top rail: TRESPASSERS PROSECUTED.

I climbed over the gate and took to the track, guiding myself by the occasional flash of light from my covered torch. There were truck-tyre tracks, fresh and heavy in the mud. A minute or two's walk brought me to a building which, like the sign out front, had an abandoned feel to it. This must be the mill. I ran a hand over the handle on the front door: it was locked fast and covered in dust. There was a sizeable workshop behind it, but there was no sign of recent human activity: no motors humming, no lights glowing. I risked a quick glance with the torch. There was grass in the roof gutters and holes in the skylights, heavy machinery lying dormant.

Flinders was getting the hang of this investigation business. He ran to the left, then the right, had a sniff and a bark and led me to a track that wound down into the valley. I walked for thirty seconds then spotted the truck down there, parked near a creek. Alongside it was a backhoe, busily working by floodlight.

I needed to get closer. I followed the track for a hundred metres, keeping one eye on the worksite below. I saw somebody on the back of the truck roll a drum forward and drop it into the bucket of the backhoe. A cloud of greasy diesel fumes floated over the scene, a portable generator rumbled. I was maybe two hundred metres away when the men suddenly stopped what they were doing and turned their eyes in my direction. I dropped to the ground. Had they heard something? Was there an alarm? One of them swung a spotlight in the direction of the track I was on and traversed it over the grassy slopes.

A flurry of wind ran down the valley. I was on an exposed track in a bare paddock, a dangerous position, but as the spotty moved on I caught a glimpse of a patch of dogwood further across the incline that would offer a level of protection if I could reach it. One of the men walked to the edge of the circle of light and gazed in my direction. Then he was joined by another man, this one, I was troubled to note, wielding a long rifle with a night scope. The operator of the backhoe? He raised the weapon and swept the slopes. I grabbed the dog and buried my face in the dirt, wondering what to do if they spotted me. Run like hell and hope the guy was as shithouse a shot as he was a toxic waste disposer?

The mud was a shitty mixture of diesel, grease and whatever was in those drums.

When the light moved away I took off, crouching as low as I could. I was relieved to reach the dogwood. I crouched in the bushes and looked back at the scene below. The workers had disappeared but the backhoe had resumed operations. Then I heard the truck start up and realised I'd left myself exposed in yet another way – my car was still out on the road. They may have had their suspicions that they were being spied upon, but if they spotted the car as they left, they'd know for sure. Maybe they'd even be able to tie it to me. Had Burstill taken note of my vehicle? My rego number? Wilde Wastes doubtless would have had security cameras, given the shifty business it was running.

The vegetation thinned out as I worked my way uphill, but it still made for some painful moments. I could feel scratches and welts opening up across my face, bites and stings on my hands, creepy-crawlies in my pants. When I heard the truck change gears for the run up the hill, I increased my pace. Finally I reached the fence and scrambled through. The dog was hot upon my heels. I dashed to the car, jumped in, drove without lights for a short distance then waited and watched. The truck red-lined it up the slope, hit the road and turned right, going back the way it had come.

I headed for home, one eye on the rear-view mirror.

## CHAPTER 25

Ilit the fire, fed the dog, made a quick pesto pasta and sat at the hearth eating slowly and trying to work out what I'd gained from the day's exertions. A host of questions, some suspicious characters and activities, more avenues to explore. First thing in the morning I'd give Vince Tehlich a call and fill him in on Wilde Wastes' after-dark activities. Did the benevolent cousin even exist? Burstill would have been disqualified from operating a business for years. Like any self-respecting swindler, surely he would have had a stash stored away for a scenario like this? As a financial advisor, he would have been a dab hand at setting up a company under a false flag. I had no idea what was in those drums, but it sure as hell wasn't orange juice.

Could the illicit dumping be connected to the Wycliff killing? It was possible, but the best chance of uncovering the truth would be by means of a proper police investigation, something Vince Tehlich was better placed than me to pursue.

I felt exhausted, my eyelids clanging down, my head nodding, but when I went to bed sleep refused to come. There were too many questions swirling around my brain. For want of anything better to do, I had a go at the old Bakelite radio beside the bed. To my surprise, it still worked. All I could pick up was talkback. The callers had all been around when the radio was made, their average age about eighty, their IQs similar. A few minutes of that and I fled for the comfort of my Spotify playlist, drifted off to sleep listening to Strauss's *Alpine Symphony*.

Sometime during the night I was woken by a sharp bark and a flurry of paw scratches. Did the dog want to go out? I found my torch. Flinders was sniffing about the north side of the room. The weather had deteriorated yet again. Apparently that was a permanent state of affairs up here. The rain had returned and the wind was ripping at the roofing irons, rattling the windows. No wonder the dog was agitated. I was a little agitated myself. I listened carefully. There was a discordant chorus of odd sounds coming through the walls and ceiling. Rats in the roof? Possums in the trees? Owls in the chimney? I heard scratches and rustles, shudders and squarks, screeches, thunks.

Thunks? That didn't fit. They had the hollow sound of metal on wood. An axe. I frowned. Did the rats have axes? Or was Rocco across the road up and about early? Had he run out of firewood, decided to do a bit of late-night chopping? Weird. Another thunk, this one with a definite echo to it. I dragged myself out from under the covers and took a look through the front window. Nothing. Layers of darkness, low flying clouds, yellow moon, mad mauling winds.

I opened the front door and inspected the night with my torch. No sign of Rocco – no lights in that direction.

Another thunk, this time from the northern side of the house, then a tearing sound that sent a bolt of fear through me.

Through the skylight, in a fragment of reflected torchlight, I caught a glimpse of sudden movement. Something was heading my way, fast. I hurled myself out the door. I rolled off the verandah and huddled on the stone steps as an avalanche crashed around me.

Time whirled. Space crumbled and collapsed. The roof was rent asunder with an explosion of stars and leaves and the almighty crash of tons of wood, maybe a massive branch, maybe an entire tree, one of the big bastards. Disintegrating beams, crumbling corrugated iron, roaring winds. Odd spears pierced me in odd places. My mouth was full of debris and dust, my ears were ringing. Then things settled down. I tried to crawl out of the rubble, had trouble doing so. I was half buried under a pile of iron and wood, the remains of the verandah.

I glanced to the north, caught sight of a light bobbing towards me. Was that Rocco, coming to help out? No, wrong direction. It was the killer coming to finish me off. I braced, got ready to defend myself, though that was easier said than done. It felt like half the house was on top of me. I was in a cavity protected, in part, by an array of fallen boards and beams, but that could change in an instant. The light came closer and I tensed, waiting for the right moment. My usual dexterity was much reduced, but the anger stirring inside me might have been compensation.

I heard a set of footsteps slushing through the mud, and I saw a shadowy figure that appeared to be a man. He drew closer. He angled the torch into the wreckage, sweeping it across the shattered building. I caught sight of a boot – black with a blue flash down the outside. I was only going to get one chance at this. He stepped onto the remnants of the verandah. The moment he came within range I threw out a hand, seized an ankle and attempted to whip him off his feet. But the rubble shifted as I moved, pressed down on me, left me with neither the balance nor the reach to launch a proper attack. A boot heel slammed into my shoulder. By the time I struggled out from under the debris he was gone. I caught a glimpse of light back in the bushes from whence he'd come.

I moved in that direction, then heard a car start up, saw a set of headlights illuminate the trees. The vehicle spun for a moment in the mud, then swung out onto the road and thrashed away.

Should I set off in pursuit?

Another thought brushed everything else away: Flinders. I felt ashamed. I'd spent too many years living on my own, given insufficient thought to the welfare of my fellow creatures.

I ran back to the shack and whistled. Heard a pitiful whimper in response. I grabbed an axe from the woodshed and slammed my way through the wreckage. I found my torch, then the dog, over near the window. He was alive, but terribly knocked about, his eyes bewildered, beseeching. His back half appeared to have been crushed by an errant branch.

The tree had carved a swathe of destruction through the building, smashing the bed, cupboard and dresser. The kitchen bench was still intact, except for a layer of debris. I found my keys and phone. Where was the nearest vet? Windmark. I raised the branch, eased the dog out from under it and carried him to the car. I nestled him into the front seat and set off at speed.

The surgery advertised itself as providing a twenty-four/seven service, and the claim wasn't far off the mark. While we were waiting, the dog rested his head against my thigh and shuddered. His big brown eyes gazed up at me. He must have been in agony.

'Sorry, boy,' I whispered, my heart filled with a fear that I was watching his life slip away.

I thought about that falling tree and ground my teeth. Somebody would pay for this. Things had just ratcheted up a lot of notches.

A car rocked up and the vet appeared, introducing herself as Hayley and frowning sympathetically when she laid eyes on Flinders. As we carried him indoors, another car drove into the car park, a woman at the wheel. Charlie, the nurse. They took him into the surgery. The pair spent half an hour working on him, then the vet came out into the waiting room and said she had to confirm I was the dog's owner.

'I'm responsible for him at the moment.'

She told me his back right leg was shattered and would need to be amputated at once. The left was broken, but there was a chance it could be saved. No promises: if the operation failed and infection set in, he'd have to be put down. I cursed myself. The poor creature hadn't asked to be involved in my misadventures. He'd saved my life, been good company for a few days. Hayley asked if I was willing to consent to, and pay for, the surgery, to which I readily agreed, all the while looking forward to putting down whoever was responsible for this. She said that, even if the operation was successful, they'd have to keep Flinders at the clinic for a few days' recovery and rehab.

I thanked them both, shook their hands, paid the deposit and sat in the HiLux contemplating my next move. It was after seven now: office hours, at least by rural police standards. Five minutes later I turned into the drive of the Windmark Police Station.

# CHAPTER 26

Vince was in residence. He scowled when I told him about the house and the dog, scowled some more when I told him about the toxic waste on Heffernan's Lane. I gave him all I had on Wilde Wastes' nocturnal activities – the location of the dump, the number of the truck – and he said he'd contact the Environmental Protection Authority straightaway, arrange surveillance and a raid on the property.

The scowl on his face was just about frozen into place by the time I told him what I wanted to do next.

'The guy's retired, Jess. Can't you let him enjoy his autumn years in peace?'

I explained my thinking: Dan Starcevic, Nash Rankin's old boss, clearly knew him better than anybody else I'd encountered thus far. He was the only person in this entire investigation who'd been described as close to Nash. He could well hold answers to the questions that had been bugging me for days.

Vince still had his doubts, but eventually he came round. The fact that somebody had gone to the trouble of trying to kill me – with a falling tree, no less, the same method they'd used on Raph Cambric – clearly suggested there was more to this case than met the eye. He said he'd get in touch with Dan Starcevic and find out if he was willing to speak to me. He insisted on following me back to my shattered home.

He clicked his tongue and shook his head when he saw the trail of destruction the branch had carved. 'Widow maker,' he muttered. I'd heard the expression before; it was what they called eucalypts out here. They could drop massive branches or upper trunks at any time, often with fatal consequences for those below. It was more than a branch. Virtually half the tree had shorne off and crashed down.

I showed him the rubble I'd been under when my assailant came in to deliver the coup de grâce. We examined the tree from which the branch had fallen. There were a couple of marks that could have come from an axe, but it was difficult to be certain, given the general deterioration of the branch. There were signs of root rot, of termite infestation. Whoever did this knew their timber. They'd chosen a tree which could well have fallen anyway. The incident would have passed off as an accident had I not spotted the axeman and lived to tell the tale.

We examined the dirt track on the north side of the house, where the vehicle had parked. There were numerous tyre treads there, but one stood out: a Dunlop Sport Maxx. It was recent and deep, slewing in the mud. My years of living in the red dirt country had given me an encyclopaedic knowledge of tyre treads; by the time I left Kulara, I knew half the town by their tyres (my offsider knew the other half by their footprints).

'We gonna make it formal?' asked Vince.

I'd been wondering that myself. The danger of reporting the episode to the crime unit was that I'd have to fess up to my own surreptitious activities. Word would doubtless find its way back to Dougherty or Wallace.

'Maybe I'll keep it under the radar for now,' I replied.

Vince put a call through to the local Emergency Services, who said they'd despatch a crew to deal with the tree.

He stood on the steps and stared at the wreckage, clearly concerned. 'You be careful,' he warned me as he departed.

The wind was settling down now, but the sky was still overcast – unless that was a reflection of my mood. Seeing poor old Flinders so badly knocked about had rattled me. I shuddered to think what it would do to Nash when he found out.

Whose toes had I been treading on? The three charmers from the day before were the prime suspects, of course. It could have been any one of them, although Paul Burstill seemed the least likely. Somebody had carried out the initial inspection and prepping of the tree, and surely that would have happened during the daylight hours, while I was away? If Burstill was responsible, he was a bloody quick worker. And if there was one thing Burstill wasn't, it was quick. Mind you, he could have assigned one of his employees to shadow me when I left the recycling plant. I'd had the discomfiting feeling that I was being followed. But still, the timing seemed unlikely.

Who else? The brute who attacked me in the dark obviously wasn't Ronald Laws, but who was to say he hadn't recruited someone? How did whoever it was know where I lived? Maybe that wasn't such an obstacle. Half the population of Satellite probably knew about the female copper in the cabin on Shady Grove Road by now.

The SES crew rolled up soon afterwards, accompanied by Lance Cunningham, who stared at the ruins of my house in horror. Vince Tehlich had filled him in. He said he'd try to find me alternative accommodation, but I told him I'd stay here for now, even if it meant camping in a smashed and battered hovel. Then my neighbour, Rocco, came over to see what all the fuss was about and stayed to join the party. He was stocky and bald, well into his seventies and handy with a chainsaw. The SES volunteers were a gang of bouncy reprobates in big boots and orange overalls who immediately set to work with their axes and chainsaws. Lance pulled on a set of chainsaw chaps and joined in. The tree was chopped and largely removed in a couple of hours.

Just as they were finishing up, another mini-convoy arrived. The Kelly gang. Sam, with his son Nick, a couple of apprentices – one of them Karly Tehlich – and a truckload of building materials and equipment. Sam, a burly bloke in his fifties, stood looking at the ruins before he eventually managed a wry smile.

'When Luce told me you had a roof that needed repairing . . .'

Vince had told them about my predicament. Lucy was there, along with Possum and my father, Ben, who gazed at the remnants of my home wearily, hands on hips, eyebrows raised, mouth fallen. He was a wiry, sun-scarred fellow with brutal boots and a hat the size of a light truck tyre. I could understand his resignation and concern. There's always been a dangerous current, a riptide, running under my life. Having spent most of his own life out on the edge, he recognised a fellow traveller when he saw one and blamed himself.

My visitors worked like a mob of Amish barn-raisers on speed. By knock-off time I had a roof over my head and a set of more or less intact walls and doors. The table and bed had been crushed but Nick, a bush furniture-maker by trade, improvised a replacement of the former and my indestructible swag did the job of the latter. Some of the repair-work was rough and ready, but it would do for now. Possum turned out to be a devil with the duct tape: she used it to seal the gaps, cover the temporary wires and to stick transparent plastic sheeting over the broken windows.

It was getting on for dark when she taped a hand-drawn sign – HOME SWEET HOME, with a cartoon figure of a bandaged cabin on crutches – over the door.

We all stood in the yard and admired the finished product. I thanked them all profusely. Dad invited me to stay with him at his cottage in Canticle Creek, but I demurred. I didn't know who'd been responsible for the carnage visited upon me that morning, but I wanted to be ready and waiting for them if they came back for another go.

Lucy persisted. She said I was looking a little ragged around the edges, that there was a warm bed and a hot meal waiting for me back at the Bluehouse, the family's home in Canticle Creek. I eventually came round. Maybe the universe owed me a bit of TLC after the tribulations of the past few days. The counterattack could wait.

## CHAPTER 27

We headed back to the Bluehouse, twenty-five kilometres to the south-west. As we walked from the car, I took a moment to admire the reconstruction work they'd carried out over the past couple of years. The new house was a substantial dwelling of mudbrick, recycled iron wood and radially sawn timber that seemed to have somehow grown out of the earth and shaped itself to the contours of the surrounding slopes. Sam Kelly definitely had a touch of the homespun genius about him. God only knew how you got natural, solid materials like timber and stone to curve and flow the way they did here. They'd painted the doors and window frames blue in honour of the house's predecessor and namesake.

After an excellent meal and a convivial fireside chat I headed off to the spare room I'd been given. I popped into Possum's room to say goodnight. This was a risky exercise at the best of times: Possum's room was a zoo. Her current guests included an ant farm full of jumping jacks, an injured baby possum and a Mexican walking fish. There was a magpie named Pendles, currently out of sight but generally perched in the tree outside her window. I remembered a previous occasion when I'd sat on a chair and discovered a baby snake beneath the cushion.

She put her book aside and looked at me directly.

'You wanna talk about it?' she asked, her eyes bright.

'About what?'

'Whatever you've been doing that's got somebody so riled up they're dropping trees onto your house.'

'Sorry, Poss. It's police business.'

'And that's another thing,' she pressed. 'I hear you're not quite police these days.'

'Just a temporary misunderstanding. I'll be back in action soon.'

She licked her lips. 'I also hear you got yourself a man – at last!'

I groaned softly. Was there no such thing as privacy round here?

She raised herself in the bed. 'Do tell, Jess. Who is he? Is he hot?'

'He's just a slightly mixed-up feller who lives in the hills at Wycliff – when he's not in gaol.'

'Oh yeah, I heard that. Slight complication.'

'Nash Rankin's his name. He grows apples and corn and looks after injured eagles. Oh, and he specialises in rescuing roadside turtles in dramatic fashion.'

'Sounds like my kinda guy.'

'I suspect he would be. If he ever gets out I'll bring him here to meet you. They've accused him of killing the man at Wycliff, but I don't think he's guilty. I'm trying to find out who is.'

She thought for a moment. 'Well, you're in the right place.'

'What do you mean?'

'The hills around Satellite, they're full of wackos. Always have been. Have you been to the Saturday market yet? It's like the *Star Wars* bar on steroids. Shipwrecked astral travellers, gorillas in leather jackets, heavyweight hippies, featherweight drug dealers, survivalists, sovereign citizens – they're all there, treading on each other's toes. It's hilarious.'

'As opposed to Canticle Creek, you mean? Where you're all chartered accountants and church wardens?'

Her laughter rang around the room. 'More like church mice – as in as poor as. But seriously, Jess, Satellite's always had a reputation. Makes us look tame. If I wanted to know anything about the people of Satellite, that's the first place I'd look.'

I pressed for more information. 'Nash said he was raised in a cult that used to operate in the Windmarks. Have you ever heard of the Revelators?'

She contemplated the ceiling. 'Rings a bell. When I was at school there were a few kids whose families had been caught up in it. Those kids on average turned out pretty weird. From what I remember, they were either gibbering evangelicals or went the other way and became complete stoners. But I've only ever heard it spoken of as ancient history. The group disappeared years ago, didn't it?'

'I believe so, but there could be aftershocks running down through the generations. Nash also used to be a cop. I've been looking at people who might hold that against him.'

She rolled her eyes. 'That'd fill the MCG.'

'Maybe,' I said, suppressing a yawn.

She noticed and told me to get some shut-eye because I'd had a hell of a day. I couldn't disagree.

As I left the room, she picked up her book and said she'd ask around. I frowned. I always worried about Possum. If there was a firestorm, she'd be in there with the storm chasers.

'Don't go sticking your nose into anything, Poss. Somebody might bite it off. You hear anything, just let me know. I've got a bad feeling about this business.'

She rolled her eyes, suggested I was over-prone to bad feelings. I thought about the killer trees and toxic waste dumpers, the weirdos and wackos she'd just told me were cruising around the district and suggested sometimes bad feelings were justified. She made a face and returned to her book.

I lay in bed listening to some music. Courtney Barnett's 'Depreston', a recommendation from Possum. Eventually I drifted off to sleep, getting as close as I could to the sleep of the just, enjoying a night not interrupted by drips, dogs or lethal trees.

First thing in the morning I rang Hayley, the vet. Flinders was hanging in there. The operation appeared to have been a success, but they'd need a few more days to be sure. She was still worried about infection; he was in a vulnerable state. If he did survive, we were going to have to rename him Tripod.

I put the phone away and sighed. Poor bloody hound.

I needed a bit of cheering up, so I headed out to the mudbrick cottage the Kellys had built for my father. I knew he was in residence when I spotted his old brown boots next to the back door. They were a portrait of their owner: they bore the scuffs and scars of every mile he'd hiked, every cliff he'd climbed, every fire he'd stomped out. I found him crouching over a canvas with a paintbrush in his hand and an air of frustration about him. He was well into his seventies now and looked it. But the older he got, the more desperately he wanted to make up for the sizeable slabs of his life in which he'd been forced to do things other than art to eke out a living. He'd only started seriously exhibiting when he was in his late forties.

He greeted me curtly, then got back to work.

I looked over the canvas he was jabbing at. The outer edges were shrouded in dark mist, but the centre section hummed with colour and life. I made out a plummeting goshawk, a hunch-back orchid, a v-formation of spitfire caterpillars ploughing through the dirt.

'What are you working on?'

I made the enquiry with some hesitation. Dad never liked talking about his work, said he'd let the paintings do the talking. But this morning he was in a loquacious mood.

'You know how it goes with me, Jess. I just stuff around until something jumps out and grabs me by the throat.'

'So, what's got your throat now?'

He gave the question a moment's consideration.

'Carbon.'

'Carbon?' I echoed. He must have detected the surprise in my voice. He stood up, stretched his back and gestured at me to follow him. Outside, he led me towards a stand of trees at the back of the block. At their base was a curved, mud-covered structure, a metre wide, three or four long, burrowing into the surrounding slopes. I was surprised I'd never noticed it before, then realised it must have been buried in the undergrowth and only come to light after the fire swept through here.

'What is this?' I asked.

'It's a Japanese kiln,' he replied. 'No prizes for guessing who built it.'

The Bluehouse had originally been the home of Kenji Takada, Lucy's father, a noted Japanese potter turned artist who settled here in the fifties.

Lucy came out and joined us, caught the tail end of the conversation. She must have spotted us from the kitchen.

'It's called an anagama,' she explained. Lucy was a potter herself, had inherited many of her father's proclivities. 'Sam and I have been restoring it. We're just about ready for our first firing.'

'Have a look inside,' said Dad.

He drew a torch from his pocket and passed it over. I leaned in and lit up the chamber. It was long and sloping, with a firebox at the front and a chimney at the back.

'Here, let me open the side stokes,' said Lucy.

She removed a brick from the side of the kiln. As the natural light flooded in, I saw that the floor was littered with shards of rock and pottery. But what really caught my eye were the walls. They were covered with a thin layer of molten green-gold glass. Those luminous surfaces were works of art themselves; you could discern frozen rivers and craggy mountains, lonely pine trees, long-legged birds. I picked up a fragment from the kiln floor. It was only a couple of inches long, but its vitreous yellows and greens formed the perfect image of a tree.

Lucy thought so too. 'Looks like a golden wattle.'

'Do you mind if I keep it?' I asked. 'I know someone who might appreciate it.'

'Of course not,' she said. 'It's yours.'

I slipped it into my pocket.

'I remember the firings from my childhood,' said Lucy, folding her arms and gazing into the shadows of the kiln. 'We'd often take the shards, turn them into something beautiful: necklaces, bracelets, odd little toys. Once a year, Dad and his friends would load their pottery in, fill the firebox with acacia wood and light it up. Clouds of smoke and jets of flame would come billowing out the chimney. He'd say we were watching the dragon breathe.'

'Fascinating, isn't it?' added Dad. 'But what really got me thinking about the role of carbon in all this—'

'In all what?'

'In all of . . .' – he waved a hand at the surrounding hills – 'everything, was this tree.' He gestured at a big old she-oak nearby. 'Look how healthy it is. That's because it was nourished by carbon from the smoke and ash in its early years. Carbon's essential to the cycle of life and death. It forms compounds with other elements – calcium, potassium, phosphorus – and ignites the systems of the forest. It's shape-shifting, indestructible, and its medium is fire.'

I was suddenly keen to take another look at the painting he'd been working on, curious to see how closely it aligned with what he'd just told me. The three of us walked back to the studio. I stood in front of the canvas and soft-focused my eyes. 'Has it got a title yet?' I asked.

'The Black Spark.'

Typical. An oxymoron. I realised the blackness that ran around the outer edges of the painting was somehow central to its geometry. It glimmered like the desert sky at night. It was beautiful, except for a peculiar section in the upper left corner. The shadows there were of a different order, as deeply dark as a bog hole swallowing a wombat. Or a black hole swallowing a star. Looming over it was what looked like a rocky outcrop, or a human skull, deeply incised into the darkly impasto paint. The overall effect was almost demonic.

'Why does this bit send a shiver through my bones?' I asked, pointing at the corner.

Dad grimaced and scratched his whiskers.

'Where there's life, there's death.'

'What?'

'Not everybody round here is as welcoming as the good people of Canticle Creek. I was pottering around the ridge country up along the northern end of the Wiregrass Valley a few months ago when I spotted an outcrop on the escarpment that intrigued me. It was on private property, so for once in my life I thought I'd do the right thing and ask the owner's permission before going in. There's this big house looming over the road like a medieval fortress. And bugger me if the bloke on the front gate doesn't tell me to sod off. I ignored him, of course. Drove a little further down the road – past all the TRESPASSERS PROSECUTED signs – then nipped in the back way. But somebody must have spotted me. Next thing I know there's this bloody great hellhound coming after me. I ran off, but it still took a chunk out of my arse. Had to scramble up the escarpment to get away.' He shook his head. 'Nice people. Thought I'd honour them with a mention in the painting. It was worth it, though. The outcrop was granite, like I suspected, but when I got up there I saw it was studded with xenoliths.'

Xenoliths I knew. Rocks with a different origin from the igneous mass in which they were embedded.

I was settling in for a discourse on the formation and distribution of xenoliths – Dad was a scientist before he became an artist, and a gasbag before he became either – when my phone pinged. It was a text from Vince Tehlich. 'Starcy will see you.' Vince's old copper mate, Nash's boss. 'Number and address attached. He's already had one heart attack don't give him another.'

# CHAPTER 28

The address was in the tiny town of Rufus, an hour to the south. That must have been the retirement shack Vince had spoken of.

I rang the number, received a curt reply and precise directions to Starcy's place. Over the phone at least, he had the air of a feller who didn't fuck about with formalities and small talk. I drove down to Rufus and found the property where he said it was: five minutes out of town, ten isolated acres on the shore of a lake with a pair of white-faced herons at the water's edge. There was a fibro shack with a LandCruiser in the carport and a tinny on a trailer in the yard.

As I cruised down the drive, the front door opened and a man emerged. He came towards me, limping. Old coppers are like old footballers: they limp a lot. He was tall, heavily built, wearing black tracky dacks, a blue lumber jacket and a green beanie. He carried himself with an air of authority, despite the years and the gait.

'Jesse,' he said, engulfing my hand in his. He had cracked nails, bent fingers, calluses on his calluses. 'Come round to the fire. Need some warmth on a day like this. On a subject like this.'

He led me to the far side of the house, gasping a little as he walked. There was a pair of metal chairs looking out over the lake and a lively fire upon which a billy was simmering.

I paused to take in the view. The breeze blowing off the lake was icy and light, the greenery on the opposite shore luminous.

'You live here on your own?' I asked.

'Mostly. Since the wife died. Still got a place down the city, but I like the peace out here. It's the antidote to forty-five years of wading through the human sewer.'

'Sorry to disturb it.'

He brushed my apology aside. 'If it'll help the boy . . .'

Nash wasn't exactly a boy, but maybe when you got to Starcy's age, we all looked like boys or girls. He threw a chunk of red gum onto the fire, poured me a pannikin of tea, gave me a lamington from a packet.

'So,' he said, lowering his glasses and raising his eyebrows. 'Vince Tehlich tells me you're in a relationship with Nash.'

'I seem to be.'

'That'd be a first for him, at least in my experience. You must be an adventurous soul. I didn't even know he was in trouble again until Vince told me yesterday. Don't have that many contacts still in the job. Better for my mental health to steer clear of the brotherhood. I'll try to get down and see him. Not supposed to be driving right now, but I got a mate who's happy to be my chauffeur.' He stretched out his right leg and gave the knee a massage, then looked me in the eye.

'You seriously think Nash might have been the victim in all of this? The patsy?'

I tried to explain the reasons for my suspicion. I told him I'd been looking over Nash's old cases, had interviewed the priest, the towie and the swindler.

Starcy's upper lip curled. 'Must have been like a bloody enema, having a chat with that lot. What did you make of Neddy Kursk?'

'Bit of a pig, but there's no law against that.'

'We had a good look at him as an accomplice to his brother's trail of mayhem and blood, but there was no direct evidence of any involvement. Plenty of suspicion, but no proof.'

'Interviewing Burstill was just as bad,' I said. When I explained that I'd sprung his crew dumping what I presumed to be some kind of toxic waste in the Windmarks, he glared out at the lake and frowned. I got a hint of how he must have made the villains cringe in his younger days.

We both looked around as a bird call echoed across the water. The herons moved through the shallows, their necks extended, their lethal beaks poised.

Starcy turned back to me.

'I was pleased to hear you're doing this,' he said. 'I'm just about past it myself – got a dicky ticker and titanium hips, but when Vince told me about Nash's latest trouble, I thought he must have been cursed. There are still things about that first conviction that puzzle me.'

'Such as?'

'It just didn't feel right. I might not have the education you young smart-arses have today, but I know when someone's selling me a pup. I was with Nash the morning of the incident.

He told me he was going up to Horse Thief. Said he had an old friend who was troubled about something, wanted to talk.'

'He didn't say what about?'

'No, but there was nothing in his eyes to suggest he was going there to punch anybody out. I'd seen him angry and he didn't look angry that morning.'

I pressed Starcy for more details about the incident and he obliged. Much of what he told me I'd heard before: the neighbour, the fight, the fatal shot.

But when I asked him what Nash had to say in his own defence, he was more expansive than anybody else had been thus far. Clearly the episode had weighed upon his mind for years. Nash said that when he got to the house, the door was open and Glazier was laid out on the floor. He went in to assist but, as he knelt down, he was attacked from behind. He didn't see who by; he said his attacker was dressed in black, the room was half-dark. When he came to he found Glazier dead and the sirens wailing. The investigators believed him at first, but then they started having doubts. They could find no trace of anybody else in the house, even after an intensive examination. Then they went through Nash's computer and found he'd come across evidence that Leon Glazier was involved in trafficking sexual images of minors. Offences like that had always raised Nash's hackles, though he denied all knowledge of the images. Then they got wind of the weird behaviour he'd been displaying in the weeks leading up to that day – he'd been confused, aggressive, dizzy. One time he blacked out in the station, cracked his head against a desk.

'Vince Tehlich told me about that,' I said. 'He told me Nash even thumped you.'

'Puh!' Starcy rolled his eyes. 'That was nothing. It happened a couple of weeks before. Nash was so mixed up for a while there, he thought he was punching the wall. I barely even noticed it, but there was another senior member of staff there and a report had to be made. Nothing came of it at the time, but when the investigators heard about it, they saw it as part of a pattern. They began to wonder if Nash hadn't shot Glazier during a psychotic episode. They asked me more questions about him: Was he using drugs? Was he having some sort of breakdown? They obtained a statement from a Family Services psychiatrist who'd been involved with Nash since he was a kid.'

That caught my attention. Nobody else had mentioned this. Of course, I assumed various health professionals would have been involved with Nash's case, given its outcome, but I hadn't realised the psychiatrist who gave evidence had known Nash since his childhood. I asked Starcy if he remembered the doctor's name.

He scratched his scalp. 'Rush, I think it was. Damien Rush. He wasn't a bad bloke; it was his evidence that saved Nash from a twenty-year stretch. He said the boy was suffering from psychosis and PTSD, that if he did kill Glazier, he more than likely wouldn't have known what he was doing.'

I thought about Nash's isolated bush home, his attachment to wild things, his quirks and eccentricities. Gaol or custodial supervision, incarceration of any form would be hell for somebody like him. He'd said as much to me that night at the Wiregrass. He needed the calming influence of the bush to keep his head level. He needed to smell peppermint and wood smoke, to watch bees floating over flowering gums, eagles over mountains. He needed ant bites, winter chills, the rough texture of wild honey.

Starcy rose to his feet, picked up a cane and asked if I'd like to accompany him on his hourly walk. He explained that he had a litany of hip and knee problems. Regular exercise was his only way of staying out of the old folks home.

The two of us set out on a narrow track that wound its way along the northern edge of the lake.

## CHAPTER 29

As we walked, I asked Starcy how long he'd known Nash and he ran a finger across his chin, thinking.

'Must be twenty-five years,' he replied.

I did a double take. Had I been mistaken about Nash's age?

Starcy noticed my reaction. 'First time I came across him he was only thirteen.'

I listened, intrigued, as he told me how he'd met Nash Rankin.

'I was the sergeant-in-charge at Montgomery, down in the valley,' he said. 'Drove into the car park one morning and there's this teenage boy hunched up on the front step. He was dark-haired, wild-eyed, wearing dirty jeans and a torn jacket.'

'I've come to report a crime,' were his first words to Starcy. 'A company of criminals.'

'Whoa there,' Starcy had said. 'Who are you and where are you from?'

He said his name was Nash Rankin and that he came from the Patmos Centre.

Starcy knew a bit about it. The Patmos Centre was a church-based organisation delivering drug rehabilitation programs in an old boarding school up along the Windmark River. They'd been there for five years, kept to themselves, never caused any trouble. The leader, Reverend John Patmos, had worked his way into a position of authority among the local clergy, despite what some thought of as an over-enthusiastic approach to religion. They did have occasional services at the centre, and the church's hierarchy resided there, but their operational headquarters, and the ultimate source of their prosperity and power, was a vast mausoleum down in Greendale, to which as many as a thousand people were drawn by Patmos's Sunday morning sermons.

When Starcy asked Nash what crime this 'company of criminals' had committed, the boy reported that the 'Revelator' had killed his sister.

I felt a pang of sympathy when Starcy reached this part of the story. His sister, Shiloh, was the only member of his family I'd heard Nash mention with affection. I remembered his story of how they'd sit up in the golden wattle and sing along with the birds. I instinctively reached into my pocket for the little pottery piece I'd retrieved from Lucy's kiln, and held it in my fingers.

'What the hell is a Revelator?' Starcy had asked the teenage Nash. It was the first time he'd heard the word, though when the shit hit the windmill, it became the name by which the organisation was generally known.

'It's what we call the leader of our church,' Nash had told him. 'Reverend Patmos. He forces the young girls to have sex with him.'

A couple of weeks ago, the boy said, Patmos had subjected his fifteen-year-old sister to what the church elders called 'purgative redemption'. It was rape. She'd fled the community, desperate, distraught, and had ended up sleeping rough on the streets of Melbourne. The night before, Nash had got word that Shiloh had hanged herself in a Preston park. That was what had driven him to the station that morning. He pleaded with Starcy to get up there and arrest them all, said the place was a nest of iniquity, its leaders a pack of dangerous animals.

When one of Starcy's team, Constable Alice Hurley, arrived for work, he told her what was going on. They took the boy in, gave him hot food and drinks, called in a police family liaison officer to look after him.

Starcy reported the matter to his superiors in Greendale, who agreed to launch an immediate investigation, but he decided he'd go up to the property himself and have a pre-emptive look around.

Now, walking by the lake with me, he paused to contemplate a bustling ants nest for a moment then looked me in the eye.

'Worst decision I ever made,' he said.

I waited for him to continue.

'Alice and I drove up the valley, but we were pulled up at the gate by some goon in a uniform. Bit over the top for a church, I thought. Still, maybe it was necessary, working with addicts and all that. We got sent up to the big house and were honoured with an audience with the man himself, John Patmos. A more silver-tongued prick you could never imagine. He was tall and broad-shouldered, with thick white hair and teeth. What you might call ruggedly handsome. His office was all polished marble and bevelled glass, fitted out with armchairs you could stable a horse in.'

Starcy took a swig from a flask in his pocket. I'm not much of a drinker, but I could have done with a swig myself, a thirst that only deepened as the story unfolded.

'I began,' Starcy continued, 'by saying that we'd picked the boy up. Patmos said he was relieved to hear it. Nash's mother, Rebecca, was one of the live-in staff. She was already shattered by the death of her daughter, had been worried sick about her son. It would be a relief for all concerned if we could return Nash to his family as soon as possible.'

Starcy slowed down, clearly troubled. The conversation was costing him. I sensed he'd survived as long as he had by sweeping things under the carpet, but you can only do that for so long. There comes a time when you have to bring in the industrial vacuum cleaners.

We came to the end of the track, then turned and made our way back to the shack. 'By this stage,' said Starcy, 'I'm thinking this is outta my league. We should have waited for the Sex Crimes Squad or the Child Abuse team – somebody used to interrogating snakes – before we set foot in the place.'

He crunched his knuckles and stared at the gunmetal sky. 'Then in she sweeps. Mrs Patmos. Guin. She's even more charming and confident than he is: attractive, in a silicon sorta way, smooth as silk with buffed-up hair and flashy nails. She dishes up tea and cake on a silver tray, tells us about the work they do, how brilliant their results are, the lives they've saved, the crackheads they've pulled back from the brink. I've spent my life learning to detect bullshit, but even I'm entranced.'

He paused, then shuffled uncomfortably, his right knee obviously playing up. 'But then I ask a question about Shiloh and something strange happens. Patmos looks grief-stricken, starts talking about the girl, the tragedy of it all. Then I glance at a mirror on the wall and catch a reflection of Guin behind me. Patmos is a big, beefy guy. Guin's small, kind of scrawny, but just for a moment, she seemed to tower over him. Over us all. She's warning him to shut his fucking mouth in case he blows it. I realise she's been controlling every word of the conversation from the moment she entered the room.'

We reached the house and resumed our seats. Starcy stirred the fire with a heavy poker, turned over a log. Flames shot up as the ambient oxygen reacted with the carbon. He closed his eyes and let the warmth wash over him. Looked like he needed it.

'John Patmos was the face of that organisation,' Starcy continued. 'He was the Revelator. He had the presence, the handshake, the name. He's the one the press got their fangs into when it all came out. But Guin, my god – she was a force of nature. Something's not right, I thought. I knew it in my bones. This woman's a monster. Nothing she's involved in could be in any way decent. Whatever she's doing, it's all about her. I asked if we could have a look around, but the atmosphere had changed. "I'm afraid not," she said. She warned me there were some troubled young souls there, the sight of a police uniform could set them back months. I suggested maybe we could just have a look around the outside areas, not enter the residences or workshops, but her lips tightened. "Not without a warrant." Then she smirked in a way that made me feel like she was pissing on me from a great height. My offsider, Alice, felt it as well. She said later she felt nauseated, just being in Guin's presence. She also noted the woman had had more plastic surgery than a flock of reality television wannabes.'

Starcy and Alice left soon after that. Back at HQ, things were moving quickly. The investigators in Melbourne located a friend of Shiloh's who confirmed the essential facts of Nash's story, that the girl had been in a pit of despair and shame after being raped by Patmos. The police raided the Institute the next morning. They were packing warrants and battering rams, armed to the teeth with social workers, sniffer dogs and family liaison officers, but they were too late. The rats had scuttled. Maybe they got a tip-off, maybe Starcy's visit put the wind up them. Whatever the reason, the Patmoses had skipped the country. They'd been preparing for an eventuality like this for years, fleecing some of their followers, blackmailing others, amassing a fortune, shoring up their fortresses. They had homes all over the world, millions of dollars squirrelled away on treasure islands or buried in bank vaults, all of it protected by a crew of cut-throat lawyers and tiger-eyed accountants. Eventually Interpol tracked the couple down to a luxury villa in the Caymans.

VicPol set up a task force and launched a major investigation into what rapidly took on all the god-awful attributes of a hardcore cult. Without the Patmoses there to eliminate dissent and stifle questions, the scales came off. Whistle-blowers and wounded acolytes came out of the woodwork and a more comprehensive picture of the organisation emerged. In Starcy's words, what a maggoty shit-show it turned out to be. Nominally Christian, but with the usual carry bag of cults everywhere: a dash of apocalyptic gibberish, a pinch of Revelation and Eastern mysticism, lashings of traumatising narcissism and a vicious riptide of sex and death. All of it tax-free, much of it funded from the public purse.

The outer suburban church was the usual band of weak-minded happy-clappers, but it was in the more secluded confines of the rehab centre in the Windmarks that the real horrors were perpetrated. What the organisation called 'addiction therapy' was mostly Guin and her little coterie screaming at tormented teenagers to repent their sins and expel their demons. Anybody who stood up to her was thrown onto the street. Guin had an uncanny ability to separate the gullible from their money. She'd use doctors and nurses to sniff out well-heeled invalids on their deathbeds. She could alter wills by telekinesis. She could charm her followers into making ongoing donations for churches that were never built, missionary ventures that never happened.

For Patmos himself, salvation came at the point of his prick. He helped himself to the young women, subjecting them to his 'purgative redemption'. That was bad enough, but what shocked Starcy to the core was the discovery, confirmed by numerous sources, that Guin was a voyeur. Of epic proportions. She'd get off watching her husband, or anybody else who was on heat or horny – the dog if there were no other options – perform. She had a cubbyhole adjoining the 'master bedroom' which was equipped with two-way mirrors, lights, thermal cameras and microphones.

I listened to Starcy's tale, aghast, wondering how such a nightmare could have flourished so wildly then faded so swiftly from the community's memory.

'How did they get away with it?' I asked, aghast.

'The Patmoses had an army of experts – doctors, accountants, even coppers, rumour had it – who were ready to do their bidding: carry out autopsies, forge papers, bury the evidence and cover their tracks. Some of them were genuine followers. Others?

The Patmoses had perfected the art of blackmail. They'd use young girls – or boys – to seduce some sucker they thought they could use and film the results – then they had 'em by the balls.'

I shook my head.

'So, what happened to Nash when the cult was broken up?' I asked. 'He was still only a kid.'

'He spent some time with his mother, but that didn't work out. She was totally hooked on Patmos and the movement, one of their earliest converts. When it fell apart, so did she. She drifted back into the inner Melbourne drug scene, OD'd six months later.'

'And his father?'

'We never were able to find out who the father was. He was listed as "unknown" on the birth certificate. I did ask Rebecca once – all she'd say was he was the devil who got her on to the drugs in the first place. Nash was raised from then on by his grandfather. He left school early, spent most of his time on the land, in the bush. I kept in touch as best I could. Used to visit him and his grandpa, Matty.' He smiled fleetingly. 'They always gave me a box of apples.'

'Did anybody else keep in touch?'

'Not that I saw. They were a damaged lot, the Revelator refugees. That was Guin's speciality: she'd drag the weak and the wounded out of the gutter, fleece them and leave them weaker and more wounded. Make them dependent on her and her husband. On the cult. I think Nash did catch up with some of the other kids from time to time, people he'd grown up with . . .'

'Like Leon Glazier?'

'Like Leon, yeah, Nash was a leader to them, especially early on. But they all had loads of baggage and layers of psychological scarring. Mostly Nash just lay low, found a peace of his own working with wildlife. Nobody was more surprised than I was when he asked if he could use me as a referee to join the police. Apparently he'd been thinking about the force as a career ever since that first morning on my doorstep. He was keen to help people in situations as desperate as the one he'd been in. He wanted to do something decent, he said, be a catcher in the rye. I tried to tell him the characters he'd be dealing with were more likely to be on the rye than in it, but he was determined. I had my doubts: he was isolated, fragile, maybe suffering from PTSD. Then I thought about it some more. Thought about the way he'd come down to the station that first morning and reported the leaders of the only home he'd ever known to the authorities. I've worked in law enforcement all my life, seen some real feats of courage, but that stands out for me as the bravest. I recommended him for the job unequivocally. And it worked well – until suddenly it didn't.'

I sat there morbidly entranced as Starcy finished the tale.

John Patmos was eventually extradited back to Australia, but he never paid for his crimes. He died of an aneurysm while he was on remand.

'And Guin?' I asked.

'She's dead as well, thank Christ. Never saw the inside of a gaol, of course. The shithouse rats never do. She had a ring of attack lawyers around her, ready to bark and bite at her command. But even they couldn't keep her going forever. She died of cancer five years ago. I was here at the shack when

I heard the word. Came out and lit a bonfire to celebrate, burned a rag-doll effigy and raised a fuck-off toast to the old bitch.'

Fair enough, I thought. Another question sprang out of nowhere. 'What happened to all the money?'

Starcy flipped his hands. 'Better minds than mine have tried to unravel that one. There were various family members and a pack of desperate hangers-on and victims trying to suck what they could out of the corpse, but I gather it all sank into the quicksands of international justice. Our forensic accountants did what they could, but in the end they didn't think there was much left, not after all the bribing and hiding and litigation – and plastic surgery – was paid for.'

He leaned forward and revved the fire a little more. I rose to my feet and walked down to the lake. The birds edged away through the silver water making tiny ripples. They were like delicate brushstrokes in a Chinese winter landscape.

By the time I got back to the house, Starcy was up and chopping wood. He placed a log on the block then turned and caught my eye. There was something dark in his gaze. Anger? Remorse? Impossible to say, but he muttered a single sentence.

'You find out what happened, Jess. That boy's been through enough.'

He raised the axe then swung it down and split the wood with an energy that generated sparks.

# CHAPTER 30

As the town of Rufus disappeared in the rear-view mirror, I thought about the story Starcy had just given me.

Jesus, what a mess. What a life Nash had endured. No wonder he'd chosen to lose himself in the isolation of the bush. Eagles and apples and rolling green paddocks were a much less toxic environment for him, less likely to trigger the symptoms of his illness.

He'd endured years of abuse and struggled to rebuild his life, not just once, but twice: first by joining the police, then by working with wildlife, only to have it all fall in on him both times.

Now he was stuck in isolation in the remand centre, with the very real prospect of a much longer stretch dangling over his head. From what Starcy had told me, I was the only person who cared enough to try and break that isolation – and I was forbidden from having anything to do with him. Starcy had said he'd try to get down to see him some time soon, but given the old policeman's age and infirmity, not to mention his inability to drive, I couldn't see much help coming from that quarter. Nash would be wasting away in a prison cell, uncertain of whom he could trust, torn away from the wild things that were his only form of therapy.

Maybe not though. According to Starcy, at least one other person had been there for Nash in the past, and would perhaps be willing to step up again. The psychiatrist, Damien Rush. He'd spoken in Nash's defence in court, had apparently kept up a relationship, even if only a professional one, since his teenage years. But I knew nothing about the doctor, not even whether he was still alive and compos mentis, or still practising.

I pulled over, got on to my phone and spent a few minutes trawling the internet. Rush kept a low profile, but eventually I found him, or at least a psychiatrist of that name. He was based in a private hospital, the Nexus, in the upper-middle-class Melbourne suburb of Ivanhoe.

I checked the time. Three thirty. I could be there in an hour. Whether or not I'd get to actually meet the man was another matter. Given the state of the nation's mental health – wasn't a quarter of the population on psychiatric medication at any given time, and weren't they just the ones well enough to realise they needed help? – I presumed that, if Dr Rush was there, he'd have patients sitting on each other's laps in the waiting room. The last thing he'd want was an unannounced visit from the not-quite-partner of a former patient.

But what did I have to lose? I drove down to Ivanhoe and located the hospital: a double-storey building with the name Nexus under a crown on a sign at the door. The waiting room in the mental health department was about what I'd expected: crowded, jittery, nervy, with a nimbus of anxiety and depression lowering over it. There must have been several doctors on the go at once; the patients came and went at a rate of knots.

The receptionist looked at me, aghast, when I said that no, I didn't have an appointment, that I wasn't a patient, that I was here on behalf of a friend and hoping for a few minutes of Dr Rush's precious time. I thought about telling her it was a police matter, but I'd been stretching that line to breaking point of late and was worried about what would happen when it snapped. Sooner or later, if I kept flashing my ID around, word was bound to get back to my bosses. The receptionist said she'd give the doctor a message but she doubted he'd be able to see me. She asked if I wouldn't like to just leave my details and she'd pass them on, but I said I'd give him a written message now and wait for a reply.

She gave me a notepad. I decided to lay it on the line. This guy, after all, was a shrink; if I laid it anywhere other than on the line, chances were he'd spot it. I wrote that I was a friend of his old client Nash Rankin's, that Nash was in deep trouble and needed Dr Rush's support, that I was desperate and could see no other options.

The receptionist left me alone for a couple of minutes while she went into the doctor's rooms, then came back and resumed her seat. The crowd thinned out. At around six thirty the receptionist closed down her computer, stood up and pulled on a coat. Then she took another look at me, must have taken pity. She said she'd see what she could do to move things along. She went through to the office then came out and said Dr Rush could see me – briefly – when his current patient left.

Not long after she departed, the internal door swung open and two men appeared. The first was a frazzled character with a ragged beard and yellow teeth, gaunt, in his sixties. The other was clean shaven, bouncy, brisk, with a bright red bow tie and a confident gaze. I was surprised – though maybe I shouldn't have been, given the crowded room and the fact that psychiatrists spend their lives poking around other people's neuroses – when the doctor turned out to be Mr Frazzled. He bade the patient farewell, introduced himself as Damien Rush then told me he could spare five minutes but that he had an important family conference up in the wards at seven.

He led me into an office fitted out with plump chairs, an overflowing desk and crowded shelves. The walls were covered with calming works of art and framed degrees from sandstone universities. The first thing he said when he closed the door behind us was that, for reasons of patient confidentiality, he couldn't discuss his former patient's medical condition. I assured him I wouldn't have expected any less and asked if he'd been in touch with Nash Rankin in recent years.

He shook his head. 'I'm afraid I haven't had a private conversation with him since I testified on his behalf in court seven years ago. I'd already been treating him for some time.'

'He came to you as a private patient?'

'I was a member of the crisis-management team Family Services put together after the authorities broke up what the press took to calling the Revelators. I saw Nash on a semi-regular basis, though the appointments became less frequent as he grew older. I thought he was coping well with his condition. Working as a police officer seemed to suit him, give him a new sense of purpose, but then there was that terrible relapse that saw him charged with murder. I was pleased to be able to testify for his defence. He's a singular young man with a strong altruistic streak. If he did commit an offence, I doubted he was aware of it.'

'You haven't heard anything about him lately?' I enquired.

He frowned and waved a hand at his dishevelled office. 'There's an epidemic of anxiety rampaging through society right now, especially since Covid. There are stressed or depressed people everywhere you look – even more in places you might not think to look. Those of us on the front line can get a little overwhelmed.'

'Tell me about it. I'm a police officer when I'm not running round after Nash.'

He raised a brow. 'I'm sorry, what was your name again?'

'Jesse Redpath. Leading Senior Constable.'

He leaned back in his chair and stroked his straggly beard. 'Then I'm sure you understand the situation.' He sat up straight. 'So how can I help you today?'

'Nash is back in custody,' I said. 'Accused of killing a neighbour up at Wycliff Rise.'

Rush sighed, shook his head, said he was saddened to hear that, but not especially surprised.

'I see patients like Nash every day of the week,' he explained. 'They may not all kill someone, but for far too many of them such a tragedy is only a missed medication or a traumatic episode away. I don't imagine I'm breaching patient confidentiality by admitting that Nash was suffering from severe psychosis – it was all over the news at the time of his trial. When he was having an episode, he was incapable of distinguishing hallucination from reality. Like so many patients, he was reluctant to stay on his meds; he felt they were affecting his consciousness, giving him what he called brain fog. That may have been so, but the alternative – as I fear Nash is now discovering – can be infinitely worse.'

That was all cheery news, especially for someone who, like me, was involved with Nash.

'The thing is, Doctor, Nash needs help. Now. He's so isolated. He's got very little in the way of family or friends. I've only met him a few times myself, so I suppose I can't even say we're that close. But I do want to support him. Desperately. From what I can gather, I'm about the only one.'

Rush nodded thoughtfully, then asked if I'd visited Nash in prison myself.

'Ah, there's a slight problem. As I said, I'm a serving police officer. My bosses think I've become a little too close to him.'

'How close have you become?'

'Too close for comfort.'

He leaned back in his chair and studied the ceiling. 'You do realise,' he asked, 'that a relationship with an individual like Nash Rankin is going to be fraught with long-term difficulty? There's a reason so many patients with psychological profiles like his end up living and dying alone. Sometimes solitude is their preferred mode of existence. They find human relationships too intimidating. Too dangerous, for all involved.'

'I understand that,' I said, though I was struck by the negativity of the comment. I'd never been to a psychiatrist, but if this was the best the profession had to offer, I wouldn't be in a hurry to seek one out. 'The thing is, Doctor, I'm worried about him, but I've been formally warned off having any direct contact. I'm under suspension at the moment. They think I helped him evade arrest.'

He sighed sympathetically then nodded. 'That does sound awkward. And he has no one else?'

'Not that I've been able to find. There's a couple of old friends from the force but they're mostly out of action these days. I was wondering if there was any possibility of your taking him on as a patient while he's on remand?'

He looked doubtful. 'I'd honestly love to help, but that could be an extremely difficult process, given the parlous nature of mental health treatment in the justice system today.'

He fashioned his fingers into a little church. I noticed there was a slight tremor in his hands. Old age, I wondered, or the manifestation of some underlying condition?

'Excuse me for a moment,' said Rush, turning his attention to his computer. 'At Wycliff Rise, you say?'

'That's right.'

I couldn't see the screen, but I assumed he was doing a review of Nash's recent activities. He shook his head and gave the occasional click of his tongue. Then he turned back to me.

'A terrible story,' he said, to which I readily agreed.

'You must understand,' he continued, 'I can have very little direct input into his treatment unless I'm formally appointed as his healthcare specialist. And the wheels of justice grind so slowly. Just getting to that stage could take months.'

I said I was worried Nash might not last that long, to which the doctor proposed a temporary solution.

'I'll do what I can to visit him, although it will only be on a personal basis at this stage. A familiar face could do a lot to lift his spirits and improve his mental wellbeing. I presume he's in the remand centre?'

'Last I heard.'

'That's good. I have had other patients in there. Access is a little smoother, provided he's not in isolation. I should warn you, though, not to get your hopes up. Anything I can achieve in a visit or two will be no more than the first steps in a journey that will take years, possibly a lifetime. I'll try to see him next week, though I can't promise anything. This is a busy facility. We regularly get overwhelmed by emergencies.'

I thought about Nash's face as he was led away to the ambulance, his isolation in the hospital, his hunger for wilderness.

'Doctor, I'm pretty sure Nash is one of those emergencies.'

He smiled a thin, troubled smile that barely bothered his beard.

'We'll see what we can do.'

He stood up and ushered me to the door.

As I made my way out to the lifts, I experienced a pang of disappointment. This was the bright spot on Nash's horizon? His best option for succour? A medical expert who looked overdue for retirement and who said he would do his best but couldn't promise anything other than a possible visit the next week.

Nash was in a bad way.

I needed to do more.

When I reached the foyer I pulled out my phone and dialled Starcy. He answered straightaway. I asked if he was still planning to visit Nash.

'Course I am. I said I would.' That didn't surprise me. If Starcy said he'd do something, he'd do it. But then he added: 'Might have to make it by taxi though. My mate can't drive. His knees are playing up as well.'

'What is it with you old coppers and your knees?' I asked. 'Must be all that kicking you used to do.'

His laughter rang out through the foyer.

'I was wondering if I could give you a lift down to the remand centre?' I continued. 'I can't go in myself, but I could drop you off and wait outside.'

'Sounds bloody marvellous. I can teach you a thing or two about kicking villains on the way.'

'Can't wait. How's tomorrow work for you?'

'Works well. Bring your ID. I'll see if I can get you in.'

# CHAPTER 31

Starcy was out on the verandah, ready and waiting, when I pulled up in front of the shack. He was wearing a good – if a little, like forty years, out of fashion – suit, walking with a cane and carrying a battered briefcase. Something about the eagerness with which he hobbled towards the car suggested he didn't get away from the property very often. Or maybe it was just the old law-and-order hormones stirring.

'Off into the bowels of hell,' he pronounced, jauntily waving his cane in the direction of the city.

'You really think you can get me in?' I asked.

'Still got a few connections,' he said.

We drove through the town of Rufus and out onto the highway, heading west. It wasn't long before the tall towers and greasy clouds of Melbourne loomed in the distance. The conversation between Starcy and I flowed easily. Perhaps it was his enthusiasm at being back in the saddle, but some of the hardness had evaporated from his face. He asked me about life in the Territory. He'd never been there. His main conception of it was as a place where villains went to bury the loot – or the bodies.

I assured him it wasn't all like that, that there were plenty of long, boring days, drives and people to be endured. I did give him a few – slightly embellished – Territory tales, though, to whet his appetite. I told him about the camp cook who turned out to be a hit man on the run, the diamond-driller who was caught burying stolen gold in a pit toilet, the camel that ate the local drug dealer's stash and was last seen dashing off into the desert with the dealer in pursuit.

Starcy returned the favour by passing on some tips about police life in country Victoria. He'd worked all over the ranges. He knew which roads the smugglers and rustlers were likely to take, and which members of which families were likely to be taking them. He told me about the ways in which the seasons – particularly the footy one – were reflected in the local criminal activity.

We discussed the death at Wycliff Rise. He knew my three suspects, of course, gave me little snippets he thought I could use. He told me Ronald Laws had a cousin who could be worth a visit. The cousin owned a bar in Greendale, had occasionally strayed onto the wrong side of the law and could be leaned upon for information. He told me Paul Burstill had been addicted to coke and used to get a little hyper when he hadn't had a snort for a few days. Neddy Kursk was his deepest concern. They'd always suspected he'd been involved in his brother's atrocities, but could never prove it. They'd also had reason to believe he'd been cooking and distributing crystal meth, but again, they'd never caught him in the act. Starcy had always had a bad feeling about the man, warned me to watch my back.

Pretty impressive, I thought, for a feller who'd been out of the job for ten years. He'd obviously kept a finger on the pulse, despite his claims of trying to steer clear of the brotherhood.

It wasn't until we were inching our way through the inner city that the conversation took on a darker tone and turned to Nash. Maybe it was the gridlocked traffic, maybe it was the dirty old town around us reminding Starcy of why he chose to live in the bush.

'So what's the plan for today?' I asked as we waited at the lights on Punt Road.

'I spoke to a mate who spoke to a mate who happens to have another mate who's the shift supervisor today. We just have to follow the normal visiting procedures and he'll bury any record that you've been there. Hopefully word won't get back to anybody antsy enough to do you any harm.'

'Like Ed Dougherty.'

Starcy clicked his tongue and rolled his eyes. He didn't seem to have much time for my boss. 'Always been a pain in the arse, young Ed. Such a stickler for the rules, he loses sight of the reason we're all here.'

We pulled into the car park in front of the remand centre. I'd never visited it before, but it looked like the usual hellhole of red brick and iron-clad despair. There was a prison officer named Burr waiting for us at reception; Starcy's reputation obviously preceded him. Burr greeted Starcy with deference and escorted us through the various levels of security. It was as smooth a ride as you could hope for, but my heart was in my mouth from the moment I stepped through the front gate.

The doors clanged behind us, our footsteps rang with a heavy echo. If it was this bad for me, I shuddered to think what it must be like for Nash.

We had to wait outside the visitors' centre until they were ready for us. Finally Nash appeared, looking wary. He was wearing green prison overalls and a face full of fresh bruises and wounds. Starcy was thoughtful enough to wait outside while I went in. Nash's eyes lit up briefly when he spotted me.

'What have they done to you?' I whispered as I hugged him.

'I got careless,' he answered. 'It's all right, I can cope. But I'm amazed to see you. Vince Tehlich told me you'd been barred.'

'Friends in high places.'

We sat at a table and I asked how the meeting with his lawyer had gone.

'She was good,' he said. 'But the judge wasn't. Bail refused. I'm in here until we go to court. Exactly when that will be, I've got no idea. Could be months.'

I didn't know what to say in response to this news, so I reached into my pocket and pulled out the little piece of pottery I'd found in Lucy's kiln and passed it over to him. He glanced at it, momentarily confused.

'You told me how you and your sister used to climb the golden wattle and sing along with the birds,' I explained. 'I couldn't bring a real tree, but I hope this might be a little token of it, something you can hang on to when things get rough.'

He swallowed.

'How'd you get it past the guards?'

'Starcy's mate gave us the red carpet.'

'Starcy?'

'Your old boss.'

'I know who he is, but what's he got to do with it?'

'Look over at the door window.'

He turned his head, and Starcy gave him a wave.

'Good god,' Nash said.

I took his hands in mine. 'You've got people on your side, Nash. Don't despair. We'll get you out of here.'

I was trying to raise his spirits, but I couldn't see much evidence of success. His situation was bad and we both knew it. The refusal to grant bail was a blow. It suggested they had a stronger case against him than we knew. It was a difficult conversation, its difficulty somehow underscored by the desperate environment in which we found ourselves. It didn't help that one of his first questions was about Flinders. I couldn't bring myself to give him all the gory details, just said that the dog had had an accident and was recovering at the vet's, would be bouncing around before we knew it. We talked about the farm. He said I was welcome to help myself to the fruit, but when he said it would be ready to pick in February, I shot back at him.

'My god, Nash, we'll have you out of here before then.'

Starcy came in soon afterwards, greeted him confidently, assured him that the ongoing investigation would establish his innocence. But when I told him I was looking over his old cases, he frowned.

'You don't want to go stirring up what's dead and buried, Jess.'

'Even if the ghosts are still floating around?'

'Especially then.' He shook his head. 'You're running around after the likes of Neddy Kursk? For god's sake, be careful.'

He appeared so troubled by the news, I regretted sharing it with him. I reminded myself that he was a man who'd had everything he ever cared for snatched from him. He was still looking traumatised, though trying to disguise it, when we left.

'Just take it one day at a time,' were my last words to him.

'Is there any other way?' he replied.

As Starcy and I made our way back through the various levels of incarceration, the bolts and bars and heavy metal doors, I felt a tear running down my cheek.

Starcy noticed. 'Cheery places, aren't they?' he said, gesturing at the echoing walls around us. 'I'll do what I can to get him some protection. Outrageous that he's getting bashed in here.'

We walked back to the car, slowly and moodily.

Half an hour into the return journey Starcy glanced at a road sign and stirred in his seat.

'Neddy Kursk,' he said, apropos of nothing. 'You said he had a place down in Bloomfield?'

'He does.'

He proposed we drop on him unannounced, have a sniff around. The visit to Nash had clearly got his dander up. He wanted to do more.

'Smash and Grab,' he muttered with a shake of the head when we pulled up in front of the towing company. 'They're not even trying to hide it.'

We were about to go in when we spotted a man walking out from the main shed and moving towards a four-wheel drive in the car park. He was in his forties, with gravel-rash skin, an oily quiff, a weak chin and prominent teeth. It was the fellow I'd thought bore a faint resemblance to Margaret Thatcher.

'That's bloody Rev McQueen,' Starcy said.

He was out of the car before I had a chance to ask who bloody Rev McQueen was. Starcy swung across the yard, leaning heavily on his stick but moving at a surprising clip. I followed. McQueen caught sight of us, looked alarmed and picked up the pace. He reached his car and climbed into the driver's seat.

'Stop there,' Starcy yelled with a voice that rattled the gravel.

McQueen started the engine and began to back out. Starcy raised his cane and thrust it through the open window and into the spokes of the steering wheel. McQueen was still trying to remove it when Starcy reached in, turned off the motor and whipped out the keys, all in a single, fluid motion that belied his age and physical condition.

'Hello there, Rev,' he said.

McQueen looked around, searching for an escape route. Quickly came to realise that speaking to Starcy was the only one.

'Sergeant Starcevic,' he grunted. 'Long time no—'

'What are you up to, Rev?'

'Just trying to earn an honest living.'

'That'll be the day. You still running with the Rowsills?'

McQueen shook his head. 'I'm out of that scene now, Sergeant. Driving a tow truck.'

Starcy stepped back and surveyed the yard. 'Aye, that's one thing I'll grant you. You always knew how to drive.'

McQueen was growing increasingly anxious, glancing back towards the office.

'If I could have the keys back, Sergeant. I got an appointment.'

'Who with?'

'My dentist.'

'Are you hawking a load of stolen nitrous oxide?'

'I got a broken tooth, it's giving me hell.'

Starcy stared at him, hard. Then he straightened up, withdrew his cane and handed over the keys. He looked exhausted.

'Nice to catch up, Rev.'

McQueen didn't share the sentiment. He threw the vehicle into reverse, swung around smoothly and barrelled out onto the road. We heard the V8 roar as he hit the bitumen.

Starcy sniffed the air.

'Dentist my arse,' he said. 'That guy hasn't seen a dentist in years.'

I asked about McQueen and Starcy explained that he was a career criminal who'd spent most of his life behind bars. Back in Starcy's day, he'd been a driver for the Rowsills, a crew of semi-crazed drug dealers who controlled much of the outer east. He was in general a hopeless human being, but he did have one skill at which he came close to genius: he could drive. Anything. Quickly. Put him on a Harley-Davidson or behind the wheel of a road train and he could handle it with ease and speed. He was a man who saw hurdles where others saw walls, opportunities where others saw roadblocks.

I glanced at the office and saw a curtain move.

'We going inside?' I asked.

Starcy shook his head. 'I've seen enough. Too much. Don't know what these guys are up to, but if Rev McQueen's involved, it can't be good. He's not a leader's arsehole, but he's a faithful follower with an eye for the main chance. I'll get a mate to ask some questions, but right now I haven't got the stomach for it. Or the energy. They wear you down, these bastards. They're like that game my grandkids play – Whack-A-Mole. You smash one and a dozen others take their place. Look at these guys, cruising around the fleshpots while Nash is getting hammered in the slammer. Think I just want to get back to my white-faced herons. They're the only people I trust.'

We trailed back to the car. As we were getting in, I noticed Neddy Kursk had come out onto the verandah of the office and was staring at us with his hands on his hips and a baleful expression in his eyes.

# CHAPTER 32

It was well after dark when I turned into my drive and realised with a slight sense of trepidation that I was being followed. The trepidation only intensified when my follower flashed a set of blue lights at me – something I'd done myself when I wanted to put the wind up someone, but I didn't like being on the receiving end. Who the hell was it? Lance Cunningham? Did he think I was speeding in my own driveway? Or maybe it was Neville Wallace playing silly buggers?

I got out as the car doors opened. The passenger was a tall, hard-faced officer busily putting on his hat and adjusting his tie. He didn't look familiar, but the tie was a worry, as was the folder in his hands. A man on a mission. He was trouble enough, but the driver was worse. Inspector Dougherty.

I got out and waited. Dougherty came up and loomed over me, as he tended to do.

'Redpath,' he said.

'Boss.'

'This is Sergeant Kurt Giddens,' he said, indicating the other man.

We shook hands. It was like wrestling a set of Stilsons.

'To what do I owe the pleasure?' I asked hopefully. There was always the possibility that there would be some pleasure involved, although I suspected – given the amount of extra-curricular activity I'd been engaging in of late – it would be all theirs.

'Chilly out here,' said Dougherty.

'Come in and I'll put the kettle on.'

I unlocked the door and went in. As I turned on the light, I remembered Rupert. I prayed he'd have the decency to lie low.

No such luck. The little bastard popped his nose out of the teapot, scuttled across the bench, hit the floor and headed for the ceiling by way of a convenient wall. My visitors watched, drop-jawed, until he disappeared into the rafters.

'Think we'll skip the refreshments,' said Dougherty.

Giddens didn't say anything, but he looked like I'd just offered him a cup of arsenic. He gazed at my humble abode with an air of stern disapproval. The barn-raisers had done an amazing job, but a battered shack is still a battered shack, whatever way you look at it. My home had always been a modest affair, even before the tree fell on it.

'Just give me a minute to light the fire,' I said. 'Get a bit of warmth happening.'

'Don't worry on our account,' said Dougherty. 'We won't be staying long.'

'Well at least have a seat,' I said, sweeping some of the debris from the sofa. I touched the fabric; still relatively dry, amazingly. Dougherty sat down, but Giddens stood with his back to the non-existent fire. He wasn't saying much, either with his mouth or his body. He had the appearance of one of those Aussie blokes who find it easier to crack a ball-bearing than a smile.

'How's suspension treating you?' asked Dougherty.

'Can't complain. Been catching up on the home repairs.'

The wind picked up outside and rattled the plastic sheets on the windows. Possum's HOME SWEET HOME sign wobbled and hit the floor with a crash.

'Mind you, they're mostly still at the planning stage,' I expanded. 'Had a tree fall on the house.'

Dougherty's gaze shifted around the room, doubtless taking in the mismatched boards and beams, the temporary walls, the improvised handiwork.

'They do that,' he said. Then his voice took on a more pointed tone. Here we go, I thought. 'Sergeant Giddens here is with Professional Standards Command.' I may have died a little in the arse. Had they heard about my visit to remand? 'He needs to give you a letter, ask a few questions.'

Giddens reached into the folder and came out with a fat yellow envelope. 'We wanted to make sure you got this personally,' he said. 'It's a statement giving official notice of the interview concerning the complaint that's been made about your performance. The interview will be conducted in the Greendale station at nine am Wednesday week. I've also included contact details for the Victorian Police Association, who'll accompany and support you, should you request it.'

He passed it over and I put it on the coffee table, unsure of the protocols for handling such a document. I'd never been suspended before. Was it like a birthday present? Was I meant to open it now or save it for later? My guests weren't giving me any hints.

I stood up. 'Right-oh. If that's all then . . .'

'No,' said Dougherty. 'It's not all. I've got some questions myself. We've had another complaint, couple of complaints, actually. Sounds to me like you've been running round the countryside investigating Nash Rankin's old cases. Surely that can't be true?'

I sat back down.

'Investigating?' I replied with all the lightness I could muster. 'I wouldn't call it that. There may have been a bit of local banter here and there. I do live in this town. I have to engage with the locals. Word seems to have gotten round that I've been suspended. People are going to ask questions.'

Dougherty glanced at Giddens then turned back to me. 'Sounds like more than local banter. You haven't been accessing the LEAP database while under suspension, have you?'

The Law Enforcement Assistance Program? I shook my head, thanking the lord I'd hidden Vince's files in the bottom drawer. If I was going to go down, I didn't want to take him with me. I could only pray he'd been discreet, had obtained his information from trusted sources. I was confident he would have; despite the genial country cop vibe, Vince was a sharp operator. He was connected. He'd cruised the shark-infested waters of regional police politics for twenty years and hadn't been eaten yet.

My visitors gave no indication they wanted to search the place. There'd been no mention of a warrant, no warnings issued. Not yet, anyway. This was just a shot across the bows.

I didn't like that last question, though. The conversation was starting to feel like an interrogation. I wanted it over. I turned to Dougherty.

'Can I ask who the complaint was from?'

'You can ask.'

Giddens gave a sharp little smile. Kurt was a good first name for him.

'Have you learned anything you'd like to share with us?' continued Dougherty. 'From all this banter with the local hayseeds, I mean. What are people saying about the Wycliff death?'

'Not much, boss. They keep to themselves round here.'

Dougherty pinched the bridge of his nose then leaned forward, elbows on knees, feet spread.

'I gotta tell you, Jesse – you're skating on thin ice here. There are people who think we should never have taken you on. They said you were a wrecking ball. You got talents, sure, and you're determined. You're smart. But you're dangerous. They said we got systems and procedures, and you're the sort of person who ignores procedures, tears systems apart.'

He rose to his feet.

'I wasn't one of those people, I should add. I was willing to give you time to prove yourself. And like I said before, the night of the storm, you performed well. Really well. I was telling Sergeant Giddens about it on the way here. You rescued that woman from the river without concern for your personal safety. You spotted the truth about Raph Cambric's murder in a way that most of us wouldn't have in a million years. But sometimes you gotta hold your mouth and follow the rules. This isn't the wild west – or the Northern Territory. We've got systems.

Protocols. And you gotta work with 'em, woman. Otherwise they'll chew you up and spit you out.'

A heavy silence settled over the room.

Dougherty put on his hat and moved towards the door. Giddens followed. Before the inspector disappeared into the darkness he caught my eye and fixed me with a slow-burning stare that gave me a hint of why he'd risen to the heights he had.

'Are you hearing me, Jesse?'

'I'm hearing you, boss.'

I stood on the verandah and watched them leave.

Somewhere in the night a bull bellowed.

# CHAPTER 33

I woke the next morning with Dougherty's words still resonating in my head. Skating on thin ice. I looked out the window, at the frost-covered paddocks and cracked, dirty puddles in the yard. You'd be hard-pressed to put your foot out there without stepping on some ice, thick or thin.

It was Saturday. I remembered Possum's comment about the farmers' market in town and I decided to wander in and check it out for myself. A bit of light relief, some friendly – or at least interesting – faces and fresh food wouldn't go astray after all the dramas of the past few days.

The market wasn't hard to find: a burst of exotic colour and movement – red and white tents, silky blue dresses and scarves, fluttering banners and Tibetan prayer flags – in a landscaped grove beside the pub. I ambled around. There were potatoes and pumpkins with the frost still on them, there were cupcakes and honey, sourdough seed bread, second-hand tools, essential oils. There was an Egyptian herbalist selling figs, frankincense and prune-like objects that turned out to be vultures' testicles.

The crowd was a bustling, sizeable one, and, as Possum had promised, a more eclectic collection of misfits you'd have to travel a long way to see. There were scratch bands and Bolivian buskers, pot-bellied bikies and landlocked pirates. There was a bloke who looked like he'd just ridden down from the Snowies eating a falafel and a herd of hungry yuppies in North Face jackets. A pair of dreadlocked hobbits in Rasta hats sat on a low branch rolling joints and cackling hysterically at each other's jokes – or, more likely, their own.

I said hello to the odd character who recognised me, ignored the regular whiff of weed or patchouli. I bought a few implements for the home – a heavy metal poker and a mattock – some handmade soap and a Thai curry. I stopped and watched a game of footy on the adjoining oval, took pleasure in the slap of wet leather on heavy boots, the flying bodies, the long, beguiling arms plucking the ball from the sky then sending it spiralling into the forward line.

I wandered along the back of the market until my attention was caught by a small, purple tent bedecked with long vines of jasmine, transforming it into a kind of bower. The sign over the entrance read: CRYSTAL VISION. I glanced into the opening and the jade-green eyes of a woman in a flowing red dress seated at a folding table. It was hard to give a more detailed description than that, given that the interior was swathed in shadow and her face was partially covered by veils.

I would have walked on by, marked it down as one of the odd little enterprises designed to separate fools from their money which spring up at events like this, but then I noticed the array of crystals laid out on the table.

Blame it on my upbringing if you will – my father was fascinated by geology – but I'm a sucker for a quality crystal and there was some quality on display here.

The woman flashed those fierce green eyes at me and invited me in. I did so warily.

She swept a hand over the crystals. 'Which one would you like me to read?' she asked.

I didn't want her to read any of them, at least not without telling me how much I was going to be slugged for the pleasure. There were maybe twenty crystals of varying shapes and sizes spread across the table. I was struck by their diversity: there were the usual flashy blades-of-light quartzes and amethysts, but there were other, more subtle, specimens I could only identify because my father had enjoyed testing me with such displays – rocks and minerals of every description – when I was a teenager. I gave them a cursory glance and identified feldspar, aquamarine beryl, peridot, serpentinite, lapis lazuli.

Despite the array of colour, clarity and planes of symmetry before me, it was a modest little chunk of pegmatite rock on the right, the crystals embedded in it viridian, lustrous, that caught my attention. I hesitated for a moment, then touched it.

'Interesting,' said the woman. 'What made you choose that one?'

'I used to live in a street called Scheelite.'

Her brows rose. 'Ah,' she said. 'So you know your crystals.'

'Some.'

She took the rock and gazed into it. Almost of its own accord, my bum found its way into the chair in front of her.

'You've come a long way,' she said.

'Not that long. I live on the outskirts of town.'

'But before that. I see a wild, sparse country where the minerals are laid bare and their messages radiate out to those of a mind to hear them.'

I was momentarily taken aback. Then I relaxed. It wasn't exactly a secret that I was the new cop in town and local gossip could well have spread the word that I'd come from the outback.

But then she went on.

'You're on a journey,' she said. 'A dangerous journey.'

Yeah right, I thought. Who isn't on a journey and aren't we all fellow passengers to the grave?

'But you need to be careful,' she intoned. 'There are dark forces out there and they're watching you closely.'

Well, when you work in law enforcement, you do have the odd encounter with lawbreakers and they have been known to post lookouts. Maybe she'd heard I'd just had a tree fall on my house and was playing to my underlying fears. Something about this woman, though, was starting to make me feel uncomfortable. If she was a bullshit artist, she was a bloody good one.

She returned her attention to the scheelite but I'd heard enough. I made to rise. I was reaching for my purse and wondering how to get out of there without getting too badly stung when she spoke again, this time with a definite edge to her voice.

'I see brutal spirits and bitter winds. I see a woman lost and drowning in the black bog hole of her own kin. A horseman attempts to rescue her but he, too, is dragged down into the depths.'

I froze. I couldn't see much of the fortune teller's face, but what I could see was enough to tell me she was genuinely horrified by what she was looking at.

'You're stepping into dangerous waters,' she continued. 'Be careful. You don't want to end up like that poor woman. These people can kill you with a look, whisk you away from the face of the earth.'

I rose to my feet. I'd had enough of this woo-woo.

'Where do I pay?' I asked.

'You don't,' she replied. 'Just take care of yourself – that will be payment enough. The devil walks in a multitude of masks and guises.'

I put twenty bucks on the table and left. Why was my heart pounding?

I bought an espresso and a chocolate cookie from the coffee stall and took a seat at the top of a natural amphitheatre near the creek. There was a string band playing down on the little mound at the foot of the slope.

I took a slug of the coffee and a bite of the biscuit, still trying to shake the veiled woman from my mind. That had been a strangely disturbing encounter. Not only did it sound like she knew more about my activities than I did myself, she seemed to be speaking in a circuitous manner about the death at Wycliff Rise. Was the horseman Raph Cambric? If so, then who was the drowned woman? And what did the fortune teller mean by brutal spirits? Any of the men I'd visited the other day – the creepy priest, the stroppy tow-truck operator or the toxic waste dumper – could fit into that category.

I really should go back and ask the woman some more questions. If she had information about the Wycliff incident I needed to know about it.

# CHAPTER 34

So distracted was I by these considerations, it took a few minutes before I realised that the singer in the band below me was Annie J, my friend from the pub. She had a raunchy voice and an earthy stage presence – not that there was much in the way of stage. I listened as the band belted out a powerful rendition of 'Zombie'. Still in a Cranberries state of mind, they balanced the ledger by performing the mellifluous 'Dreams'. When they took a break Annie came over to say hello.

After a compliment or two from me and a minute's banter between us, Annie mentioned that Carina Whitaker was at the market that morning.

'Who?' I asked.

'You were asking if there was anybody around who knew Leon Glazier, the victim up at Horse Thief Creek. Carina did. She went out with him for a while. She's a regular here – got a stall selling leather goods – handbags, belts and whatnot. There is a slight problem though.'

'What's that?'

'There's no way she'll talk to a cop. When I asked her if she'd mind answering a few questions from you, she told me to sod off. She runs around with a pretty edgy crowd: hairy-nosed anarchists, lefty sceptics, professional misfits. Said she'd never trusted the police and was even less inclined to do so after Leon's death.'

That made me even more keen to speak to her, Inspector Dougherty's warnings notwithstanding.

Annie gave me directions to Carina's stall then said she had to get back to the band. I set off through the bustling alleyways and in a couple of minutes I came across a woman sitting on a log with a selection of leather goods laid out on a blanket in front of her.

She didn't exactly have a high-powered sales technique: she had a coffee on a rock beside her and was eating from a bag of roasted chestnuts. She seemed more interested in reading her book – Ursula K. Le Guin's *A Wizard of Earthsea* – than in making a sale.

'Carina?' I asked.

She looked up at me and her eyes widened. She was around my age, with platinum hair, a black silk dress and a blue cashmere jumper.

'Jesus,' she said, clearly recognising me straightaway.

It took a little longer for me to recognise her. The last time I'd seen this woman she was shivering and soaked through and I'd just pulled her from a flooded creek.

'How you doing?' I asked.

'Better than I would have been if you hadn't come along when you did. I never thanked you properly – so thanks.' Then she narrowed her eyes suspiciously. 'You know my name . . . You aren't the cop Annie said wanted to talk about Leon?'

I fessed up and introduced myself. She reached into her bag, pulled out a pack of rollies and studied me.

'Why are you interested?' she asked.

I wondered how much to tell her, decided to go with the pared-down version.

'You heard about the murder at Wycliff Rise?'

'Of course.'

'And Nash Rankin's role in it?'

'Yep.' She rolled a smoke.

'I just wanted to be sure it happened the way they said it did. And to do that, I need to know more about the earlier incident, at Horse Thief. I'm new in town. Most of my colleagues seem to think I'm a nuisance, just for asking about it. Makes me think there's something not quite right.'

She lit up and took a heavy drag.

'I try not to talk to cops but in your case I'll make an exception. Thank god somebody's interested. I was never convinced we got the full story of Leon's death.'

She had a throaty, smoker's voice and skinny fingers. Her hard-bitten demeanour was disrupted by the occasional low laugh.

'So what do you want to know?'

I sat down beside her. 'Whatever you want to tell me.'

She frowned. 'One thing we need to get out of the way before we start. You're not being completely honest. Annie told me you've hooked up with Nash.'

'If you can call it hooking up when the pointy end of the hook's in gaol.'

Carina laughed, took another drag and watched as the smoke drifted away. She seemed to be deciding she didn't mind me, my profession notwithstanding. The fact that I'd rescued her from the flood presumably helped.

'Sounds like me and Leon,' she said. 'Bloody Nash Rankin. I never even met the bugger, but I heard Leon talk about him often enough. I was stunned when I found out Nash was responsible for his death. As if Leon hadn't had a tough enough life already, then Nash puts an end to it like that. Terrible. But the more I heard about it, the more I began to wonder if somebody hadn't got their wires crossed. Leon didn't have many friends and he'd lost touch with his family. Nash was one of the few people he did have time for. They'd been in this weird church together as kids. You've heard about the Revelators, I suppose?'

'I have.'

'Bunch of fucking creeps. That was what made me sceptical of the official version. The cult experience bonded those kids. What the fuck could Leon have done to rile Nash up so much he'd want to kill him? They tried to tell me Nash was crazy, but he was the one who saved them all when they were young. That doesn't sound crazy, it sounds heroic. I wondered if they'd arrested the wrong person, or if maybe Leon's death might have been an accident – or a set-up. The cops – present company excepted, maybe – are a fucking brotherhood: step out of line and they'll burn you. Maybe Nash stepped out of line. But nobody was interested in hearing what I had to say and Leon was never a friend to the people who own this country. He'd been an activist for years.'

'What sort of activist?'

'The usual anarcho-syndicalist schtick. Overthrow the system, hang the oppressors. Good luck with that, I'd say to him. He was arrested a few times. Chained himself to a coal train once, joined an occupation of the head office at BHP.'

When I reminded her that the investigators reckoned Nash had found evidence that Leon was involved in distributing child abuse material, she flared up.

'No way! Any hint of child abuse, anywhere, in any shape or form – some randy priest in handcuffs on TV, that pervy prince, the smug cardinal – and Leon would go off his nut. Those boys were survivors of abuse themselves.'

Carina offered me a roasted chestnut. It was delicious, perfect for a midwinter morning.

I was still trying to get a better picture of Leon Glazier. I asked her if the two of them had been together at the time of his death.

'I'm not sure we were ever exactly "together",' she replied. 'He was a hard person to get close to. We had a bit of a fling for a few months, but he'd learned not to trust people, not to open himself up to anyone. Only thing he seemed really interested in was his political activities – and his work.'

'I heard he was in IT.'

She said he was self-employed, providing technical support to local residents and businesses. 'Mind you,' she added, 'I was never quite sure whether he was working or not. He spent an awful lot of time sitting in his room staring at a screen, and his income was sporadic at best. Even his political activities were mainly online, one army of keyboard warriors yelling at another. He was a hacker and a web-head from way back – off exploring conspiracy theories, secret societies – not to follow them, but to expose them, debunk them. To laugh at them. He loved looking into cults, cabals, keyboard crazies, online wack-jobs of every description.'

This was all news to me, and it opened up new lines of enquiry.

'You don't suppose he could have stirred up the crazies so much they came after him?'

She shrugged. 'Anything's possible. I'd be suspicious of you if you hadn't pulled me from the flood. But Leon? I dunno. He was super careful about his privacy online, hiding behind a VPN, always changing passwords, user names. He knew a lot more about that world than I ever did. He was like a kid, and the crazies were his playground – especially cults. He'd troll them, send his dog down their rabbit holes, try to show 'em up for the bullshit they were. He would have had a ball with Q-Anon if he'd lived to see it. He talked about setting up a podcast, but that never got far. I always figured his interest was because he'd been a survivor of a cult himself, he wanted to save others from them. That's what I told myself, but as time went by I realised how much his crusade was taking over his life. It didn't leave room for anything – or anyone – else. We just drifted apart and I started seeing someone else. But there was nothing hostile about the split, and I hope he still thought of me as a friend. I certainly thought of him as one.'

A pack of teenagers on BMX bikes whizzed past, spraying an arc of mud all over us. Carina jumped to her feet.

'Boys!' she yelled. 'No bikes in the marketplace!'

They ignored her, kept going until they turned right onto a track that disappeared into the bush. The one bringing up the rear glanced back at me. He had a full helmet on and was moving fast, but I recognised the hostile glow in his eyes. It was the crossbow boy. Bailey. I reminded myself to check with Lance, see if he'd found out anything more about the family.

'I'll let you get back to work,' I said to Carina, standing up. 'Speaking of which – I've been meaning to get a new bag. What would you recommend? I'm looking for something small and tough.'

She spent a few minutes showing me her wares. In the end I picked out a beautiful Moroccan leather bumbag. I thanked Carina for her time and told her to keep in touch. I gave her my number, suggested she not do any more late-night swimming in flooded creeks.

The crowd was thinning out. The stall holders were starting to pack up the tables and pull down the marquees. The food sellers were laying out their last-minute bargains, the cars were lining up at the entrance. Before I left, I went back to ask the fortune teller if she knew anything about Raph Cambric and to remind her that withholding information about a crime was a crime itself.

But when I reached the back of the market her tent had disappeared and there was no sign of her.

# CHAPTER 35

The sun sort of rose on yet another icy, mist-woven morning. I stood for a moment on the front porch. My fingers were red-raw, frozen. A pair of sluggish kangaroos drifted across the lawn, footprints in the frost, tails wet. Winter up here in the high country was relentless. It was as if all the things that mark you as human – movement, breath, the very spark of life – were slowly being subsumed into an all-conquering, blood-numbing cold.

I lit a fire, enjoyed the heft of my new poker, made a pot of coffee.

I rang the vet, got the nurse, Charlie. She said she'd fallen in love with Flinders. 'Those eyes!' she exclaimed. She said he was doing well, but they wanted him to stay there for rehabilitation. That suited me. I would have had trouble caring for a disabled dog just now.

I decided to go down to the monster mall at Greendale and pick up some of the essentials I hadn't had a chance to buy yet: more bedding, blankets, a good winter coat.

I didn't last long at the mall. They wore me out, those places. After purchasing the thickest coat and warmest bedding in the store, I went in search of food. Couldn't find much: it was all pretend. Food from the land of the bland. That didn't seem to worry the lumpy proletariat, who were lumbering through the food court swilling slurpees and shovelling carbs into their cakeholes. I bought a nori roll and fled.

On my way back to the car I noticed a woman in a green jacket unloading a trolley into a grey Subaru. She looked up as I walked by. She was tall and well-rounded, with a lock of blonde hair falling over her sharp blue eyes. It took me a moment to place her. I'd only seen her from a distance, but there was no doubt.

'Excuse me – Marcie, isn't it?'

Raph Cambric's sister-in-law, last seen wrangling a mob of kids into the house on the farm at Wycliff Rise.

She knew me straightaway, said I'd made quite an impression on her husband. He'd been having second thoughts about his brother's death since my visit, had tried to come up with alternative explanations. Hadn't come up with anything, mind you, but he was wondering if they'd been too quick to follow the party line. She said she'd always liked Nash Rankin, had chatted with him over the fence from time to time, but he'd held his cards so close to his chest that she never felt she knew him.

There was a cafe on the other side of the car park. I asked if she had time to join me for a coffee. She said she could give me an hour but no more. She had to get back and rescue her husband from the kids.

'I've seen them in action,' I said. 'Better not be late. They'll tear him apart.'

We found a table close to the window, ordered coffee and cake and engaged in a few minutes of exploratory chatter. She'd lived in the Windmark Ranges all her life, worked as a teacher before she married Jared. She told me some of the newcomer things to do – the best waterholes and wineries, the hidden cross-country ski runs. Not that she did many of those things these days. Raising the kids and running the farm took up most of her time and energy, especially now that Raph was gone.

She leaned forward, fixed me with a firm gaze.

'Which brings us to . . .'

'Yes,' I admitted. 'I'm still trying to work out what happened to him. If Nash was responsible, he'll have to deal with whatever the legal system dishes out to him. But if he wasn't . . .'

I let the words drift off into the beams of winter light streaming through the glass panels. I suspected Marcie and I were sharing the same thought: if Nash had been wrongly charged, there was a killer out there somewhere.

'You seem like a sharp observer,' I continued. 'I thought you might have some ideas to add to the mix. I've heard rumours – from your husband, actually – that Raph might have been seeing someone.'

She scoffed at the comment. 'More than that, if I'm any judge of human behaviour. He was a man transformed for a while there. He was a lovely guy, Raph, but not what you'd call outgoing. He just moved through life at his own quiet pace – maybe that was something he picked up from growing apples and handling horses. But then, a few months ago, he changed – dramatically.'

'How so?'

She thought for a moment, then dabbed at a piece of cake with a fork.

'His face lit up. He began making quick-fire jokes at the dinner table, played more with the kids. Some sort of nesting instinct, I suspected. My first thought was: he's met someone. But it was more complicated than that. There was something else going on. Hard to say what, but it sure as hell wasn't all wine and roses. I started seeing darker emotions in his eyes. Anxiety. Doubt. Maybe even fear – not for himself, for someone else. It made me wonder if perhaps that someone was a person he couldn't be seen with. Otherwise I didn't understand why he didn't just bring her home to meet us.'

'What if she was a he?'

She frowned. 'That wouldn't have worried us. Despite what you might think, we're not hillbillies up there.'

'And you've got no idea who this mysterious lover could be?' I asked. 'You and Jared never speculated?'

She shook her head, but then added she'd been thinking it might have been somebody connected to his farrier business.

'We're pretty isolated out on the farm,' she explained. 'But Raph travelled all over the place, met a lot of people. He used to do the horse work on Fridays – a regular time so we knew when he'd be off the property. And a couple of times I swear he had that spring in his step – or the shadow in his eye – on a Thursday evening.'

She took a sip of coffee and stared out at the busy Sunday car park, the fat four-wheel drives squeezing into spaces designed for Mini Minors, the wandering shopping trollies.

'A few weeks before Raph died,' she continued, 'something changed. The anxiety came to the surface, took over. He was moody, downcast. He spent a lot of time pacing back and forth down in the paddock, phone in hand, where nobody could hear him. He seemed to be doing a lot of ringing, but not getting much in the way of answers.'

She lowered her head and rearranged the froth on her coffee. 'They're so damned bottled up, these bush blokes. When me and my girlfriends get together, we tell each other everything. But the men! They keep it to themselves, bury their emotions – especially their fears. If Raph had just opened up, we might have been able to help him.'

I nodded in appreciation of the picture she was painting. 'Jared told me Raph disappeared for a while.'

'He was gone for a week. But when he got back he wouldn't talk about it. Wouldn't say where he'd been, what he got up to. Just said he was cruisin'. Like that's something we do out here. We don't cruise – we work. I assumed the trip was connected to this mysterious relationship, but that was as much as I could guess.'

'And you've no idea where he went?'

She looked away, almost guiltily. 'Hate to seem like a stickybeak . . .'

'In my line of work, we love stickybeaks.'

She finished her coffee. 'When I was putting out the recycling, the week after he returned, I noticed some receipts in the bin. One of them was for food and fuel – in Dubbo.'

Dubbo. Outback New South Wales. What the hell was he doing there? I pressed Marcie for more information, but she had little to add. There were no family or other connections she knew of in Dubbo. She did wonder whether the mystery person might have gone there and Raph had set off in pursuit, but that was pure speculation.

I wondered if she might have anything else she could share with me. Maybe she knew more than she realised.

'Do you know how I could find out more about his farrier work?' I asked. 'I don't suppose he kept a list of his clients?'

'It was mostly word-of-mouth, cash-in-hand. But I might have seen him with a little address book sometimes. He had an office of sorts, at his home. You're welcome to have a look around it if you want.'

'I'd appreciate that. When would suit you?'

She checked her watch. 'No time like the present.'

I jumped at the offer. I presumed the Homicide investigators would have already been through the place, but we would have been searching for different things.

We drove out to Wycliff in our separate cars. Marcie dropped into the main house and had a quick word with Jared, then led me down to Raph's home. It was a neat, single-bedroom cottage near the packing sheds. She told me it had originally been the overseer's quarters.

The two of us spent a good hour going through the building. It bore all the hallmarks of a single man's cave: a bathroom redolent of Old Spice and mint toothpaste, a kitchen of pizzas and stew, a row of old footy trophies on the mantle. From the look of those, Raph had been a goal kicker of some local renown. There were several objects which Marcie told me were of sentimental value: an empty rum bottle, a bronze telescope and a tiny sculpture of a boy on a buffalo.

There was a row of framed photographs on the dresser: Jared, Marcie and the kids; an elderly couple; a boy I realised must be the young Raph going over a high jump on a black stallion. I found the last photo heartbreaking; his face was beaming with all the energy and dreams of youth. I couldn't help but compare that image to the brutal tableau of his death. The sight of Raph crushed in his tractor would live with me forever. There was a more recent photo of him at work on a horse's hoof, an expression of deep concentration furrowing his brow, a couple of nails clenched between his teeth. He was an attractive man: sharp lines, firm jaw, mellow eyes. Generous eyes. There were no photos of a woman with long, dark hair.

At the rear of the house was a corrugated iron shed which apparently served as a tack-room/office. It was packed with oilskin jackets and hats, saddles and blankets, an array of tools mounted on a wall: hammers and tongs, hoof nippers, rasps and knives. The room had a not unpleasant scent of oiled leather and sweat.

Over in the corner was a metal filing cabinet, upon it a pile of books. The top one was called *Hickman's Farriery*. The others were in the same vein: horses and their care, farm skills, car and equipment manuals. We looked through the filing cabinet, and I was pleased to see he was a fellow who had yet to catch up with the digital age. More for me to look at. There were files on insurance, vehicle maintenance records, tax returns, invoices, receipts, all the bits and bobs of a travelling tradesman's life. He was a member of several professional associations, including the Master Farriers' Association and the Australian Fruit Growers. I took a closer look at the files, but found little of interest. The receipts were what you'd expect for a working farrier/farmer and there was no sign of anything from Dubbo.

But as I closed the drawer I noticed an imprint in the dust on top of the books, as if there'd been a smaller one there at some stage. I lifted the pile aside and came across a small black book that had slipped down the side of the cabinet.

It was an address book, a little frayed and falling apart at the edges, well thumbed, oil and dirt stained. I suspected it had been knocked from the pile when the police were searching the place. There must have been a hundred names in there, Raph's contacts and customers from all over the region. Too many to be useful. But as I flicked through it a small piece of paper – a beautifully rough-textured, creamy cardboard – slipped from the back cover. I picked it up and read a handwritten sentence in a delicate black script:

*something inside me weeps black tears*

There was no signature, but below the final word was a deft little sketch of a flower – possibly a rose, from the shape of its petals and stem, although it was uncoloured and difficult to identify with any certainty. Marcie, standing beside me, read the note then looked at me darkly.

'That,' she said, 'must be about the saddest sentence I ever read.'

It wasn't just the words on the page. It was the atmosphere around them. Their anonymity and isolation, the fact of their being discovered among a dead man's effects. The card radiated heartbreak.

'You don't recognise the writing?' I asked.

'It's certainly not Raph's.'

'Or the artwork?'

'Same.'

She gazed out the open door, her mind elsewhere.

'Any ideas?' I pressed.

She shook her head. 'I miss my poor, dear brother-in-law. His life – especially the last few weeks of it – must have been a hell of a mess. I wish I'd known.'

We trailed back to the cottage, sat at the kitchen table and worked our way through the address book, seeing if Marcie's local knowledge could offer any insight into the authorship of the mysterious note. Some of the names were clear: Hanrahan, Ted. Billy Leotardo. Donna and George, Canticle Creek. Others were harder to read. They were more shorthand, reliant upon local knowledge: Fritzy, tree bloke, Wednesday. Paul the plumber. Raffles neighbour – the strawberry roan – Hettie?

I told Marcie how their neighbour, Stefan, had said he'd seen a woman riding pillion with Raph, that she was dark-haired and slim, in her late thirties. That helped. Marcie could discard some names at a glance: too old, too young, too fair, too heavy. By the time we finished, we'd eliminated maybe half the people in the book, but that still left me with around fifty names – who may or may not have had anything to do with the laughing passenger on the pillion.

Still, it was something, another part of the picture.

I asked Marcie if I could take the notebook with me, to which she readily agreed. I put it in my bag. We exchanged numbers, and she promised to give me a call if she came across anything new. She said she'd ask around, contact friends and family, make some discreet enquiries of people she knew and trusted. Do her best to find out who the woman was. She walked me out to the car, wished me good luck and left me with a kiss that surprised me with its affection.

# CHAPTER 36

I was rolling home from Wycliff Rise when my attention was caught by a solitary figure walking across a bushy paddock on the outskirts of town. She was wearing blue jeans and a grey jacket and carrying a straw basket in one hand and a long stick in the other. She had her back to me and was gazing at the ground, but I recognised her straightaway. She stopped, scraped at the ground then knelt to examine something.

I pulled over, got out and climbed through the fence. Lost in her thoughts, or her search, she didn't notice me until I drew near.

'Hey, Lucinda,' I said.

She spun round and stood up. Her eyes narrowed, then turned to the horizon. Looking for an escape route, or making sure we were alone?

'Hello, officer,' she replied.

'Jess will do,' I said. 'What brings you out here?'

'We're just fossicking around.'

'We?'

'Bailey's out there somewhere,' she said, nodding at the bushland at the back of the paddock. The comment sent a little shiver down my spine. The memory of that arrow still rattled through my brain.

'I saw him at the market yesterday,' I said. 'Hooning around with a bunch of boys on bikes.'

She scowled. 'I'm sorry about that. I try to keep an eye on him, but he slips away. He's going through a stage.'

I took a closer look at the basket in her hands. As well as a number of natural history specimens – cicada shells, fungi, a snake skin – there were several items that suggested she was doing more than mere rambling: a hand lens, a plant press and a field guide to fungi.

'Looks like you mean business,' I said, gesturing at the contents of the basket.

Her face came as close as I'd seen to lighting up.

'We're always trying to learn about the local ecology,' she explained. 'The botany, the bird and plant life. Even under-ground – the mycorrhizal network is amazing.'

'Mycorrhizal?'

'Where the fungal roots interact with a plant's.'

I should introduce this girl to my friends at Canticle Creek, I thought. They might find they had a few things in common.

I indicated the surrounding countryside. 'And is this all your land?'

She frowned. 'Are you going to arrest me for trespassing?'

'Just asking. You sound like you know your way around the place.'

She nodded. 'It belongs to our neighbours. The Chambers. But Mr Chambers knows we're here. He's given us permission to come and collect specimens. Our family puts a lot of emphasis on understanding our environment, being able to look after ourselves. To live independently, if we ever have to.'

'Hence Bailey and his crossbow?'

She looked at me with knitted brows.

'I wasn't joking when I said if he'd wanted to hit you, he would have. He's got an excellent eye.'

'Have you asked him why he chose me for a target?'

She shook her head, seemed a little lost for words. A black wind whistled through the upper reaches of the trees that lined the paddock. I noticed a blur of movement in the bushland adjoining the paddock and Bailey stepped out into the open. He was maybe a hundred metres away, but that was enough for me to note, with some concern, a bow in his hands. Not the crossbow, thank god. A traditional recurve hunting bow. At least it was by his side, not raised and ready for action.

Lucinda read my face.

'Don't worry,' she said. 'He's only using light arrows. He likes to practise with them, but he knows not to kill anything when he's with me.'

She called him over. He came closer, suspicion in his every move. He stopped when he was about halfway, close enough for me to read the hostility in his expression.

Lucinda sighed and said quietly, 'Bailey's been a bit hyper lately.'

I asked her if she went to school locally.

'No, I'm down at Presbyterian Ladies, in year eleven.'

I wasn't surprised to hear that. Everything about her – the house, the voice, even the natural history interest – said private school.

When Bailey finally joined us, his sister insisted he greet me. He did so grudgingly. He had a handful of objects – feathers, eggs, a bird's skull bone and some fungi – which he placed in her basket. I tried a joke about dropping into their place for a mushroom omelette but he wasn't amused.

'We didn't have time to thank you the other day,' said Lucinda, maybe trying to compensate for her brother's rudeness. 'That was kind of you, not telling our father about Bailey.'

Kind or stupid, I thought but didn't say. If Bailey got into more trouble, did something even worse, it would be my fault.

'Does your father have any idea of what actually happened that day?' I asked.

'I certainly wasn't saying anything,' said Lucinda. 'But, after you left, he asked a lot of questions.'

'About what?'

She frowned. 'You.'

'Do you think he believed my story? It was the best I could come up with on the fly.'

'You did brilliantly. You're obviously an accomplished liar.'

'It's one of the skills you develop when you're a woman trespassing in a man's world.'

She almost laughed, but then a look of alarm shot across her face. I followed her eyes. A car had just pulled up on the road that ran along the far side of the paddock. It was a maroon BMW.

'Oh my god,' she muttered. 'He was coming to pick us up, but he's early. Maybe he won't have recognised you,' she said hopefully. Both of us knew that was unlikely. 'You'd better go.'

She waved at the BMW then joined Bailey as they walked across the paddock to meet their father. I turned away, head low, hands in pockets. I returned to my own car, thinking, again, that there was something discomfiting about that family. I resolved to drop into the Satellite Police Station the next day and see if Lance had done any follow-up on them.

As I drove home, I tuned in to Radio National and a familiar song came on, one I knew from my time in the Territory: Kev Carmody, singing 'On the Wire'. It was a song about Country and connection. Country, connection. I wondered how they fitted into my investigation. There was no question they did. They underlie everything, fitted everywhere. I thought about Bailey and his father. I thought about some of the other characters I'd encountered in recent days: toxic waste dumpers, drug runners, midnight assassins, a grief-stricken poet. They were all manifestations of their environment. Hardscrabble, lightning-struck country produced hardscrabble, lightning-struck individuals.

# CHAPTER 37

When I got home I decided it was time to clean out the cobwebs. I changed into trainers and trackpants and set out for a punishing run through the bush. I felt fresh and keen and made good time. I was sprinting up the home stretch, opposite the neighbours' place, when I was stopped by the sight of an axe-wielding mad woman charging at me.

The woman was storming down Rocco's drive with a wild expression on her face and the axe held high. She was heavily built, maybe in her early fifties, wearing blue gumboots and a red beanie.

This is going to be interesting, I thought. Fight or flight? I figured I should be able to outrun her, given her gumboots and build, but I couldn't let her rampage around the neighbourhood with an axe. She may have just dismembered Rocco, for all I knew. I would try to disarm her, hoping that she didn't disarm me in the process.

'You little bugger,' she yelled, waving the weapon around like a berserker.

Bit rude, I thought. Not that little; 173 centimetres last time I checked. Then I heard a squawk and noticed a sleek red fox with a hysterical rooster in its mouth slip out of the bushes that lined the drive and set out across the adjoining paddock. The woman changed course and took off after it. She shouted again and put on such a burst of speed that the fox decided discretion was the better part of dinner. It dropped its victim and shimmied off into the forest. The rooster picked itself up, shook itself off, did a wobbly wander then started pecking at imaginary bits of grain.

The woman drew to a halt, took a deep breath then leaned over, gasping.

'Get on home,' she ordered the bird, which puffed its chest, spread its wings and began to wander off in the same direction as the fox.

'Not that way, you bloody moron,' she called, steering it back towards the chook shed with a well-aimed boot. Only then did she notice me standing on the other side of the road.

'Hello there,' I called, relieved to find that I was dealing with a feisty woman defending her flock and not an axe-wielding maniac.

She did a double take and looked around warily. She was wearing a bulky mohair cardigan and a flowing green dress.

'Jesse Redpath,' I added with a neighbourly smile. 'You'll be Mrs Teller then?'

'Meg,' she said at last. I came closer and shook her hand. She turned away, reluctant to look me in the eye. Her own eyes, I noticed, were a deep shade of green.

'How's business?' I asked.

She looked puzzled.

'Rocco told me you sell eggs.'

'I see. Yes, it's going okay. Be going better if the bloody foxes would leave us alone. Just about impossible to produce free-range eggs with them on the prowl. Look at that one,' she exclaimed, nodding in the direction the recently departed rooster-thief had gone. 'Snatching them in broad daylight.' She looked back up the drive, down which her husband was now walking. 'Anyway,' said Meg, 'you'll have to excuse me. I'm late getting started on my deliveries.'

'Hey there, Jess,' called Rocco as he drew near. 'How's your poor little bashed-up house coming along?'

'Keeping the weather out – thanks to you and the rest of the team.'

'Happy to come over again,' he replied. 'Just let me know when you want a hand.'

Meg was already on her way, walking back towards the shed. She glanced back at me and I was struck, again, by the brilliance of her eyes. And I realised where I'd seen them before. Last time we met, Meg had been sitting in a purple tent with her face veiled and an array of crystals laid out before her.

'Just a minute, Meg!' I called out. 'Could I have a quick word?'

'I really have to get going. I've got customers waiting.'

'It will only take a—'

But she was already halfway up the drive, head forward, long legs swallowing up the metres until she vanished into the back of the property. Rocco seemed a little embarrassed. A few seconds later a van came round the corner of the house and headed down the drive. Meg was barely visible through the tinted windows. She gave us a curt farewell wave as she turned out onto the road.

'Bye, love,' Rocco called.

We stood there watching until the van disappeared down the road to town.

'That was a dramatic appearance,' I said. 'Started with a fox and finished with a getaway car.'

He looked at me apologetically. 'Meg gets a little anxious around new people.'

'Probably sensible. Tell me – does she ever put on a silk scarf and go reading crystals at the market?'

Rocco emitted a sigh and cleared his throat.

'Aye, yes, she's been known to do that. She's a spiritual explorer, our Meg. The hills around here are full of groups who think of themselves as spiritual explorers in one way or another.' He smiled. 'I should know: Meg's been in most of them. She was evangelical Christian when I first met her, but that all went to the shithouse. Since then, she's been playing the field. Buddhism, astrology, witchcraft – Wiccan, they call it. Inner Totem Pole Chakra journeys. Vipassana meditation. Crystals are the latest, but maybe they're the best. Or the least harmful.'

'What do you mean?' I asked.

'When I first met Meg, she was in a bad way. That's probably why she was happy to pair off with an old codger like me – I was something solid, with a steady job and a warm house. I was even responsible for the crystals.'

'How so?'

'I used to be a gouger up in Coober Pedy, had a box of 'em in the shed. She used to do things with them: clean and polish them, cut them open to highlight the colour. After a while she started to say they gave her peace of mind, told her things.

And who am I to say they don't? At least a crystal doesn't come with a pack of priests in pulpits trying to protect their turf.'

I had to agree with him there. 'Yes, that's my trouble with organised religion: the demarcation disputes. That and the homophobic fellers in dresses. But tell me something, Rocco. When I met Meg in the tent, she said something about a drowning woman and a dying horseman. Do you know what that was about?'

He shook his head. 'Never said anything like that to me. But if she said it, she meant it. People think she's away with the fairies, but she's sharp – dismiss her at your peril. And she gets around. Sometimes I think the crystals are just a front, her real power is in those deadly green eyes. She's like Sherlock Holmes: she notices things other people miss.'

'Does she know I'm a police officer?'

'That's an example. She was the one who told me, the day you moved in.'

'She seemed rather keen to be out of my company just now.'

'Like I said, she's anxious around people until she gets to know them.'

'Yeah, but she's happy to sit in a tent and read the fortunes of strangers.'

'That's because she's in disguise. She's like an actor: a different person when she's on stage.'

If Meg really was that well attuned to local developments and knew I was a cop, maybe she'd been trying to warn me of something she'd picked up in her travels, to give me information without making it too obvious where it had come from.

'Can you do me a favour, Rocco?'

'Sure.'

'When Meg comes back, could you tell her I'd love a little chat? It can be as private and confidential as she wants.'

Rocco had a disarming smile.

'Of course.'

# CHAPTER 38

It was late afternoon by now. I'd had enough dramas for one day. I drove into town and had a counter meal at the pub. People were definitely getting to know me. Maybe the rumour that I'd been suspended for shagging an escapee gave me a little more bush-cred.

I enjoyed a game of pool – several games of pool – with the boisterous boys in the back bar. As the night wore on and the booze kicked in, the decibels went up and the quality of the wit went down. I was called upon to adjudicate in an argument about the best ways of avoiding a hangover and a DUI charge (orange juice). I was a member of the crew who stepped up to help old George Watson push-start his '74 LandCruiser ute. When the ute took off at speed, we all fell about laughing.

As George rumbled away in a cloud of blue smoke, I reflected upon the way so many of these old bush characters and their vehicles come to resemble each other. They understand each other's faults and foibles, they know which bits are rusty and ready to fall off, they make allowances for the passing years.

They were both held together by ockie straps and bandages. Put George at the wheel of a Lexus and he'd be at sixes and sevens.

I was heading for home when the phone jangled. The jangle had a disconcerting edge to it. The name on the screen had an even more disconcerting edge to it: Neville Wallace. I pulled over to take the call.

'You're going over Nash's old cases,' were his opening words.

He wasn't beating about the bush and it wasn't a question. Nothing unusual there; Wallace was more likely to run over a bush than he was to beat about it, and he was more given to statements than questions. Dougherty or his Professional Standards mate must have blabbed.

'I may have made some discreet enquiries,' I admitted.

'You harassed Ronald Laws at his place of work.'

'I asked him a few questions, yes.'

'Well done. You killed him.'

I thanked god I'd already pulled over. Otherwise, I might have driven off the road.

'Our inspector got a call from Laws' employer this morning,' Wallace continued. 'The guy was screaming blue murder, threatening to take it to the media, the politicians. Said Laws had a visit from a Constable Redpath who interrogated him in a – quote – "unnecessarily aggressive" manner that stirred up his demons so bad he went home and hanged himself.'

Stirred up his demons? I'd heard that phrase before. The boss. George Hawley. I shrank back into the car seat, regretting that I couldn't just keep shrinking and disappear. This was serious.

'You were bloody warned to keep your nose out of this, Jess,' Wallace continued. 'You were meant to be out looking at eagles or fucking strangers or whatever it is you do in your free time, not interfering with an ongoing investigation.'

I turned my gaze to the dark waving bushes and trees that lined the road. I closed my eyes and took a deep breath, exhaled heavily.

'You still there?' he growled.

I swallowed and asked what was going to happen now. He said the complaint had been passed on to the Professional Standards Division and would doubtless come into play at my interview next week.

'It's out of my hands now, Jess,' he said in closing. 'You'll be lucky to survive this.'

Fair enough, I reflected as he signed off. What a mess. What an A-grade fucking mess. I couldn't muster much in the way of sympathy for Ronald Laws, but maybe I could have been a bit less heavy-handed with him. Although I didn't think I'd been all that rough. The guy was already a walking disaster zone, with his tics and grimaces and his flickering eyes. His crimes were appalling, but who knew what had happened in his life to turn him into the monster he became? He may have been abused himself, may have been completely delusional, may have actually thought he was helping troubled teenagers through dark times. Maybe my unannounced visit was the last in a long line of traumatic events? Maybe he was carrying a load of guilt for something else? We'd never know now. Bloody hell. He might have been on the edge of a precipice before I interviewed him, but I was the one who tipped him over it. It would be on my head.

What was the future like for a disgraced ex-cop? Bleak. Maybe Annie would give me a job at the pub. Or I could take over growing Nash's apples. Nash! Shit. That was the worst part of this disaster – for all my blundering about, I'd achieved precisely nothing that would get him out of gaol.

I drove home slowly. I pulled up in front of the house and sat there staring at it. The plastic windows were flapping. What a dump, I thought. The dump looked back at me, cold, dark and lonely. An echo of my mood. My life. What a mess. By god, I needed a little warmth. I decided to light the fire, make it a big one, a blazing inferno. I couldn't see myself getting much sleep tonight. I tried the porch light but it wasn't working. I got out my torch, gathered an armful of the wood I'd stacked on the verandah and pushed the door open with my knee.

I caught a glimpse of movement to my left, heard a pair of heavy boots rush across the verandah floor.

Some monstrous force slammed into my left side and sent me spiralling into the house. The torch flew from my hands, swivelling flickers and flashes of light across the roof and walls. I fell to the floor, instinctively trying to regain my balance, to take a defensive stance, but my assailant delivered a massive kick to my guts that left me gasping for breath. There wasn't much light in the room, but there was enough for me to recognise my attacker: Neddy Kursk. The bastard was in his element: his eyes glittered like feldspar, his nostrils were quivering like a pig's. He was finding this immensely satisfying.

I tried to rise, but he dropped a knee into my back, put his hands around my throat and squeezed. I felt his red-hot breath upon my neck, came close to throwing up. The room started to fade and spin. Don't go there, I told myself, that would be a death spiral. I managed to raise a leg and hurl myself to one side, attempting to break his iron grip. Succeeded in part. I hit him a glancing blow in the ribs but he countered with a punch to the face that left me reeling. I parried a couple of blows and sort of found my feet, but he grabbed me by the collar and sent me spinning across the room. Somewhere mid-whirl I caught a glimpse of something that might prove useful. I crashed into the hearth and he moved in and stomped on me again. The pain ripped into my ribs like a chainsaw's teeth.

As he raised his boot to deliver the coup de grâce I seized the poker I'd spotted as I flew and rammed it up into his groin with all the poise and power I could muster. A shock wave of pain lit up his body's circuitry. The sharp metal tip must have gone in ten centimetres. His face twisted and crumbled. The first time I met him I thought he had a head like a rocky outcrop; if so, it had just suffered one hell of a landslide.

He stumbled onto me, one hand reaching for the poker, the other for my throat. I punched the former, bit the latter, struggled out from under him. He seized the poker and screamed as he wrenched it free. Blood spurted every which way. What a tough bastard, I couldn't help but think; no way could I have done that. Then again, he was a dumb bastard, too – from what I knew of stab wounds, he'd just accentuated the blood flow. I punched him in the head to slow him down but he barely noticed. My little fist was the least of his concerns.

I ran to the door, slammed it behind me, jumped to the side and waited. A moment later he wrenched the door open and came out roaring, tripped over my outstretched leg and fell to the foot of the stairs. I bounced round him and ran for my car. The keys were still in my pocket, thank Christ. As I started up, Kursk came lurching down the path and threw himself at the windscreen, arms flailing, face a vision of twisted fury and black blood that would haunt my dreams forever.

I threw the car into reverse and he slid away. I completed a whirling circuit of the yard, pointed the vehicle at the road and floored it. As I raced to town, I spotted a set of headlights in the mirror. Was that Kursk already? Maybe he had an accomplice, or perhaps time was playing tricks with my head. I powered a hundred metres down the road then slowed, deciding that a wild ride wasn't a wise move when you'd been battered, bashed and half strangled. I slowed some more, keen not to wake up and find myself smashed into a tree with Neddy Kursk grinning down at me. My ribs were throbbing, my body was a mess of festering agony, my face was slick with blood – mostly my own, I figured, but maybe not all. I thought for a sickening moment about that poker burying itself in his flesh, the splatter as he yanked it out.

I reached the Satellite Police Station. No sign of life there, the building bolted and dark. The pub was a different story. The lights were glowing gold and warm. I drove towards it, drooping onto the wheel, got out and found myself on all fours. How did that happen? I crawled up the front steps.

A row of liquor-logged faces stared at me when I staggered in through the swinging doors. Their mouths were a mass of empty circles, their beers frozen over. Annie bolted across the room to try and catch me before I fell.

'Any chance of an ambulance?' I may have murmured, then the room decoupled from reality and I hit the floor.

I woke to find a worried Lance Cunningham kneeling beside me. A couple of Highway Patrol bruisers hovered in the background, hands upon their weapons. Their expressions reminded me of that eternal truth: when there's a crisis, cops come together.

Somewhere a long way off a siren screamed.

'Who the hell did this?' Lance's cheeks were burning with anger, his eyes with concern.

'Neddy Kursk.'

'Where?'

'My place.'

He nodded at the Highway guys, who promptly left.

I gave Lance what he later described as a madwoman's breakfast account of the attack, a scattered explanation interrupted by the arrival of a pair of paramedics. They began a brutal examination, but, mercifully, I passed out before they got far. By Annie's later account, Lance refused to leave my side until he was sure I wasn't going to cark it, then he set off to join the hunt for Neddy Kursk.

# CHAPTER 39

I lay in the hospital bed, staring up at the ceiling and trying not to move. Every shuffle or adjustment I made drove another salvo of pains out of the woodwork. My scattered agonies: they'd rear their ugly heads, run around my body and go back down. Even having a wee was agony. A crap would have been nice but the mere prospect scared the shit out of me, which may have amounted to the same thing.

I'd been here for a couple of days, mostly drifting in and out of sleep, or consciousness. The dark was not a pleasant place to be, infested as it was with red-bearded spiders with fists like sledgehammers and boots like jackhammers. Nothing broken, apparently, but my ribs may have begged to differ.

I felt like Kursk had unleashed a herd of wildebeest to stampede across the Serengeti of my skull. Concussion, the doctor said. My tongue, swollen and bloody, gently probed the hole where my top right incisor used to be. The bastard! I'd had quite nice teeth, if I do say so myself. The doctors assured me the dentists could give me another as good as new. My most satisfying moments came when I lay back and fantasised about my next encounter with Neddy Kursk, when – hopefully with the help of a few colleagues to even the odds – I'd do what I could to rearrange his own teeth.

People came and people went. Once I was vaguely aware of a man who would have looked a lot like Neville Wallace if he hadn't seemed so worried. His face was traversed by sympathetic grimaces or smiles – it was hard to tell which was scarier. I decided to find out if he was real.

'What's cooking, Nev?' I asked.

He glanced at the half-eaten mush on the table beside me and sneered. Soup and mush had been the order of the day after the damage Neddy Kursk inflicted upon my mouth. 'Something that'll make your hair turn green.'

I grunted, still unsure of whether he was a dream, then floated away.

I had a vague recollection of other people dropping in: my mother picking at the buttons on her cardigan and fretting, asking why I ever joined the force, why couldn't I find a nice, respectable job? My father crunching his hat and grunting. At least they weren't arguing, which they tended to do on the rare occasions they bumped into each other. It wasn't until late the second day that I was able to manage a halfway decent conversation. Maybe it was more of an interrogation and not particularly decent – it was with Neville Wallace. He asked how I was with an air of concern that puzzled me. I had no idea he was such a brilliant actor.

He wanted to know if I was ready to talk. When I said I was – just – he pushed for more information about the attack. I gave him as much detail as I could manage. I told him about

Kursk's hiding place round the side of the house, the fire-wood I'd been carrying, the details of the fight. I answered his questions as best I could, given the missing tooth and the unpleasant memories the discussion was stirring up. That poker, that blood, the hammer-horror vision of his face smeared across the car window.

Nev listened carefully, then said everything I'd given him tallied with their own reading of the scene. They had a cigarette butt Kursk had flicked away as he waited, the blood-stained (twelve centimetres deep, he was keen to inform me) poker, the scattered logs, fingerprints on the light globe.

He asked for more details about my previous contact with Kursk, but when I fessed up to my earlier visit to Smash and Grab, he already knew about it, of course. He said the other employees of the company had corroborated my story. The investigators had found CCTV footage of me entering the property. The drivers confirmed that my visit had left Kursk pissed off and punching the walls. They said he was never more than a punch away from a free-for-all. Then I asked what Kursk himself had had to say.

'Not much,' Wallace grunted. 'But then you wouldn't expect him to, him being dead and all that.'

'Shit. What happened to him?'

'You,' he said dismissively.

I dropped back into the pillows. Somewhere beyond the window a big winter bird ploughed a lonely furrow through the sky. I'd had a few dust-ups during my career, but I'd never actually killed anyone. All things considered, Neddy Kursk wasn't a bad place to start.

'They found him at daylight,' Neville continued. 'On the road to Greendale. Went over an embankment and hit a tree. Not sure whether it was the crash or the poker that killed him. Bit of both, I imagine. He was making a run for it after you got away. Tried to staunch the blood with rags, made a mess of it. Looks like he lost consciousness, blacked out, bled out.'

The multitudinous medical devices attached to my body clicked and pinged. I imagine the BP monitor was going haywire.

I asked if they'd figured out why Kursk wanted to kill me.

'Still putting the pieces together,' he answered. 'Working hypothesis: he was an accomplice to his brother during his killing spree, wanted to relive the glory days. Apparently you really pissed him off.'

'He had a poker up his arse long before I put one there. Are you looking at him for Raph Cambric?'

'We are. We've discovered he was at the scene at Wycliff.'

I tilted my head, and raised a brow. 'I didn't see him there.'

'Yes you did. He was driving the tow truck.'

I ran a hand across my temple. How unobservant of me. I remembered the driver now. He'd been hunched up in a jacket with his cap low and I'd had other things on my mind, but I should have recognised him when I spoke to him at Smash and Grab.

'That's how he got the tow job,' Neville said. 'He must have been waiting in the vicinity. We're thinking he wanted an excuse to be at the scene legally, in case we picked up evidence of him being there.'

I lay back in the bed and gazed at the flowers on the table.

'Why would he want to kill Raph though? Where's the motive? His brother was into killing women, not apple growers.'

Neville shrugged. 'We're still speculating. Maybe Raph spotted him trying to snatch someone from the side of the road. We're checking the missing person reports, but there's been nothing in the vicinity so far. We do know Kursk was engaged in other illegal activities: we found packets of meth, a pistol and a stash of cash in a safe in his office. Maybe Raph came across a lab in the bush, threatened to report it. Kursk had worked around there for years. Operating as a towie was the perfect cover for a distribution network. He even knew some of the local police, through the job. He must have heard Nash Rankin lived nearby. He'd had a grudge against Nash since his brother's trial, figured he'd make the perfect patsy.'

That all made sense – sort of. Still plenty to be untangled but better minds than mine were working at that. Maybe we'd never know. Most crimes leave unanswered questions of one kind or another.

I did have one more question, though, and it was an important one.

'What does all this mean for Nash?'

Wallace smiled. Maybe he was just being friendly, maybe he was embarrassed by the fact that I'd been proven correct – sort of. Maybe neither of those; as a general rule, Wallace was neither friendly nor embarrassed.

'Charges are being dropped. No way the prosecutor will be able to mount a case now that such an obvious alternative candidate has appeared. Have to run it by a judge, but Nash should be out in a day or two.'

I breathed a sigh of relief, an exhalation tinged with joy. That had been my goal all along: to see Nash set free. I wished

he were here; I'd have loved to see the look on his face, to kiss
the look on his face.

But then I had another thought.

'What about the Professional Standards investigation into,
er, yours truly?'

'Ah. Right.' Wallace shuffled uncomfortably. 'That's not so
easily dealt with. You barrelled through an ongoing investigation
like a runaway road train, drove a suspect to suicide – allegedly.'
He stood up. 'Maybe they'll go easy on you. I'll certainly put in
a good word. You seem to have solved Raph's murder and saved
the taxpayer the cost of a trial and a lifetime's board and lodging
for his killer.'

He offered another scary smile.

'Some of us think you did the world a favour.'

# CHAPTER 40

Around the middle of day three I received a visit from Vince Tehlich. He came bearing flowers, grapes and a selection of magazines. I took a look at the magazines.

'Surfing?'

'All we had in the station. Katie's into it.' Katie? Ah, yes, the new constable and kitchen whiz, she of the drizzled chocolate cookies.

'Glad you didn't go to too much trouble.'

'She thought you'd like 'em. She also sent these.'

He pulled out a bag of the cookies.

'Now you're talking,' I said. 'Props to Katie.'

'We heard you were having trouble eating.'

I flashed him a gappy smile.

He took a seat and we had a conversation much like most of those I'd had with my visitors over the past couple of days: the quality of the food, sleep, wounds and views. I assured him they were all pretty ordinary. I told him the doctors had said I should be discharged the next day, which suited me fine. I was keen to get out of there.

Vince did have one significant piece of information: Nash would be out tomorrow as well, all charges officially dropped.

I was thrilled, but I also felt a slight tremor of anxiety. I was rapt that Nash was getting back to his apples and eagles, and pleased to have been able to make a contribution to his release. But what did it mean for me? For us? So obsessed had I been with gaining his freedom, I hadn't given a moment's thought to what it would be like to hold him in my arms again – if it got that far. We were an odd couple, a pair of hard-bitten eccentrics whose eccentricities may have flowed in the same direction from time to time, but were just as likely to spark each other up like a set of errant jumper leads. Each of us was accustomed to the pleasure of our own company. From what I'd learned of his past life, it was obvious he'd be a hard man to live with. Rumour had it, I wasn't all peaches and cream myself.

'Any idea what time tomorrow?' I asked.

'Depends on how thick and twisted the red tape is – or the people charged with untangling it. But they generally get out early afternoon. The Police Association's got a peer support program. They're gonna pick him up and bring him home.'

'That's decent of them.' Nash was going to need all the peer support they could muster.

I'd been wondering if I should go down to greet him at the remand centre but this would be better. I decided I'd go home as soon as possible – this afternoon if they'd let me. First thing in the morning I'd go to his house and get it ready: give it a sweep and a clean, light the fire, repair the door. Maybe I could even pick up the dog. Flinders and I could hobble out to greet him together. I was surprised to find myself almost shyly looking forward to holding Nash in my arms again. I really liked that man – maybe could even come to love him – and was nervously hoping he'd feel something similar for me. I caught a glimpse of myself in the bedside mirror and groaned, again, about my missing tooth. Jesus! I finally get a reason to make myself presentable and some bastard goes and smashes me in the mouth. Ah well, Nash could like it or lump it.

I asked Vince if he'd mind giving me a lift back to Windmark, to which he readily agreed. It took us a couple of hours to get the paperwork sorted and to pick up the selection of pills and potions the doctors insisted I consume, then we were on our way. I rang Dad to tell him I was going home, then a couple of minutes later I received a call from Lucy Takada, insisting I stay at the Bluehouse. A warm house, hot food, friends and family to check up on me in case I carked it in the night – how could I say no? I could head up to Nash's place first thing in the morning.

Vince dropped me off at the Bluehouse an hour later. Lucy and Sam, Possum, Dad, even Karly, all came out and gave me the sweetest welcome imaginable. I was given the seat of honour – the royal blue armchair by the fire – and tea and scones smothered in cream and Possum's legendary blackberry jam. The culinary highlight of the evening was the sourdough bread pudding Lucy had whipped up in my honour. Alas, I couldn't do it justice. I wasn't even halfway through the dessert when the traumas of the past few days began to catch up with me: my head was throbbing, my chest aching. I winced once or twice when I raised the spoon.

Lucy was keeping a sharp eye on me and insisted it was time for bed. No objections from me. Bed was bliss, especially compared to some of the crappy sleeping experiences I'd been enduring of late: wet blankets, cold swags, nights disrupted by falling trees, noisy nurses and bovver-booted killers. Here it was all flannel sheets, thick doonas and hot water bottles in soft covers. I was asleep almost before my head hit the pillow.

## CHAPTER 41

When I awoke, I was troubled by the strength of the light stealing in through the gap in the curtains. How late was it? I checked my watch. Not too bad. Just after nine. It had been a long few days. I climbed out of bed warily. There was some general soreness in my back and some evil bruising across my right thigh, but none of the fainting fits or nausea I'd felt on the first days after the assault. I experienced a shooting pain in my ribs when I breathed too deeply, but that was okay – I wasn't planning on breathing too deeply. Maybe that would change if things with Nash worked out better than expected.

Lucy was cooking porridge. They lived on porridge round here, especially in winter. Dad came in and the three of us chatted as we ate. I asked if I could borrow a car, but he wasn't happy about me driving, insisted on taking me back to Satellite himself. I agreed, though after taking my prescribed painkillers and antibiotics, I was feeling good, at least by my lousy standards. I rang the vet, got through to Charlie, the nurse. Flinders was getting used to hobbling about on three legs, but they'd prefer to hang on to him for another day or two; they were still worried about infection. That was probably for the best. Nash might benefit from a prior warning about his truncated hound.

Dad drove me up to Satellite and dropped me off at the pub, where my car still sat in the car park. I went in and thanked Annie and Libby for the flowers they'd sent me and grabbed the keys. Dad followed me all the way home and insisted on entering the house first, lump of wood in hand, just to be sure there weren't any more killers lurking within. There weren't. He helped me restore some order to the place – wood stacked, blood mopped, furniture back where it belonged – then left me to it, said I should get some rest.

As soon as he'd gone, I set out for Nash's house in Wycliff. As I approached the community I noticed a lonely chimney standing out in a paddock alongside a patch of winter daffodils blooming in what must have once been a cottage garden. I pulled over and picked a bunch, figuring Nash might appreciate a burst of honey-scented yellow when he walked into the lounge room.

As I resumed the drive, I wondered again what the future held for us. Would we remain a couple of hermits who got together for the occasional buddy-fuck or would we be something more?

I pulled into the driveway and looked around. No sign of his car. Had Forensics taken it away? Or had he come home early and driven off somewhere? I prayed it hadn't been stolen. That would really make his week.

I walked to the front door. Locked. The police must have repaired the damage they'd inflicted. But I found a side door that was unlocked. It gave an eerie creak as I pushed it open and entered the room. My boot heels echoed off the wooden floor, the fridge hummed.

It was only a couple of weeks since I was last here, but the house appeared to have visibly aged. The cold, the silence, the lack of occupation – it was nothing like the snug abode I'd stepped into that first night.

I walked across to the lounge room window and gazed out over Nash's farm. This was the first time I'd had a good look at it in the light of day. There was an orchard of budding apple trees, a pile of chopped wood in an upturned water tank, bits of machinery and equipment poking their noses out of a steel shed. The sky was relatively clear, but the western horizon was roiling with those never-ending storm clouds. From the look of them they were still a couple of hours away.

I could see nothing resembling a vase, but there was a pitcher on the kitchen bench, so I put the flowers into that and placed them on the table. They looked cheerful and bright. I took a dishcloth from the sink and began to wipe away the dust that had accumulated. There was a broad shaft of light slanting through the big bay window, but the building still felt uncomfortably chilled. Should I light a fire? Maybe not a wise move until I knew for sure what was going to happen. I had no idea when Nash would be here, how he'd be feeling. But setting the fire, making sure it was ready to go as soon as he arrived, I could see no harm in that.

I went across to the fireplace and noticed an envelope sitting on the mantelpiece. I took it down and saw my name on the front.

I opened it with trembling fingers and a sinking feeling in my chest.

There was a folded sheet of paper inside, on it a handwritten note. It was as bad as I'd feared.

*Sorry Jesse need some time alone, Nash.*

I'd been half expecting it, but still, the message knocked the breath out of me. He must have been released earlier than expected. He'd anticipated my arrival, not wanted to see me. He'd been and gone. I leaned against the mantelpiece and sighed. That's what you get, I told myself, hooking up with an unstable recluse. What had Dr Rush said about people with psychiatric profiles like Nash's? Solitude can be their preferred mode of existence. They find relationships too intimidating.

I willed myself not to be judgemental. He couldn't have known what I'd gone through to get him out of gaol. He was weird, but – what the fuck – we're all weird. He was a self-centred arsehole, but who wasn't? He had a better excuse than most of us – traumatised from childhood by a bunch of crazy cultists, stitched up by a serial killer. And, I told myself, never forget that Nash had acted heroically in his youth and brought down the Revelators, an astonishing achievement for a thirteen-year-old boy. The universe owed him a bit of breathing space. Incarceration must have been a nightmare for him. He clearly wanted peace and quiet, not a complicated relationship with another rogue cop. Probably a wise move on his part. I wasn't partner material.

I flopped down into an armchair, feeling exhausted, deflated. And slightly cross. He could have written a longer note. Or been a bit friendlier. Maybe even had the guts to tell me to my face.

Let it go, I told myself. Some people – you included – aren't built for long-term relationships. For love. I wondered where he'd gone. Somewhere out bush, I presumed. Maybe up to the Wiregrass and his little hide and his precious bloody eagles.

Fair enough, I told him. It's your choice.

I found a pen and wrote a message of my own on the back of the envelope:

> *Nash,*
> *Understood.*
> *Happy to catch up when you feel like company. Flinders is at the vet's –*
> *leg injured but he's doing okay. I'll take care of him until you're ready.*
> *Call me sometime.*
> *Jess*

I added my phone number, assuming he didn't have it.

I put the envelope back on the mantelpiece with no idea of when he'd get it. Maybe days, maybe weeks. I walked towards the door, my footsteps – and my heart – heavy.

Then I paused, my downcast eye caught by a flash of metallic sheen in the dust on the floor. It was a feather, long and brown, with dark stripes and a pointed tip. Nash's eagle. As I bent to pick it up, I noticed the hat from which it had fallen, upside down, partially crumpled and concealed under a chair.

What the hell were that feather and hat doing here? I knew Nash had them with him when he was lifted into the ambulance – I'd put them on his head myself. The guards would have taken them when he was signed into the remand centre, and returned them when he was released.

Nash needed that hat, that feather. He'd risked his freedom – his life, really – when he snuck back home to retrieve them. The feather was his lucky charm. He'd even been wearing it in the middle of the storm when I first met him. If he was heading off to spend some time alone in the bush, surely he would have taken it with him?

A volley of questions helter-skeltered through my head, threatening to overwhelm me. I felt desperate. Who could help me? No one. I had to figure this out myself. For reasons I couldn't explain – something to do with the speed at which things were happening in this case – I sensed that time was of the essence. Whoever these people were – if they even existed – they reacted at lightning speed.

But it wasn't just time I was lacking. It was perspective. I was desperate to work out what was going on, but I just couldn't. I couldn't see the bloody thing. I felt like a crow caught in a tornado. I needed distance, balance, a bird's-eye view.

I stared at the feather then turned my gaze to the distant bush.

The answer was somewhere out there. I could feel it. My trouble was that I didn't know the country round here well enough. I was still finding my way.

I thought back to my last days in the Territory. Elsie Napanangka and a couple of her little old lady friends had invited me on a drive to some of their important places. The four of us travelled quietly through the Tanami Desert for days. At night, they'd sit by the fire and sing. They weren't just singing about the places we'd been to, they were singing them up. Manifesting them in song. So intimately did they know that world, to them it was alive, interconnected.

That was my problem now. I didn't understand the country and its connections. I needed a lens to look at the matter objectively.

I needed to rise above it. How was I going to do that? I wasn't a bloody eagle.

For some reason, a song I'd heard recently came to mind. Kev Carmody's 'On the Wire'.

I hummed a few bars of the song, then knew what I had to do. I stood up and strode out to the car.

# CHAPTER 42

I raced up to the Wiregrass, pedal to the metal, until I reached what I'd come to think of as Nash's gully. I grabbed my bag and binoculars and walked into the hollow. There were no indications of recent activity. It didn't look like he'd been here. I worked my way past the campsite then came to Nash's hide. I clambered up into it, but again, there was no trace of occupation, unless you counted possum and chough shit. Something had nibbled at the Vita Brits, but I couldn't imagine Nash was that hard up.

My eyes swept across the valley below, then travelled up the escarpment and settled upon the other significant local player in this drama: the mountain ash. It loomed over the slopes like a monarch, powerful and imposing. The eagle's nest still appeared to be empty.

I caught sight of Nash's climbing equipment on the wall.

Have you got the nerve? I asked myself.

I grabbed the equipment, scrambled across the slope until I came to the foot of the ash and gazed up into its upper reaches in awe. From my rough calculation, it looked to be about sixty metres high. It could have been worse. Apparently this species – eucalyptus regnans – is the tallest flowering plant in creation and can grow to a hundred metres. The first fifteen metres were clearly the toughest: there were no lower branches angling off, nothing to cling to.

But there was another option. The golden wattle closest to its base. It had branches and boughs spreading in every direction. Maybe I could use it as a ladder to tackle the first few metres then swing over to the ash? Only one way to find out.

I attached the spurs and harness, grabbed the ropes and scrambled into the lower limbs of the wattle. I worked my way up through the understorey, gingerly pushing through a gauntlet of sticks and spikes and foliage. I was halfway up when the branches began to thin out and bow down under my weight. I assessed the distance between the trees: time to have a go.

I took hold of my throw-line and crept out onto a branch. It was weaker than it looked and bowed down precipitously. Suddenly it gave way and I was dangling upside down, perilously close to falling. I threw a hand out and grasped one of the nearby branches, but that tore loose as well and I performed a mid-air jig until I seized a third branch, this one strong enough to hold me. A searing pain shot through my damaged ribs. I did what I could to breathe into the pain, to rise above it. I paused to regain my breath, steadied myself then lobbed the throw-line into the ash. It held at the first attempt, and I swung over. I spat out a mouthful of bugs and bark, gathered myself together and resumed the ascent. The spurs were invaluable; they gave me purchase, a measure of stability. I crawled around the eagle's nest, relieved to confirm that it was empty.

As I ascended into the crown I began to understand why botanists call the upper canopy the eighth continent. It was another world up there. The higher you got, the more things changed. Birds and beetles looked at me, astonished. The background noise took on a different tone, a low, persistent thrum. A swarm of strange insects – caterpillars, green ants, weevils – crunched and crawled through the leaf-work. A spider floated in from god-knows-where and ran its web across my face. A big-eyed praying mantis froze, millimetres from my nose, scrutinised me then slowly backed into a camouflaging branch. I wondered if I was the first human ever to be here.

Looking down at the forest below, I was struck by how tessellated its structure was when observed from this angle. The trees maintained their distance from each other but worked in groups, gathering in geometrical patterns, maximising their exposure to light, minimising wind. There's a term for this phenomenon: canopy shyness. I'd heard of it, but I'd never seen it so clearly before.

I was maybe forty metres from the ground when I decided the branches above me were starting to look treacherous and I was getting tired. Not a healthy combination. My ribs were throbbing, my head was spinning. Maybe this'll do, I said to myself. There was a comfortable-looking fork just above me. One last effort and I hauled myself into it. I hooked in the harness, leaned back against the trunk and closed my eyes, getting some air into my lungs, some strength into my limbs.

Then I looked out over the Wiregrass Valley.

This is it, I decided. This is why I'm here. This is as close as I'm going to get to a bird's-eye view.

I could see all the way down to the Windmark Valley. There were sporadic vehicles crawling along the road beside the river, a scattering of bridges and bed-level crossings running over it. A column of bikies roared up the valley like a black wind. I raised the binoculars, my gaze drawn to the various human endeavours of the district: vineyards, timber mills, berry farms and quarries. Distant chimneys emitted silver smoke. Ice-blue horses cantered over emerald paddocks.

I turned the glasses up on to the closer Wiregrass Valley and lost myself in contemplation of the more mysterious works of nature: rock and waterfalls, stretches of mud and snow, a patchwork of blue bush and green leaf. The sky was dark and ominous, the approaching thunderstorm unsettling the atmosphere. Then a strange thing happened: the sun emerged through a gap in the clouds and illuminated a rocky outcrop on a spur in the slopes opposite my own, on the far side of the Wiregrass Valley.

The outcrop was transformed into a fleeting image: a woman's head, her hair composed of darkly forested slopes, her face of granite blocks stained by dark vertical lines – fissures? streaks of manganese? – that resembled tears. Her eyes were downcast. The light shifted and the woman's mouth appeared to move. Some words came to mind: *something inside me weeps black tears*.

It was as if the woman was speaking directly to me. I heard her voice trickling like a high-country creek through the back-woods of my mind. Maybe it was just my imagination, but, even if that was all it was, I needed to listen. The face in the rocks was thin, quiet, intense, dark-haired, dark-eyed. Lost and lonely.

*something inside me weeps black tears*

Why did it look familiar? The answer came in a flash. Lucinda. Who must have resembled her mother. I thought about the necklace Lucinda was wearing the first time we met: a gold pendant with a red flower – a rose – upon it. It bore a striking resemblance to the flower that had been so deftly sketched on the card in Raph's address book. Had the necklace been a gift, from mother to daughter?

Lucinda had mentioned her mother was away in Queensland. I remembered the shadow that flew across her face when I asked about her. Was she the missing woman? I thought of Meg, my crystal-gazing neighbour's prognostications and shuddered: the drowning woman, the dying horseman. The brutal spirits abroad.

*something inside me weeps black tears*

I wasn't seeing everything here, that was obvious. But I was getting a sense of it. It was extensive, interconnected, an underground forest, like Lucinda's mycorrhizal network. I suspected there was more going on here than a jealous – even murderous – husband.

*something inside me weeps black tears*

I didn't know what had happened to the woman who wrote those words. I didn't know what had happened to Nash Rankin.

But I felt afraid and angry for them both.

# CHAPTER 43

I needed information – fast. Nash had already been missing for hours. God only knew how long he had left. Maybe I was already too late. Whoever had taken him, assuming someone had, they worked swiftly. I pulled out my phone and rang Lance Cunningham. I thought about Annie's comment about how Lance had refused to leave my side when I'd been mangled by Neddy Kursk, the genuine concern I saw in his face when I came to. My instincts told me I could trust him.

He answered straightaway, seemed surprised to hear that I was out of hospital.

'Where are you?' he asked.

'You wouldn't want to know, but thanks for your support,' I said. He and Wendy had visited me in hospital, gave me some lovely rhododendrons and a sweet card. 'I'm afraid I have to ask for a little more.'

'Jess, you should be resting.'

'I am – kind of. I'm lying down. I just want to tie up a few loose ends.'

'Yes?'

'The crossbow boy and his family. Did you get a chance to follow up on them?'

'Been flat out – half the staff are away – but I did speak to Bill Chambers, the neighbour. He said they kept to themselves but they were okay, never caused any trouble. Except for the boy, Bailey. He's a bit wild. Bill had to tell him off once for shooting close to the livestock with his bow.'

'Did you get the father's name?'

I heard him shuffling about in his papers, then he said: 'Yep, it's Hawley. Craig Hawley.'

I went quiet for a moment, trying to weave that strand into the web that was spreading in my mind. Hawley and Sons, the medical practice managers and employers of the late Ronald Laws. Craig was one of them. His daughter had said he was a hospital CEO. Presumably he was managing one of the hospitals the company owned. I asked Lance what he knew about the mother.

'Bill heard she'd gone to Queensland to care for a sick relative.'

Again, that tallied with what Lucinda had told me.

'Did you get her first name?'

'Hang on, yeah, it's here somewhere.' Another pause as he riffled through his notes, then he said, 'Rosa.'

I still had Raph's address book in my bag. I took it out and flicked through it until I came to the Hs. There they were: *Hawley, Rosa and Craig.* Raph definitely knew her. Was Rosa the woman who signed her intimate messages with a rose? I suspected she was.

I experienced a pang of sympathy for her. Maybe it was just my imagination, but I had a fleeting vision of her romance with the farrier: the subtle glances and shy smiles while he was shoeing the horses, the laughter, the brush of hands, the electric response. Rosa had been a nurse, had married the head of the hospital, found herself trapped in a loveless marriage with a controlling partner. Raph Cambric represented freedom. She was reluctant at first, terrified – but when she fell, she fell hard. She took to slipping down to his cabin in the late afternoons, hungry for his embrace, his bed. Did she eventually find the courage to tell her husband? Or did Craig Hawley discover the affair himself?

I had so many questions, but I could only guess most of the answers. What happened at the end? Had she and Raph decided to run away together? Had he been left wondering why she didn't turn up at the rendezvous? He'd been told, like the kids, that she'd gone to Queensland to care for a sick relative. Dubbo was on the way. He'd gone to track her down, discovered she wasn't where they said she was. He came back, deeply troubled and desperate. What then? He'd asked too many questions, set their antennae twitching, triggered a brutal response.

It was all speculation, of course. The ravings of a crazy woman in a tall tree. I needed proof. Hard evidence.

Lance's voice boomed out of the speaker. 'You still there, Jess?'

'One more favour, Lance.'

'Yes?'

'Keep your phone handy this evening. I might need back-up.'

There was an uncomfortable pause, then he asked me why. I said I couldn't share anything yet. I didn't know exactly what my plans were, but there was every chance they would involve a little breaking and entering. The less he knew, the less likely it would rub off on him if it all went tits up.

'They were right,' said Lance ruefully.

'Who were?'

'The people who told me it wouldn't be dull when you got here.'

# CHAPTER 44

When he signed off, I sat there for a few more minutes, thinking. Somewhere in the mass of information I was gathering was the golden thread that tied it all together, but for the life of me, I couldn't see it. I considered a number of keys for cracking the code but in the end could come up with only one: Nash. How did he get involved? How was he connected to the Hawleys? I returned to my phone, entered his and the Hawleys' names into the search bar and skimmed the results. There were items about Nash's trial and conviction, his sentence, his incarceration. I read his doctor's opinion, the comments of his senior officers. I found a good deal about Nash, but nothing that intersected with the Hawleys.

Until I opened an article from *The Age* by the crime reporter, John Silvester, a man with a sharp eye for the eccentricities of human behaviour. His piece mentioned that Nash had been raised in a cult led by John Patmos. That much I knew, but then

Silvester went on to say that Patmos was a bullshit stage name. The original John of Patmos was the early Christian author of the Book of Revelation, the playbook of charlatans and religious grifters for millennia. The man who came to be known as the Revelator had been born Claude Hawley, in 1930s Marysville. 'No surprise that he changed it,' Silvester wrote. 'Claude Hawley was hardly a name to galvanize the masses.'

Hawley's name change came in the fifties, around the time he took to calling himself a pastor and married Guin Wilson. Guin's father was a fire-breathing church elder-cum-cattle farmer, her mother a woman who spoke to ghosts in the street and who spent the latter half of her life in the state asylum.

I remembered Starcy telling me there'd been a couple of offspring. I'd met them both now: George and Craig. They were staging a comeback, taking over the family business, stripped of the religiosity bullshit.

I felt that old, familiar stirring in my brain as the fragments flew together, driven by some centripetal force. That force was something I'd never understood, something I'd been born with.

What was going on? Various scenarios ran through my head. Were the brothers staging a comeback, taking over the family business, stripped of its bullshit religiosity? Maybe. What had Carina said about Leon Glazier? He was a hacker with a fascination for cults. Had he discovered that the Revelators were back in town? That they'd never gone away, they'd just gone underground. That they'd resuscitated a family-owned company and gone back to all the business was really ever about: power and wealth. Whatever Leon had found, it was enough to get him killed and Nash framed. They'd neither forgotten nor forgiven the thirteen-year-old boy who brought their fiefdom down about their ears. These people were astonishing: so efficient, so ruthless. They never made a move without covering their tracks, making allowances for cock-ups and setbacks, deflecting blame, diverting the authorities. And they moved fast. I remembered Starcy's story of how the Patmoses had fled the country at a moment's notice.

I had to move faster. Maybe it was too late. Nash could already be in a shallow grave down some lonely track.

A light shower – a foretaste of the imminent storm – drifted in as I made my way down the tree. I crawled around the eagle's nest, took a deep breath and swung over into the wattle. I crashed through the branches for a metre or two, but managed to get a handhold and resumed my descent at a safer pace. A few minutes later I was back on solid ground.

I returned to my car then set out in the direction of Satellite.

I pulled over when I reached Craig Hawley's property. The front gate was locked and there were no signs of life: no lights, no movement, no vehicles to be seen. That didn't mean much, of course. They were a quiet family, any cars could be in the garage, any lights round the back. The horses moved about the front paddock, the white one skittish in the wind.

I climbed over the gate and walked up the drive. I knocked on the door, rang the bell. No response. Should I risk a surreptitious little poke around? Why not? But a quick search of the area surrounding the house revealed nothing of interest: a gravelled yard, an in-ground pool, a high-quality equestrian arena. All quiet. Nobody home.

As I walked back to the gate, I remembered Craig Hawley's comment the night I dropped into his house. He'd said he had family in the area.

My mind slipped back to my moment of epiphany in the mountain ash: the outcrop on the opposite side of the Wiregrass Valley.

Who else had said something about a land formation like that recently? My father. He'd been fossicking about the hills, had come across an outcrop on a spur that sparked his curiosity. When he asked permission from the owners to enter the property – he described a long, ominous house, like a fortress – they told him to sod off, set the dogs onto him.

Why were they so protective of that patch of bush?

I returned to the car, pulled out my map and scoured the locality, trying to pinpoint the formation I'd seen from the tree. Eventually I came across a geological feature that tallied with Dad's description. It was called Thunderhead Rock, and it was twenty kays to the north, about a kilometre in from the road.

I started the car and drove up towards the Wiregrass. Was this wise? Of course not. If I had any sense, or if there was any justice in the world, I'd be kicking the doors down with a Critical Incident Response Team at my back. But I've never had much sense, and justice is as rare as bunyip shit. I certainly didn't have enough evidence for a search warrant. The other thing I didn't have was time. I was racing against a clock I couldn't see.

I didn't know what had happened to Nash, but I was going to have to find out on my own. Quickly.

# CHAPTER 45

The country up here had been scorched by fire. I wasn't sure how long ago, but most of the tree trunks thrusting up over the canopy were white and bare, dead. Ravens peered down from the upper branches, their eyes like lasers. There were a few hardy farms scattered along the northern end of the valley: beef, alpaca, even goats. The further north I travelled, the hardier and more goat-like the farms became.

There was no mistaking the property when I rounded a bend and came to it on the northern side of the road. As Dad had said, the main building was like a fortress: long and low, almost crenellated, its dark windows looking down on a sizeable acreage below. The house was at the rear of the property, up where the farmland met the bush. The rock – Thunderhead, I presumed – loomed over the forested slopes behind the building. Dad was right about the outcrop: it looked positively creepy up there, like a human skull gazing down upon the valley. There was no sign of a woman's face from this angle: it was all granite blocks and precipitous inclines. I could see why Dad had depicted it as powerfully ominous as he had. His creative instincts had always understood more than his rational mind.

I pulled up at the front gate. It was high and heavy, black iron, clearly designed to keep the world at bay. Beyond the gate there was a gloomy avenue of windswept cypress pines leading up to the house.

The sign at the front read: THUNDERHEAD ESTATE, with FINE WINES in smaller lettering below. A winery seemed out of place up here; it was like a livid scar on pale skin, an unnatural intrusion that could only keep the surrounding forest at bay with a bevy of chainsaws and poisons. Behind the house was a network of white brick and metal-clad sheds with solar panels and massive air-conditioning vents on their roofs. I presumed that would be the cellars and labs, the bottling plant.

I got out of the car, collar high, hat low, wondering what sort of security they had. Cameras? Motion sensors? Alarms? All of the above, I had to assume. I hunched lower into my jacket. The gate was closed, but I gave the lock a quick shake. Tight as. No jumping over this one.

It was getting on for dusk now. There were lights on in the main building and a squadron of SUVs and four-wheel drives in an attached carport.

I walked back to the HiLux and drove a kilometre down the road, past all the TRESPASSERS PROSECUTED signs my father had spoken of. I pulled into a side road and parked the car in a grove of tea-tree I hoped would hide me from prying eyes. I went up to the fence, studied the property from the side and considered my options.

I wanted to have a closer look at the buildings, but how was I going to do that? Knock on the door? Yeah, right. And besides, I had a suspicion that the country itself was an important element in this drama. Surely the property's seclusion was the reason they'd chosen it? They grew a few grapes, sure, but what else did they get up to? The way they'd reacted to my father's unauthorised entry suggested they were hiding something.

Maybe I could do two things in the one incursion. Use the last of the daylight to search the bushier parts of the property, and then, when it grew dark, set myself up at a vantage point behind the house and study its occupants with the binoculars. Look for any suspicious activities, anything out of place. Maybe engage in a little breaking and entering should the opportunity arise.

The sky suggested I had maybe half an hour of dim light left.

I kitted up: torch, binoculars, beanie, the folding shovel I kept for digging myself out of bogs. The storm was closing in. There was lightning in the west, ribbons and filaments of coruscation in the approaching clouds.

I climbed through the fence and walked until I came across a shallow gully. I decided to use it as a scaffold to ascend the property. It made the climb more difficult but it offered greater concealment from the house. I set out. There was a narrow creek at the gully's base, sporadic trees and rocks fallen across it. It took about ten minutes to work my way up into the bush at the rear of the property.

As I climbed, the ground grew harder, sparser, trickier to read. There were flakes of mica embedded in the black boulders strewn across the trail, chunks of granite in the sand. When I got up to where the gully ran out, I came upon a track running off to the north-west. I followed it carefully, stooped low, searching for signs of . . . of what? Disturbance, I supposed. I could see the lights of the house, maybe five hundred metres away. Whenever I came across evidence of human activity – footprints, fence posts, old drums or car parts – I crouched down and made a detailed examination of the ground nearby. I came across animal scats, wombat holes, golden orb spiders in giant night webs. A bat swooped out of the darkness, carving a wave in the vortices of its wake. I stumbled upon – not into, thank Christ – an old mine shaft at the foot of the slope. I wouldn't have minded a look down into its depths – could there be a better place to bury your secrets? – but the sides of the shaft were crumbly and dangerous and I wasn't properly equipped. At least the snakes appeared to be hibernating.

A light dusting of snow drifted in, grew heavier, settled on the surface and made the search harder. I used the torch in short, sharp bursts as the darkness set in. I spent more time on my knees than I did upright, my attention caught by the tiniest of signs: a twisted root, a clump of hair, a handprint, a tear-shaped paw print. The storm clouds were gathering overhead, but they'd yet to deliver their full load.

I'd been at it for half an hour when I came across a track with a set of tyre treads on it that gave me pause. They were Dunlop Sport Maxx. The same tread I'd seen on the dirt road near my house. Not proof of anything, of course. There could be a hundred such sets of tyres in the district. But why was it running round up here, at the back of the property? Collecting firewood? Dumping rubbish? Maybe, but darker possibilities ran through my mind.

There was a rumble of thunder and the first fat raindrops punched the ground. I had to get cracking or the rain would wash away whatever I was looking for.

I set off after the Dunlops. I lost them once or twice in the dark, but found them again with a combination of touch and torch. Eventually I reached a clearing in which it appeared the vehicle had come to a halt. There were at least two sets of boot prints heading off to the west. I followed them.

Then, where the boots ran out, I found something: a low mound of earth, recent, with a layer of leaf matter and dirt dumped over it in an attempt at concealment. Too long for a dog, too short for a horse. Whatever it was, I didn't like it. I removed my backpack, took out the folding shovel and started digging. I'd only gone a few centimetres when I encountered something metallic. I went at it for a few more minutes and uncovered an old steel and wire mesh security door. Somebody had placed it here to protect whatever was buried below. That made sense; you wouldn't want foxes digging it up and distributing fragments around the neighbourhood.

I heard a dog bark in the distance, coming from the direction of the house. I kept digging, then heard another bark. Was it closer this time? I paused, studied the night, listening. I thought of the dog that had attacked Dad. Then I heard it again, definitely closer now.

I gripped the shovel and took a few steps towards the rear of the clearing – then stopped, stunned, as a battery of portable floodlights lit up the site and blinded me. I shielded my eyes and squinted through my fingers.

What the hell . . . I hadn't heard anybody arrive. They must have been here all the time, waiting for me. A trio of figures stepped into the clearing, bright light streaming around their silhouettes. They were all holding weapons and the weapons were all aimed at me.

'Evening, Jesse,' said the man in the middle.

I took a moment to recognise him. It was his outfit that confused me: combat jacket, tactical boots, heavy equipment and gear. The last time I saw him he'd been wearing a crisp blue suit with trainers. The man who'd intercepted me at Hawley and Sons. What was his name? Kane Lochran. From Corporate Governance. He was holding a shotgun in his right arm and moving lightly on his feet, poised, ready to strike. Corporate fucking governance was right. He had a set of thermal binoculars around his neck and a portable radio in his chest pocket. Had they been watching me the whole time?

Next to him was Craig Hawley, levelling a bolt-action Winchester with a night scope at me. No surprise to see him here. It was the man on the other side who gave me a moment of despair. Ed Dougherty, the inspector from Greendale. He had a scowl on his face and a pistol in his right hand. His presence there instantly explained a lot of things: how they'd stayed a step ahead of me, how they'd known where I lived, how they'd sabotaged the investigations into the deaths of Leon Glazier and Raph Cambric. I remembered Dougherty disappearing on the first day of the investigation. Presumably he'd been planting the evidence that ensnared Nash, a move they'd been forced to make when I worked out that Raph's death wasn't an accident.

'Please don't make a sudden move,' said Lochran. 'You're trespassing, but I'm sure we can resolve this.'

Yeah, right. Whoever was in the grave behind me had doubtless heard something similar.

He pulled the radio out of his pocket and put it to his mouth. 'She was right,' he said, not taking his eyes off me or his finger off the trigger. 'We've got her.'

He listened for a moment, then replied: 'I will.'

He put the radio away.

'We wait,' he said.

We waited.

The silence was protracted, razor-edged. A distant owl hooted.

I gave Dougherty an acid stare, remembering Starcy's suggestion that the Revelators had blackmailed or corrupted cops on the payroll.

'What was it?' I asked Dougherty. 'Young girls? Boys?' He didn't strike me as the acolyte type. He had the morals of a feral cat but he wasn't stupid.

'I warned you to keep your nose out of it,' he said with a thick sneer.

Lochran answered for him. 'Inspector Ed does have an unfortunate taste for young – is women the right word, Ed? Maybe not, but, if it's any consolation, he won't be interested in an old hag like you.'

Lochran continued to move restlessly on the balls of his feet, as if he were keen to finish this. The shottie was what concerned me most. It was a weapon that didn't take prisoners, especially at this range, and he was cradling it with the air of somebody who knew how to use it. More than that: somebody who took pleasure in using it. He stepped forward, into the light, and I noticed a blue flash on the side of his boots.

'You're the bastard who dropped that tree on me,' I grunted.

'That was a warning,' he replied. 'We'd been told you were persistent.'

I could guess who told them that, I thought, glancing at Dougherty. I turned back to Lochran.

'You crippled my dog.'

'That wasn't part of the plan,' he said. A smile that said he couldn't give a shit flitted across his face.

Speak of the devil, another dog – an athletic Doberman with prominent fangs and pointed ears – came bounding into the clearing. Lochran snapped his fingers and the animal moved to his side. It stood there, panting, watching.

Jesus. Guns, dogs, fancy-dress commandos. The odds were getting longer by the minute.

A set of headlights appeared, coming up from the house. I turned to watch as a sleek black four-wheel drive drew to a halt in front of us, its powerful high beams dazzling us all. Hawley and Dougherty instinctively moved to restrain me, each gripping an arm. Lochran remained in front of us, his eyes not leaving mine, the shotgun levelled at my chest.

The driver's door opened and a man stepped out. George Hawley. No surprise there. He was wearing a long black coat, a thick scarf and an air of weary resolve, as if annoyed that I'd dragged him away from a warm fire, but supremely confident that he had the situation in hand. He was in charge here, as he liked to be.

Or was he?

He strode round to the passenger's door and opened it. A shrouded figure stepped out into the elements: short, thin, moving slowly. A woman, I sensed from the way she stepped over the snowy ground. The atmosphere grew tense. I should have been planning my counterattack, but even I was intrigued.

She moved into the floodlights' glow and pushed her fur-lined hood back to reveal a thin, brittle face, powdery pale where it wasn't rouged. She had jet-black hair and painted lips.

'Hello, Jesse,' she said.

I was speechless.

It was Guin Patmos.

# CHAPTER 46

Physically, she was the smallest one there, but her power radiated out like the energy from a collapsed star.

'How nice to meet you after all this time,' she said. Her voice was dark and commanding. 'We've been wondering when you'd make an appearance. I knew it wouldn't be long.'

'They told me you were dead,' I gasped. This situation was spiralling out of control. What next? Was John bloody Patmos about to rise up out of the grave behind me?

'Some of us are a little more resilient than others,' she rejoined.

Maybe, some inner voice whispered. But it helps if you've got a pack of doctors at your beck and call. Not only do they keep you alive, they could be blackmailed, bribed or seduced into producing fake death certificates and fake faces.

Against my better judgement, I felt curious about her. It was those eyes; they drew you in. There was a flash of lightning and a boom of thunder to the west. The storm was almost upon us. The bloody woman brought her own special effects.

'When did you come back to Australia?' I asked.

'A good few years ago now.'

'Why?'

She swept a hand out at the darkness.

'This land – it's in my blood. It's where I achieved enlight-enment.' She looked around at the bush, shivered briefly and inhaled. 'I was hungry for the scents and smells I grew up with: sassafras, boronia, chocolate lily. Flowering gums.' Just for a millisecond, I caught a glimpse of the innocent country child she must have once been. Then she added: 'But I don't suppose a Laverton girl would know such things, would she? It's all tiger snakes and thistles out there, isn't it?'

She stepped forward and pinched my chin between her fore-finger and thumb. Her nails were long and sharp. Craig Hawley and Dougherty tightened their respective grips on my arms.

'You're an interesting person,' she said. 'It's a pity we didn't meet years ago. We could have really made something of you. Tell me, was that your father sneaking around here a few weeks ago? The famous Ben Redpath?'

'I don't know what you're talking about,' I said, reluctant to give her any reason to set her hounds onto Dad.

She scorched me with those eyes. 'You're lying,' she said. 'I wasn't sure before, but I am now. That was why we arranged this little welcome party.' She swept a hand out at the floodlights and the men with guns. 'I knew you'd be along sooner or later. They tell me you come from the desert, know how to read the land. How fascinating.'

I shrivelled a little inside. Laverton, my father, the outback. This woman knew me better than I knew myself. That must have been the secret to her longevity: she planned, watched her back, eliminated threats. Looked for her opponent's weak point. She ran her nails lightly down my face then stepped back.

'Tell me, Jesse Redpath: who are you?'

'You seem to know everything – you tell me.'

Her laughter was like a slap in the face.

'You're many things,' she said. 'A demon, a thief, a trickster. But it's your spirit that burns brightest. Do you understand the danger that comes with living in the age of the apocalypse?'

'Yep – it produces maniacs like you.'

She stepped back, assayed me coldly and smiled. Her smile was more sinister than most frowns.

'What do you think this is all about, Jesse?'

'Power, of course. And there's nothing as powerful as money to a tiny mind like yours. I presume you and your sons are resurrecting the Revelators. Or at least trying to squeeze what you can out of the corpse. Let me guess: you had money squirrelled away in some safe haven and you used it to revive a company – a healthcare provider – that had been in the family for years. You're using the business to launder old and generate new money. You've dug up the dirt files and are blackmailing people into carrying out your orders and adding to your wealth. Maybe your so-called "resurrection" has even given some of your more idiotic followers a sense of your immortality. How am I doing so far?'

'It's nothing to do with wealth,' she snapped. 'This is a material world – of course you need resources for a mission like ours. But it's for a greater cause. It's for our covenant.'

I blinked. 'Your what?'

'Our direct link to the glory that lies in us all – if we choose to accept it. My husband understood that. He embodied it.' Her gaze lit up. 'You destroyed him, of course.'

'I never even met the guy.'

'You and your fellow foot soldiers of the devil, you've met him many times, in countless garbs and guises. You drove us into the wilderness. You are destruction itself.'

She stared at me and intoned a line she'd clearly used before. 'His eyes are like a flame of fire, and on his head are many diadems, and he has a name written that no one knows but himself.'

Oh Jesus, I thought, she believes her own horse shit. Is there anything more dangerous?

'I heard he was a rapist and a paedophile,' I couldn't help but say.

I wouldn't have thought the temperature could drop any further, but drop it did. An icy wave moved across her surgically enhanced face.

'There's one thing I still don't get,' I added while I had her off balance. 'Why did you go after Nash Rankin? Couldn't you give the poor bastard a break? After all you've done to him, the mess you made of his life?'

Something faded from her countenance. Had she held a faint hope that there might be a chance they could use me? Whatever hopes she held, they'd just vanished.

'This enterprise has been our life's work,' she said, with a trace of weariness in her voice. 'Our mission. We've been working at it for decades. There have been hundreds – thousands – of followers and believers. Our brethren. Our children. But that boy remains my biggest disappointment. We saw his promise early, gave him everything, and he threw it in our faces. For what? For a foolish, self-centred emotion, born of the devil. He lied to the police, betrayed the faith we had in him, the love we showed him, the truths we let him see. God only knows the harm he could have done, would have done, if it hadn't been for the doctor.'

Guin read the bewilderment on my face and allowed herself a satisfied little smirk. 'Dr Rush.'

The psychiatrist. I realised what had been bothering me since my visit to Rush. The logo in George Hawley's office: a blue crown with triple spikes. There'd been something similar at the entrance to the Nexus in Ivanhoe. Ronald Laws had mentioned that the company owned several private hospitals. The Nexus was one of them. Damien Rush had been Nash's psychiatrist since the cult was first reported to Family Services, had been treating him when he'd suffered his first psychotic episodes. They'd somehow got the doctor under their control – blackmail? I thought about the tremble in his fingers, wondered what he was on – then forced him to dope Nash with something that would induce psychosis. The bastards had used his own doctor to assault him, driven him half mad.

Guin had been trying to pump me for information, to see how much I knew, what I might have passed on to the authorities. But now she was just boasting. Even in her late eighties, standing in the snow with the wind whipping at her fur-lined coat, she had to be the one running the show. She was toying with me – and enjoying the experience.

'What about Rosa?' I asked.

'Ah, Rosa. Sometimes – for the greater good, or god – you need to make decisions that can seem harsh at the time.

I liked Rosa. We all did. But once you've been given the honour of joining the inner circle of our family, you can never leave it. She understood that. She was another disappointment. And with the farrier, no less. How degrading.'

Suddenly I'd had it with this she-devil.

'She was the mother of your grandchildren!' I yelled.

I thought about Stefan's description of Rosa riding pillion on Raph's bike, racing along the riverbank laughing, her hair blowing in the wind. I could only hope the affair had brought some happiness into her life before they moved on her.

I glanced at Craig Hawley. He was glaring at me, his cuckolded anger laid bare. I glared back at him, until he looked away.

Lochran didn't. He was enjoying this as much as Guin was. The shotgun was poised in his hands. He was just waiting for a word from Guin.

'It was you, wasn't it?' I said to him. 'Raph. Rosa. Even poor old Leon, up at Horse Thief Creek. You do the dirty work. You repair the damage when things go wrong.'

Guin spoke for him. 'My nephew has been well trained for his role. He has a special talent for making problems disappear.'

She was looking at me like I was a piece of off meat; chances were, I soon would be. I gloomily contemplated the array of weapons angled at me, wondering where to begin. Throw Dougherty at them? There was more thunder, almost upon us now, then a sprinkle of hail. A wave of rain rushed up the valley.

'We need to wrap this up,' said George Hawley.

Guin tightened her coat and stepped towards her car. Then she casually remarked to Lochran: 'Put her in the ground, next to Rosa.'

She paused for a moment, then turned, eyes widening, keen to watch what was about to go down. I remembered Starcy mentioning she was a voyeur. Of death, it seemed, as well as sex. The rain arrived in strength, a torrent of water crashing through the air, running down our backs and faces.

Lochran raised the shotgun.

I adjusted my stance, preparing to make a move.

A swift whipping sound cut through the air and a shock wave flew over Lochran's face. There was a flash of bewilderment in his eyes, then he shuddered, twisted around, threw his head back and his left arm out. His right arm jerked and the gun exploded, shredded the left thigh of Craig Hawley, who'd had the misfortune to be standing directly in front of it. Hawley went down screaming, grasping and staring at his leg in disbelief. Lochran tumbled forward. There was a fierce little bolt buried in the middle of his back.

Dougherty whirled round, looking for the source of all this devastation. Then realised, too late, that I was the more immediate threat. He swung his pistol back at me. I threw myself to one side, felt the bullet whizz past my body. I snapped an axe kick at his gun hand, a roundhouse kick into his guts. As he folded I seized his right arm, flicked him over my shoulder and slammed him into the ground. I put a knee into his back and twisted the arm until I felt something give. He groaned in agony. I ripped the gun out of his hand. He tried to find his feet, had almost found them when I swept them out from under him. I thought about the complicated situation I was in and shot him in the right leg. I wasn't sure what he was capable of but I figured that should just about cover all bases.

Craig Hawley was making a lot of noise. He'd crumbled to the ground, his thigh mainly metal and minced meat. A blast of buckshot at point-blank range will do that to you. The Doberman was trying to work out who to attack. It was clearly thinking about me, but then there was a distant whistle and it pricked its ears, turned its head and loped off into the night.

Lochran was on the ground, face down, shuddering, groping around trying to find whatever had buried itself in his back and shattered his world. Wondering what the hell had just happened.

I spun round, looking for more threats, had the misfortune to catch Guin's eye. Catch her eye? That was an understatement; there was no avoiding it. It was like being sucked into a maelstrom.

'You really are the devil,' she growled, her voice devoid of inflection. 'Hell follows you around.'

I suddenly understood that the entire artifice of her face – the pencilled brows, the painted lids, the rouged cheeks, the spidery lashes – was constructed to draw you into those eyes. They hypnotised you; if you looked deep enough, they told stories that ate away at your self-confidence. If you looked harder, you saw it all: the Bible-bashing father, as brutal with his offspring as he was with his animals. A scattergun mother on a dirt-poor farm full of slaughtered sheep and skinned rabbits, the cruelty, the callousness and cunning.

Cunning?

Jesus, she was trying to distract me. Succeeding. I caught a flicker in her gaze, followed it, landed on George, who was inching towards the front seat of his car. I ran, jumped, kicked the door into him. He crumpled. I ran round to see what he'd been up to. There was a shotgun in the rack. I grabbed it. George was groaning and trying to find his feet.

'Are there any more weapons in there?' I yelled.

'No.'

I thumped him in the head with the stock of the gun.

'Sorry,' I said as he slumped back to the ground. 'I'm sure you're telling the truth, but I wouldn't want to stake my life on it.'

I frisked him, found nothing. Maybe he had been telling the truth. Guin was standing at the front of the vehicle, one hand on the bull-bar, the other at her mouth.

'What about you?' I growled.

She said nothing, but her head was moving from side to side, trying to take on board the developments of the last few seconds. The rain was falling furiously around her. She looked like a laughing clown on a rubbish dump, with her gaping mouth and the colours running down her cheeks.

I walked towards her and she shrank away, her hands raised and moving across her plasticated face. Even now, it held the ghost of a smile, a smile would be there until the day they laid her in the ground. She gazed at the night sky, as if wondering where salvation was going to come from now, gradually realising that it wasn't coming from anywhere. I was it. She snarled at me like a trapped cat.

I stomped forward and grabbed her by the throat.

'Where's my boyfriend?' I yelled. 'And if you say he's in that grave, you won't be far behind him, you narcissistic witch.'

I tightened my grip, drew back my fist.

'Tell me,' I roared.

She flinched, faded away.

'He's up at the winery,' she croaked.

'Where in the winery?'

'The cellar round the back.'

I pushed her away. She slipped and landed on her skinny arse in the mud.

There was movement off to the south side of the clearing. Bailey Hawley stepped into the floodlights' glare, a crossbow in his hands, the dog at his side. Lucinda was on his other side, an arm around his shoulders, trying to hug him and hold him back. He was weeping and dragging himself forward, his face fraught with anger and fear.

'He killed our mother,' he gasped, gesturing at Lochran and looking at me. 'They told us she'd gone to her family in Queensland, but he killed her. I just heard them say it. He was going to kill you too.'

Lucinda was trying to console him, to little avail. They both looked around the clearing, stunned. She went across to her father and tried to render assistance. He'd gone into shock. He was staring at the dark and shivering. I took off my belt, fashioned it into a tourniquet, showed her how to maintain the pressure on his shattered leg. I made a miserable icepack out of snow and leaves, tried to slow the bleeding.

'That one,' she said, indicating Lochran, still groaning on the ground and making futile attempts to reach the arrow in his own back. 'He's an evil man. I think he killed Raph, the farrier, as well. Our friend.'

'You were there, that night at Wycliff, weren't you? I saw you on your horse.'

She nodded. 'I overheard him talking to my Uncle George. I couldn't hear the details, but just the tone of their voices gave me an ugly feeling. I tried to follow them, to warn whoever they were going to attack, but I lost them in the storm and had to turn back. It wasn't until the next day I heard that Raph had died.'

I saw the reason for her initial caution towards me when I brought her brother home. She wasn't sure what horrors her family had perpetrated, but she was doing her best to preserve something, if only for Bailey's sake. Trying to act as a mother. The last thing she wanted was a police officer poking round the house. She had to keep her fears to herself. I also understood her brother's antagonism towards me: they'd raised him to be suspicious and hostile towards the authorities who'd ruined the family. Maybe he was even being raised to be Lochran's apprentice; that's why they were getting him used to weapons and dogs.

Craig Hawley rolled over and groaned, clutching his leg. He raised himself on one arm, then slipped in the mud, flopped back down, appeared to be losing consciousness. I put him in the recovery position. 'Try to stop him shutting down,' I said to Lucinda. 'Keep talking to him.'

I stood up.

'Sorry, I have to go.'

I gathered up all the weapons and mobiles I could find and threw them into the car. Things were looking up, but I didn't want anyone in this gruesome crew calling for reinforcements.

'I'll get help,' I said to Lucinda.

# CHAPTER 47

I chose George's shotgun. It was a Mossberg 500 with four
shells left. I jumped into his car. As I roared through the rain,
I pulled out my phone and called Lance. He answered straightaway. 'There's been a shooting,' I said. 'At the Thunderhead
Estate, up in the Wiregrass. Four casualties – so far. All injuries,
no deaths. Not yet, anyway. We need ambulances. Where
are you?'

He took a moment to answer. I pictured the poor bugger
trying to piece all of that together.

'We're on the way,' he said. 'Vince Tehlich's behind me. The
Highway Patrol guys are behind him.'

'Stop anybody who leaves. Watch out for weapons. They're
armed, if a little knocked around. And Lance . . .'

'Yes?'

'Inspector Dougherty's in with them. He's injured, but he'll
try to take over. Maybe blame me. Don't let him spin you any
bullshit. Gotta go.'

I left him stewing in his own bewilderment and drove.

I followed the track until it reached the drive, then turned right. Visibility was poor, the rain heavy. As I drew near the house, a security guard with a pistol on his hip came down from the verandah and walked towards me, shielding his eyes against the glare. I recognised him: the over-zealous guard from Hawley and Sons. He gave me a wave, clearly recognising the vehicle. I responded by driving straight into him – a labour-saving exercise – and jumping out. He was writhing on the ground trying to work out which universe he was in. I added his gun to the collection I was building on the floor of the car and dragged him to his feet.

'The cellar,' I yelled. 'Where is it?'

'You just ran over my fucking leg!'

I waved the weapon at him. 'I'll run over your head if you don't take me to the cellar!'

He recognised me and his aggro faded. 'Round the side,' he moaned.

'You've got a man held captive in there . . .'

'I wouldn't know – I'm just paid fifty bucks an hour to watch the gate.'

'Is there only one of you?'

Before he could answer the front door opened and a woman emerged and stood there gaping. She was in her fifties, stick-thin, silver permed, smooth browed, with bee-stung lips and a plastomatic smile. She had a cigarette in her fingers and a wobble in her legs.

'Who the hell are you?' I asked.

'Who the hell are you?'

'I'm the police.'

She shook her head, unsurprised, deflated, as if the Armageddon she'd always expected had finally arrived. She leaned against the doorway. 'Figures. I'm Julia Hawley.'

'George's wife?'

She nodded. 'For my sins, yes. Where are the children? I was trying to look after them but that wretched boy snuck out the window and now Lucinda has disappeared as well.'

'They're okay.' Which, by the standards of this madhouse on this mad night, was relatively true. 'They're with their father.' Accurate enough for now, though I wasn't sure how much longer he'd be with anyone. What little care I had about that was purely for Bailey's and Lucinda's sake. Vicious criminal though he was, Craig was the only parent they had now.

The guard was starting to edge away.

I waved the shotgun at him.

'Cellar!'

'I've got a broken leg.'

'Good. I'll shoot the other one and Mrs Hawley can take me.'

'Fuck this,' muttered Julia Hawley, taking an almighty drag and shaking her head. 'I'm going in for a drink.'

She left, and the guard limped off in the direction of a long steel building to the right. I followed. He led me through a side door and a row of incandescent lights came on to reveal an array of racks with enormous barrels on them.

'Where is he?' I demanded.

'Lady, I dunno who you're talking about.'

'Bullshit,' I said, waving the gun at him.

He stared at the weapon, then at the floor, doubtless wondering if I was as casually brutal with a shotgun as I was with a car. 'There's a basement down the back. They come in and out of there sometimes.'

'They?'

'The Hawleys. Mr Lochran.' He looked around, his nerves taking another hit. 'Mr Lochran – where is he?'

The fear in his eyes told me he knew all about Lochran.

'He's a little indisposed just now. I'll dispose of him properly when I get a moment.'

He looked horrified. I caught a glimpse of my face in an adjacent silver tank and I was horrified too: soaking wet, wild eyed, front tooth missing. He hobbled off to the rear of the building. We came to a door, which he opened. There was a set of stairs. I told him to go first. As he did so, he stumbled in a way I didn't like, as if he was looking for an opportunity to jump me.

'I've been fucked around by this family long enough,' I snapped. 'You do that again and I'll blow your head off and say it was self-defence. My colleagues will be here any moment. Now pick yourself up.'

He picked himself up, shuffled down the stairs and switched on a light.

There was a figure on the floor with its face to the back wall. A man. He was naked to the waist, shackled to a metal bench. His upper body was covered in streaky blood and black bruises.

I glared at the guard, who raised his hands. 'This is nothing to do with me,' he whimpered, visibly shrinking away from me.

There was more equipment – shackles, cuffs and padlocks – on the bench. 'Cuff yourself to the frame,' I ordered him. He was getting the idea now, and did so without complaint.

I checked he was secure, then dashed across to the body on the floor. It was Nash. His eyes were closed and there was no sign of life.

'Nash!' He remained motionless. I checked for a pulse and found one. There was a set of keys on the bench. I picked the one that fit, unlocked the shackles and turned him over, cradling him in my arms. His face was a bloody mess, his eyes were encrusted with blood. His right ear was mangled.

'Nash,' I said again.

I heard a low moan and his lips moved, sucking for breath. Blood bubbled from a multitude of cracks and cuts across his face.

'Nash,' I yelled. 'Wake up!'

His eyes crept open, then met mine. 'Jess?'

I wiped away some of the blood with a shirt sleeve, kissed his blistered lips. He blinked.

'What are you doing here?' he whispered urgently. 'These people are a bunch of fucking maniacs. It's Guin Patmos. She's back. Get out of here. Get help.'

'Help's on the way. And don't worry about Guin,' I said. 'Last I saw of her she was sitting in the mud looking like the broken old carnival clown she is.'

'She hates me, that woman. Had her torture squad work me over. Some sadistic bastard in camo commando gear. And the sergeant from Greendale – Dougherty.'

'He's an inspector now, though he's just been demoted. What did they want to know?'

He took a deep breath and winced.

'About you.'

'Well they know now. Most of them are out in the snow trying to pick up the pieces.'

Or were they? Was I being blasé? Our situation was still precarious. God knows what the remnants of the Revelators were up to, but if they did have some sort of back-up, I didn't want to be trapped down here when it arrived.

'Can you move?' I asked Nash.

He groaned what may have been a maybe. He struggled to his knees, then I dragged him to his feet. He put an arm around my shoulders, and we staggered up the stairs. I kept the shottie in my right arm, just in case.

'What's the plan?' he asked.

'Find a secure position and shoot anybody who comes near us.'

'That's a plan.'

'Help's on the way, but I'm not sure when it'll be here.'

'What about me?' yelled the shackled guard.

'Put it in a song,' I mumbled.

We reached the top of the stairs, then shuffled out into the wine cellar. I braced myself, swept the room for threats. There were none that I could see. I went through the outside door first, gun raised and ready. Nothing. Heavy rain, floodwaters running down the gutters, across the drive.

We stood on the grass outside and listened. There were sirens echoing up the valley.

We sheltered in the darkest place we could find – a grove of cherry trees near the house – and waited until the first of a fleet of police cars came crashing and flashing up the drive.

# EPILOGUE

I put a hand out behind me and groped about. Nothing. I sat up in the swag and looked around the hide. He was nowhere to be seen. I felt a brief surge of concern, then told myself to get over it. Maybe I hadn't sailed through the traumas of the past few weeks quite as smoothly as I'd told everybody I had, but that didn't mean I was allowed to go jumping at shadows, imagining threats where there were none.

We'd come back up to the Wiregrass the night before. We cooked a meal, made love in the swag, talked into the night. Wilderness was good for him.

Nash had been out of hospital for weeks now, but he'd become so caught up with the investigation into what the press had taken to calling 'The Revelator Clan', we'd barely been able to get away from the various police stations connected to the case. I was back in charge at Satellite and Nash had morphed into a man on a mission. He'd tracked down other victims, uncovered more evidence of the cult's crimes, stared into the abyss.

One of our most productive interactions took place a few days after Nash got out of hospital. It was with my neighbours, Rocco and Meg Teller. They came to see us at the Satellite Police Station, wanted to know everything we could tell them about the destruction of the Revelators. I got the impression they were trying to assure themselves they were actually gone. It turned out that Meg had been one of the Patmoses' earliest victims – that was what Rocco had been referring to when he'd mentioned her bitter experiences with an evangelical church. It was also why Meg had never trusted the police; she'd heard the Revelators had connections there. She'd managed to break free, but she knew how dangerous they could be to anyone they perceived as a threat. It was why she'd lain low, kept her eyes and ears open, delivered her warnings in the guise of a soothsayer.

It was during the discussion with the Tellers that I got a glimpse of what Nash must have been like as a police investigator. He was extraordinary: sympathetic, sharp, intuitive, always encouraging, asking the right questions at the right moment. He was a different person from the man I'd met on the road at Wycliff or visited in gaol. People seemed relieved to unburden themselves to him. They knew he was on their side, that he had the resilience to lift them up and carry them over whatever barriers they were facing.

Rocco and I had sensed which way the wind was blowing and left them to it. We went and made a coffee – using the new, no-questions-asked DeLonghi espresso machine Vince had scored for our station, and hoeing into a tin of Katie's cookies. Nash and Meg talked for over an hour. She came out glowing, gave me a hug, said I'd never have to buy another egg.

I loved Nash for what he was doing, but I also saw the toll it was taking on him. So obsessed had he become with uncovering the Revelators' activities, he hadn't noticed how much anger it was fomenting, how that anger was wearing him down. I had to remind him, and myself, that he'd been to hell and back. The buggers had been at him all his life. He was allowed some time out.

This little excursion up to the Wiregrass had been my idea.

'Surely you can take a breather now?' I'd argued yesterday. 'The heat's off. The villains are all in places where they can't do us any harm.'

Which was true, as far as I knew. They'd all more or less survived our dust-up at the Thunderhead Estate, though for Kane Lochran it had been a close call. The ambulances had started arriving hot on the tails of the police. The Hawley brothers were currently in the remand centre, although Craig had spent most of the past few weeks in hospital and would be hobbling on a stick for the rest of his life. Guin Patmos was in the Dame Phyllis Frost Centre, where she'd been trying to convince her hard-bitten fellow inmates she was a reincarnation of John the Baptist. That had gone down well.

The Department of Public Prosecutions were confident the central figures would spend the rest of their lives behind bars. One of the murders they'd been charged with was that of Ronald Laws. A fresh examination of the evidence and the testimony of Ed Dougherty had convinced them that the Hawleys had decided their accounts clerk had become a liability and that his elimination presented an excellent opportunity to dump me a little deeper in the shit.

Dougherty, grasping at anything that might reduce his sentence, had been singing like a bellbird. Nash had been relentless with him, quickly recognising him as the weakest link in the chain. As a member of the public, Nash wasn't allowed to participate in formal interviews, but he'd worked closely with those who were, Neville Wallace in particular, and he had enough inside knowledge of the cult to know when Dougherty was blame-shifting or bullshitting. The truth was coming out in trickles and torrents. Raph Cambric had been killed because he'd been asking awkward questions about his lover Rosa's disappearance. Leon Glazier, seven years earlier, because he'd come across online evidence that the Revelators were back in business, had uncovered the Hawley brothers' identities and was going to expose them. Dougherty had confessed that they'd blackmailed Neddy Kursk into carrying out the attack on me. The inspector had evidence that the tow-truck operator had been involved in the manufacture and distribution of methamphetamines and threatened him with arrest if he didn't cooperate, but Kursk hadn't needed much encouragement. My friend Starcy had come out of retirement for long enough to organise an operation that arrested most of Smash and Grab's drivers, including Rev McQueen, with commercial quantities of narcotics in their trucks. Neville Wallace was revelling in it all – for him the exercise was like a game of blitz chess with whistles and party pies thrown in. He'd started looking at Nash like a teacher beaming at his star pupil.

Even Paul Burstill, the aspiring toxic waste king, was back where he belonged: behind bars, charged with a litany of offences that included fraud, tax evasion and illegal toxic waste dumping. The benevolent cousin turned out to be little more than a forged signature on a dotted line.

The psychiatrist, Damien Rush, had confessed to a pethidine addiction and was currently suspended from practice and under investigation by the police and the Health Practitioner Regulation Agency. The investigators believed he'd administered to Nash a drug called Levodopa, normally used for treating Parkinson's but capable of causing psychotic episodes when incorrectly prescribed. The Patomoses had been worried that Leon Glazier was getting too close to their operation and was planning on reporting them to the authorities. He'd asked Nash to come up to Horse Thief Creek to get his advice on how to make the report, whom he could trust. The Revelators had been bugging his phone. For them, it was a case of two birds, one stone.

Lucinda and Bailey were in community care. The boy was travelling badly, still having trouble with anger management and mood swings. He'd been diagnosed with complex PTSD. Nash and I had been spending time with them at the farm, planned to have them come up and stay with us in a couple of days. I was pleased to see how well Bailey and Nash were getting on. They had a lot in common. They'd gone hunting rats together – with a recurve bow – at the Cambrics' farm. They didn't actually hit anything, but I'd heard their laughter echoing up the valley from Nash's back porch. I nourished a hope that Nash would be able to give the boy the kind of support he'd never had from his own father, maybe turn his life around.

I glanced out the hide's viewing window. The sky out there was a pristine blue, as deep and clear as one of Meg's crystals.

I didn't even know they did blue down here in Victoria. I thought the state's weather was a karmic conspiracy designed to dump the maximum amount of wind and rain possible onto the heads of anybody foolish enough to expose themselves to it.

I found a sarong and slipped into it. I began to climb down the ladder, but I'd only gone a couple of rungs when I decided the morning wasn't quite as balmy as it looked from the hide. Spring had arrived, but it had yet to shake the snow from its boots. I went back to the hide and climbed into the cargo pants and woolly jumper Nash had eased me out of last night. Then, as an afterthought, I grabbed a blanket from the swag. Warm now, I made another descent.

I needed a drink, so I walked down to the creek, thirty metres away. I moved quietly, always a wise way to travel in this country. When I reached the water's edge I noticed a small deer with the same idea. It was sipping at the tumbling stream, oblivious. Then it raised its head and saw me. It sprang into the air, then crumbled into a bundle of skitters and bounded away. I listened for a moment to it crashing through the undergrowth then knelt and drank from the creek through cupped hands. Honeyeaters, fairy martins and firefinches came down to join me. Whirligig beetles and water boatmen looked up through the water with interest. A distant kookaburra call purled through rivers of silver.

There was a boot print in the burned earth on the other side of the creek and another in the grass beyond it. They weren't hard to follow: up through the ferns and acacias, the stringybarks and box greys. The first rush of spring was in full bloom: I saw spider and leopard orchids, pink bells, mosquito orchids, running postman. The flowers shone through the scrub like tiny medallions of colour and complexity in a field of grey–green. There was a scent of honey and mint in the air. I tore a strip of bark from a tree and took pleasure in its hieroglyphs and scribbled shadows, the worm trails under the surface, the rich, loamy smells that wafted up.

I followed the prints for maybe a hundred metres up the slope, then came across their maker perched on a boulder, looking out over the valley. He was wearing short pants and big boots, a blue lumber jacket and a week's worth of beard.

The three-legged hound beside Nash wagged his tail when he saw me.

Nash had the binoculars in his hands. Studying the valley below? No, I followed the angle of the glasses and guessed that he'd chosen this location because it offered a better view of the nest in the mountain ash.

'Morning,' I called.

He turned around and smiled a greeting.

'Is Pauli at home?'

'Nope,' he replied, then put out a hand and helped me scramble up onto the boulder.

I looked at the nest. It was a hundred metres away, but I thought I detected movement.

'You sure?' I asked. 'I saw something.'

'That's his mate,' he replied. 'Old Pauli's up there.'

He pointed at the sky.

It took me a few seconds to find him. No wonder Nash needed the binoculars. Many hundreds of metres over us was a black speck riding on high thermals, carving vast circles out of rising air.

Nash handed me the glasses and I watched, entranced, as the circles got lower. The eagle soon reached a point where I could distinguish the individual features of its flight dynamics: the extended wings, the shallow angle of its tail feathers, the subtle adjustments it made in response to unseen turbulence. It banked in front of us, displaying a bronzed belly and chest, revelling in the play of light and wind on its wings, the flashes of morning gold in its eyes. It launched one last swooping arc, head down, floating over a clear patch on the southern slope. Deep into the curve, it lifted lightly, appeared to hang motion-less for a moment.

Then it plummeted.

The eagle was transformed into a missile, wings back, feet forward, body barrelling down. There was a storm of talon and beak and beating wings, then it disappeared in the grass. It reappeared a moment later, completed a series of long, wing-flapping hops during which it finished off its prey. Finally the bird lifted out of the undergrowth, a small rabbit in its talons. It soared upwards, wings working hard to generate lift. When it reached the upper level of the mountain ash it gave a final flourish and gently descended into the nest. There was a flurry of activity, then the pair settled down to enjoy their breakfast.

Nash studied them for a time then glanced down at some-thing in his hand. I took a closer look. It was the little piece of pottery, the golden wattle I'd given him. He caught my eye and smiled. My father's thoughts on carbon came to mind: how it quickens and revivifies, how it holds the key to the new life rising out of the ashes. How it's elusive, eternal, impossible to destroy. There was something of that element in this man.

'Maybe it's time I cut myself loose,' he said.

'From what?'

'The past. World's full of people who've liberated themselves from some bloody thing or other. Think I'll join them.' He laughed. 'Can't be that hard, can it?'

Just for a moment I caught a glimpse of the thirteen-year-old boy who'd taken a stand and confronted the dark forces that had shaped his existence. Nash had been through the fires of every imaginable hell and come out stronger for it.

I lifted the blanket and wrapped it round us both. Took pleasure in his warmth.

'Amen to that.'

# ACKNOWLEDGEMENTS

Thanks to the Wurundjeri People of the Kulin Nation, upon whose Country I live and write. My special thanks to Aunty Joy Murphy for your kindness and friendship.

Thanks to the brilliant crew at Ultimo for their ongoing faith in my work and for the passion and care they bring to the words on the page: Robert Watkins, Alisa Ahmed, Deonie Fiford and Pam Dunne. Thanks to Josh Durham for another gorgeous cover. And thanks to James Kellow for bringing me on board.

Thanks to my agent, Melanie Ostell, for your fierce advocacy and support.

Thanks to my colleagues at the St Andrews CFA, especially Jason Earl, Chris Henderson, Jeff 'Redline' Purchase, Steve Gormley, Paul Davis and Matt Ryan.

Thanks to Martin Scuffins, both for his excellent advice on the lives of eagles and for his wonderful work at the Leigh Valley Hawk and Owl Sanctuary.

Thanks to my friends at the wonderful St Andrews Nature Facebook group.

Thanks to Sergeant Stewart Henderson, Officer-in-Charge, Warrandyte Police Station, for the inside story on how you do the job.

Thanks to Andy Knorr for the years of friendship and bush-building wisdom.

Thanks to the medical professionals who kindly shared their knowledge and patiently put up with my annoying questions: Rob Russell, Dr Simon Ruffell and Dr Kieran Thorpe.

Thanks to Debbie, Ben and the super-baristas of the St Andrews pub: Aiyana, Brianna, Dima, Emily, Karen, Kate and Wayne. A haven of warmth and cheer in the freezing Victorian winter.

As always, the last word and deepest thanks go to my beautiful family: Sally, Siena, Morgan and Kegan – and especially Kristin, whose love inspires every word I write (and who reads each and every one of those words with an eagle eye).

Adrian Hyland is the award-winning author of *Diamond Dove*, *Gunshot Road* and *Kinglake-350*, which was shortlisted for the Prime Minister's Literary Award for non-fiction in 2012. His books have been published internationally, including in Britain and the US, and translated into a variety of languages, including German, French, Swedish and Czech. *Canticle Creek*, the first Jesse Redpath thriller, was published in 2022.